Broken Vows

Marital Privileges Series
Book 4

Shandi Boyes

Also by Shandi Boyes

The Way We Were

Sugar and Spice_*

Lady In Waiting

Man in Queue

Couple on Hold

Enigma: The Wedding

Silent Vigilante

Hushed Guardian

Quiet Protector

Enigma: An Isaac Retelling

Twisted Lies *

Bound Series

Chains

Links

Bound

Restrain

The Misfits_*

Nanny Dispute *

Russian Mob Chronicles

Nikolai: A Mafia Prince Romance

Nikolai: Taking Back What's Mine

Nikolai: What's left of Me.

Nikolai: Mine to Protect

Asher: My Russian Revenge *

Trey *

Nikolai: Through the Devil's Eyes

Nero: Shattered Wings *

The Italian Cartel

Dimitri

Roxanne

Reign

Mafia Ties (Novella)

Maddox

Demi

Ox

Rocco *

Clover *

Smith *

RomCom Standalones

Just Playin' *

<u>Ain't Happenin'</u> *

The Drop Zone *

Very Unlikely *

False Start *

Short Stories - Newsletter Downloads

Christmas Trio *

Falling For A Stranger *

One Night Only Series

Hotshot Boss *

Hotshot Neighbor *

The Bobrov Bratva Series

Wicked Intentions *

Sinful Intentions *

Devious Intentions *

Deadly Intentions *

Martial Privilege Series

Doctored Vows *

Deceitful Vows *

Vengeful Vows *

Broken Vows *

Omnibus Books (Collections)

Enigma: The Complete Collection (Isaac & Isabelle)

The Beneath Duet (Hugo & Ava)

The Bad Boy Trilogy (Hunter, Rico, and Brax)

Pinkie Promise (Ryan & Savannah)

The Infinite Time Trilogy (Regan & Alex)

Silent Guardian (Brandon & Melody)

Nikolai: The Complete Collection (Nikolai & Justine)

Mafioso (Dimitri & Roxanne)

Bound: The Complete Collection (Cleo & Marcus)

Copyright

Editing: Courtney Umphress

Proofreading: Lindsi La Bar

Alpha: Carolyn Wallace

Written by: Shandi Boyes

Cover Photographer: Wander Aguiar

Playlist

Half a Heart - One Direction

I Hate That It's True - Dean Lewis

Someone To You - Matt Hansen

If You Love Her - Forest Black

28 - Ruth B. & Dean Lewis

Before You - Benson Boone

Want to stay in touch?

Facebook: facebook.com/authorshandi

Instagram: instagram.com/authorshandi

Email: authorshandi@gmail.com

Reader's Group: bit.ly/ShandiBookBabes

Website: authorshandi.com

Newsletter: https://www.subscribepage.com/AuthorShandi

Chapter 1

Emerson

Funerals suck. They're stuffy, lifeless—*obviously*—and bring out everyone from your kindergarten teacher to your second cousin's third wife. I loathe them. But I loathe this more.

Readings of wills are where crocodile tears fade, pushed aside for money-hungry viciousness.

A lawyer's conference room two hundred miles from my hometown holds as many people as the front rows of last month's nationally broadcast funeral.

I'm not surprised. Andrik Dokovic Sr. was an extremely wealthy man. The combined sum in his multiple bank accounts could keep the heat on for every family in Russia for centuries to come. He was the epitome of success.

He needed to be for anyone to see past his icy-cold demeanor.

If you can't tell, I'm not a fan of Andrik Sr. We clashed many times during the period I "associated" with a member of his family, and even with our bone-crushing love only being displayed to him as puppy love, he never let his disdain for my inclusion in his grandson's life go unnoticed.

1

That's why I'm apprehensive to learn why Andrik Sr. named me in his will.

It was probably a last-minute amendment before he croaked to remind me of my place.

"Your name doesn't belong alongside a Dokovic," were the last words Andrik Sr. spoke to me before he slid into the back of a chauffeur-driven government-plated car, taking my heart with him.

He uttered his scorn over a decade ago, but it still stings like a million wasp bites.

The hateful words of an angry, lonely man with nothing but money to snuggle with at night are easy to forget. But first love—the gooey, sticky kind that adheres to every damn surface of your mind, body, and soul—stays with you for a lifetime.

It also reminds you that hate isn't a genuine emotion. It's a façade designed to blanket your feelings in a manner appropriate for public consumption, and the only thing they give you free rein to cling to when things turn sour.

It is expected.

This, though, walking into a room that smells like old books and even older money, isn't close to the norm.

Andrik Sr. was right. I don't belong here.

If I had any other option, I wouldn't be here.

Alas, beggars can't be picky.

As my baby sister would say, you get what you get, and you don't get upset.

After wrangling through suit-clad gents and elegantly dressed ladies, I find a spot at the end of a long mahogany conference table. I hide behind a handful of attendees mingling close enough to conceal my why-the-hell-am-I-here face.

The air is thick with anticipation and another scent I can't quite work out. It is a little rancid, like everyone feels like they also don't belong here, so they're sweating as much as I am.

The thought eases my nerves a smidge, bringing them down to a manageable level.

While breathing through my nose, hoping the overspray of pricy aftershaves filling the space doesn't tickle the back of my throat, I scan the faces surrounding me. I have allergies—badly. One wrong sniff and I'll sneeze loud enough to erupt Klyuchevskaya Sopka.

If I want to remain hidden, I can't activate a volcano.

My sighting of a familiar face partway through my scan makes my quest seem almost impossible. I see Mikhail, the source of the sticky, gooey mess I mentioned earlier, seated at the opposite end of the conference room. Like his designer-clad counterparts slapping his back like he won the lottery, he's wearing a tailored suit and a fancy, show-every-inch-of-my-muscular-torso button-up shirt. He's not wearing their hideously pompous ties and has a few buttons undone, showing more skin.

He's older than the memories that broadcast like a high-budget movie anytime my heart rebels against my head by taking a trip down memory lane, but he still has that fuckboy eat-your-heart-out look that has every woman in a five-mile radius desperate for a fresh pair of panties.

Myself included.

He's the hottest guy in the room, and he knows it. *Regretfully.*

My eye roll in defiance of his cocky confidence glitches halfway around. The very essence of Mikhail's now type has entered the room, and I'm not the only one eyeballing her arrival. Mikhail waves her over with an eagerness I haven't seen cross his face in over a decade—and I've read every tabloid article printed about him in the past ten years.

He seemed happy, but not like this. This is above glee. He looks complete. Whole. Not close to the miserable, sad person I've become.

The mysterious woman is blonde, short, and gorgeous. And she has a noticeable yet still tiny baby bump that Mikhail caresses when she joins him in the premium seats.

What the?

My breath hitches in my throat as anger overtakes my curiosity. Mikhail was expected to be here and to interact with a woman with more class in her pinky finger than I have in my entire body. It is, after all, his grandfather's will reading. But this—a baby—is a slap in the face I'm struggling to ignore.

It burns knowing he's moved forward with the plans *we* made.

My back molars are nearly ground to stubs when I notice the generous rock on the blonde's ring finger. It is too many carats for her tiny finger to hold up, and it screams, "I married a rich man."

I stop endeavoring to singe a hole in the conference room table to discover if Mikhail is the man in question when the lawyer clears his throat, announcing the commencement of the will reading.

I try to focus on the meeting that stripped the last of my funds for half a tank of gas, but it is a struggle when Mikhail slips off his chair before he offers it to the blonde.

His left hand is now exposed, but too many people separate us to see his ring finger.

The crowd coos in sync when he assists the unnamed blonde onto his seat before pushing her in and standing protectively behind her.

He still has charm by the mile, and no chance in hell of utilizing it on me.

I was determined before I arrived to steer clear of him. His pretty wife and her teeny-tiny baby bump seal my resolve beneath a slab of concrete.

I don't care how attractive the package is. If it belongs to someone else, I won't even look at the packing slip to unearth what's hiding beneath its layers of tape and cardboard.

Cheaters don't deserve to breathe air.

They're on par with men who leave you at the altar.

A pang of nostalgia hits me when the lawyer reads the will. He starts at the multiple charities Andrik Sr. initiated when his campaign for office ramped up.

Not all my memories are good.

4

Mikhail shared many stories about his grandfather when we were together. They strengthened my belief that Andrik Sr. was a cruel, vindictive man with a heart of ice.

He didn't deserve his success or the utmost devotion of almost everyone in the room.

As the lawyer drones on, I glance at Mikhail, wondering if he is being hit with a similar sting of regret.

He had to abide by his grandfather's terms.

I merely had to live with the results of them.

Mikhail seems as captivated by his grandfather's charity work as the people who divide us do, but a hint of the boy I once loved remains behind his impassive expression. His left hand, now hidden in his pocket instead of beneath a conference room table, is balled, and his right hand is fiddling with a thread in his trousers that not even the world's best tailor would have noticed.

He's keeping his mind on anything but the proceedings occurring, silence still his prime go-to coping mechanism.

The room suddenly shrinks when Mikhail's eyes slide my way. As he scans the faces of the multiple people sheltering me, I ponder what he's thinking and if he's noticed my presence.

The air grows dense as memories of our past swirl around me.

No matter how large the crowd or how big the gathering, Mikhail always found me.

A smile plays at my lips as more memories load. I lost count of how often I hid from him when we went out. It was my favorite game, but it ended brutally when, on the one occasion I wanted him to find me the most, he never did.

Seeing Mikhail again has stirred something within me, something I thought was long buried. It honestly hurts remembering how close we came to happiness before he cruelly stripped it away. Our relationship was a fairy tale that became a nightmare in less than twenty-four hours, and he's now living his happily ever after with someone else.

As I wipe my cheeks to ensure they're dry, I sink toward the exit. I shouldn't have come. It was foolish of me, but desperation can lead you to act in a way you swore you never would. I had to know why they summoned me and couldn't postpone my curiosity.

I won't make the same mistake twice.

My legs are unsteady as I walk toward the door, my heart and head torn on whether I'm making the right choice.

The last time I walked away when I was apprehensive was the last time I saw Mikhail.

That was ten long years ago.

Just before I exit, my name is called. I glance at Mikhail, stupidly assuming he wants to acknowledge my presence before I leave.

The past and present collide when our eyes lock and hold. Mikhail stares at me as if he is seeing a ghost. I learn that he is when my name is repeated. It didn't come from Mikhail. He keeps his lips pressed too tightly for words to pass through. It came from the lawyer helming the meeting, from a man who announces my cowardice to the room when I slowly drift my watering eyes to him.

"Where are you going? Proceedings have only just begun. We're not close to being done yet."

"I... ah..." I return my eyes to Mikhail, and for a brief moment, understanding passes between us. It confirms my decision to leave was right and provides the farewell I was denied years ago. "I shouldn't have come. I don't belong here."

Pain stabs my chest when Mikhail briefly dips his chin, agreeing with me, before he watches me exit without so much as a backward glance.

Chapter 2

Mikhail

"What did I miss?"

After plucking Zoya from her seat, Andrik, my brother, wraps his arm around her ballooning midsection and tugs her back until she lands on his lap with a moan.

No, you didn't hear me wrong. You need to wash the filth from your eyes anytime Andrik and Zoya are in the same room, both in business and private settings.

It's gross when you learn they are parents to a five-year-old. Alas, a man forced to hold back his desires for even a second must make up for the injustice with ten times more effort.

That's why I'm so shocked about my muted reaction to Emerson's resurrection in my life.

I hadn't expected to see her today, but even if I had, I could have never comprehended this was how our reunion would turn out.

There should have been shouting, yelling, and a heap of cuss words that can only be forgiven in one way—with fire-sparking makeup sex.

That's how Emerson and I operated. Our chemistry was insane, but we clashed heads as often as expected when two people with mile-long stubborn streaks couple.

Our fights were foreplay... *until they weren't.*

With his hand possessively cradling Zoya's stomach, Andrik strays his eyes to me. Zakhar, their son, had a cardiologist's appointment at the same time as our grandfather's will reading, so Andrik suggested Zoya take his spot.

His efforts to fix his wrongs extend to *all* regions of his life. He is no longer a billionaire playboy with a long list of enemies. He's a husband and a father. The very man I thought I would become while pinning a corsage to the lapel of a recently purchased tuxedo and polishing dress shoes like they weren't brand new.

We appear to have switched roles.

The playboy title isn't the only thing Andrik has handed over. He is no longer a Dokovic, either. His wife and children will never be so fortunate as to escape the stigma associated with the name.

Only months ago, someone tarnished them with the same brush that painted my life picture thirty-two years ago. The strokes are a little less faded because the painting happened after my grandfather's death, but Andrik will need a lifetime to correct the imperfections they will inevitably cause.

I don't think he cares.

Obsession is given a new definition when Zoya enters Andrik's realm.

It was once the same for me with Emerson.

Once.

"Mikhail?" Andrik murmurs, drawing my focus back to him.

With my mind a whirlwind of emotions I have no fucking clue how to handle, I dump the task of easing Andrik's inquisitiveness onto Zoya.

The words of the lawyer dividing my grandfather's estate between multiple organizations, charities, and people I've never met before today fade into the background when I move to a window stretched across one wall of the conference room.

My heart rate kicks up when I spot Emerson's race across the packed parking lot. The wish to leave is all over her face. It starkly contrasts the expression reflecting off the tinted window of the conference room.

Ten years have passed, yet my feelings remain as strong as ever.

When Emerson's brisk flee sees her losing her grip on her handbag, she curses into the cool afternoon air before she bends down to collect her belongings.

I use the delay in her departure to drink her in. She looks just as I remember, yet different. More poised, more mature. *More beautiful.* But also more distant.

I never thought Emerson would be a woman who'd hide behind others. She used to come out swinging, no matter the crowd.

I guess even the best fighters lose strength when they realize their opponent isn't worth the effort.

Sensing my turmoil, Andrik joins me at the window. Air whizzes from his nose when he spots the cause of the angst on my face. Then words slowly trickle from his hard-lined mouth. "Emerson Morozov. I never thought I'd see the day." I exhale harshly, forcing his eyes on me. "Do you know why she's here?"

I half shrug and half shake my head, not trusting myself to speak. The weight of ten years of memories, unspoken words, and a feeling that will never fade hangs heavily on my chest.

Andrik gives me a sympathetic look. He knows how much Emerson once meant to me—how much she still means to me—because he was the first to voice concern about our plans to wed mere weeks after my twenty-first birthday.

His worries had more basis than I could have ever imagined, but at the time, I hated him for them. I didn't want to be told who I could or could not love. I loved Emerson and wanted her to be my wife and, one day, the mother of my children.

She was the one who had a change of heart.

I can't say I blame her, but I'd be a liar if I said it didn't hurt like a bitch to be dumped by the only woman you've ever loved.

My mother was stripped from my life when I was too young to

grant me a ton of memories, and although she's back now, her fragile mental health makes it seem as if she isn't.

With Emerson's items gathered and my heart in tatters, I watch her walk toward a car at the back of the lot. It isn't as flashy as its numerous counterparts, but it will get her from A to B, which is all Emerson ever cared about. She isn't about wealth and influence. She loves fiercely enough to see through anyone's flaws.

When she slips behind the steering wheel, I want to run after her and beg her to stay, to tell her to speak the fuck up and prove she isn't the coward she made out when she hid behind a wall of nameless faces, but I can't.

I must act unaffected, like seeing her again isn't ripping me apart, because it isn't her heart I'm protecting. It's mine.

My pulse thumps in my ears when Emerson looks up for the quickest second, and our eyes meet. Something flickers in her gaze, something that doubles the roiling of my stomach, but it disappears again too fast to decipher.

Andrik squeezes my shoulder in silent support when Emerson cranks the ignition of her old ride, and I force a weak smile.

"I'm fine," I lie.

I'm nowhere close to fine.

Seeing Emerson again has stirred up old feelings I've fought to keep buried for ten years, memories of what we had, what we lost, and what we could have been if we had fought harder.

We were young, so fucking young, but madly, deeply in love.

I thought nothing could tear us apart.

When she left me, I should have tracked her down and forced her to give me answers. I shouldn't have backed down without a fight or acted like I did when I sensed her presence seconds before Zoya entered the meeting under the disdainful glares of the men Andrik will end the instant I pass on their hatred to the man responsible for his wife's happiness.

The hollow emptiness in my chest when Emerson veers her car

past the window and toward the lot's exit should make my legs the heaviness of iron. I shouldn't be able to move. But before my head can shut down the demands of my heart, I sprint for the exit she bolted through only moments ago, unwilling to let another ten years pass before seeking answers.

Complicated is an understatement to describe our relationship, but it is the truth. Our lives have taken different paths, but my heart stubbornly refuses to let go.

"Continue without us," Andrik demands when the lawyer shouts my name like he did Emerson's.

Despite running at the speed of sound, I burst into the parking lot two seconds too late. Emerson is gone. Again.

Chapter 3

Emerson

As Mikhail's slumped form becomes a blip in the rearview mirror, I wring the steering wheel, my knuckles turning white. My heart aches with deep, relentless pain. I wish I could turn around and force him to speak the words he was too cowardly to say years ago, but I can't.

Mikhail left me on the day we were meant to wed.

He broke my heart.

There's no coming back from that.

As I make the two-hundred-mile trip home, memories flood my head, each one more painful than the last. I smile while recalling how Mikhail used to look at me as if I were a precious gem, and the promises we made to always be true to one another. Then I fight back a sob when I remember how it all came tumbling down with three painful words.

He isn't coming.

We had planned a future together, marriages, babies, and worldwide travels that were shattered in an instant. Nothing made sense. We were madly in love and had the world at our feet. Then, bam. It was over. No explanation. No sorrow. Nothing.

Tears well in my eyes, but I blink them away, determined not to let them fall.

I've shed so many tears over this man that there should be none left to give.

My time with Mikhail proves that not even the most stringently planned event will occur without a hiccup, but I force myself to focus on the present. I can't afford to let old emotions take over. Mikhail is my past. I am in charge of my future. This is how it must be.

When I finally pull into the driveway of my home, the gas tank almost empty, I take a deep breath and try to compose myself. I put on a brave face, masking the turmoil inside, hopeful no one will see through my façade.

As I step out of my car and walk into my house, I wave hello to my mother, who watches me from behind tattered curtains. Her skin looks extra clammy today, but her eyes are bright and filled with hope, and her sheeny lips hide a painful night of coughing.

My mother isn't well. She hasn't been for some time. That's why I attended the will reading today. Even if Andrik Sr.'s generosity is minute, it will still be better than the nothing I am currently working with.

"Hey. I'm home." I greet my family with a cheerful tone, hiding the heartache threatening to consume me.

Everyone is here. My mother, my aunt, and the gardener, whom my mother had to let go of when she became too sick to work. Even my little sister has made an appearance, which is odd, considering it's a weekday. She should be at school.

My mother defied the odds when she gave birth to a healthy baby girl in her early forties.

I'm sure she will do the same to beat her latest diagnosis.

I pull Wynne in for a hug, her groan replacing my fake smile with a genuine one. "Aren't you meant to be at school?"

Begrudgingly, she returns my greeting before peering up at me with big blue eyes. They're familiar yet so opposite to mine. She threw out my family's beloved red-haired, green-eyed combination, opting for inky locks and blue eyes.

She is the black sheep of our family, and it couldn't be more noticeable when numerous pairs of eyes stray our way, awaiting what they hope is good news.

"It was a mistake." I breathe slowly, each word consciously planned to ensure they'll pass my family's inbuilt lie detector machines with flying colors. "It was Emerson the company, not Emerson the person."

My aunt is the first to jump in. "Oh... that's a shame." I smile like my heart isn't in pieces when she joins me near the living room entryway to farewell me with a cheek kiss. "All that wasted time for nothing." She side-eyes me like she knows I'm a big fat liar before she noogies Wynne's head and exits our home. "I'll be back in time for supper."

I watch her cross the patch of grass between our homes before shifting on my feet to face my mother. She is the one who deserves my true apologies. I ran today like some of our family's financial obligations aren't my fault. It isn't fair, but if she could go back ten years and change the outcome of the decision I made for her, she wouldn't.

She knows I made the right choice when I convinced her to keep Wynne, just like she knows I'm lying.

Mercifully, she doesn't call me out on it.

"How was the drive?"

I grimace before following her slow shuffle to the kitchen. "It was fine. I guess."

My throat works hard to swallow when she interrogates me while pulling ingredients from the refrigerator. "And Mikhail? How was he?"

My fake smile is back, more tarnished than ever. "He seemed good." I repeatedly tell myself that I'm strong enough to do this while guiding my mother away from the kitchen and onto a stool. "He's married, and his wife is expecting a child."

Tears blur my eyes, but no amount of distortion will have me missing my mother's shocked expression. "He is?" When I nod, she blurts out, "Since when?" I don't have time to reply. "He was named a finalist in Russia's bachelor of the year contest only last week." She pulls out the magazine responsible for rating men on their sexiness *and* wealth before opening it to a two-page spread on the man of the hour. "See?"

I do see. I don't want to, but a nun would struggle not to look.

Mikhail has aged like fine wine. He's gotten better with age. His six-pack is more defined than it was during the years he took to grow into his lanky legs, and since his hair is no longer clipped close to the scalp, my fingers grow envious with the urge to rake them through his unkempt locks.

The photographer captured *almost* all his good points. I would have said all of them if the two-page spread had been in a limited print run Penthouse does once a year for its female readers.

As I cut the fat off a cheap chunk of meat, I say, "How many times do I have to tell you that most articles about celebrities are made-up stories? Lies sell magazines—"

My eyes snap up from the cutting board when my mother interrupts. "And destroy lives. You know that better than anyone, Emmy." Since I can't recant her honesty, since it's true, I remain quiet. "Em—"

"He's married and about to have a child, so can we please not?" I hate snapping at her. She's so sick that we're not even guaranteed years anymore. But this isn't a conversation I can have right now. My heart is too fragile. It may not survive another knock.

My mother is a woeful liar, but I appreciate her ability not to flog a dead horse when she replies, "I was going to say you should replace the onion in the dish tonight with shallots. Aunt Marcelle has been on fire all afternoon. We may not survive the night if she's served another gas-inspiring meal."

Chapter 4

Mikhail

After taking a breath, I focus on the lawyer's droning voice, trying to push aside my pain. It isn't just my heart aching anymore. My thighs are fucking killing me, and my gut won't quit crunching.

I didn't just follow Emerson's car out of the lot. I chased it for miles. My dress shirt is clinging to my body, my pits stink, and this will reading won't fucking end. I want to go home, to my penthouse, open an expensive bottle of whiskey, and get lost far from my thoughts.

Blackout drunk may be the only thing capable of stopping me from driving to Lidny and demanding answers ten years too late.

It was for the best that Emerson left me, but that's fucking hard to admit when you're standing across from your soulmate and striving to act like she doesn't exist.

My heart frees itself from the black, tarry mess Emerson's resurrection dumped it in when I finally hear my name. The list of inheritors from my grandfather's estate is endless. It's taken almost four hours to reach this point.

In all honesty, I don't want my grandfather's money. I don't need it.

I'm here to see how badly he wants to fuck with me from the afterlife and to support Zoya's slow merge into our messed-up family.

Did I forget to mention that Zoya is my sister? Unlike Andrik, she is a blood-related sibling. We didn't know that until after our grandfather lodged a bullet through his brain and left us to wade through decades of secrets alone.

If we were the type to air our family secrets, we could bring down hundreds of Russia's most elite families with us.

We're not, hence our united front at our grandfather's funeral and his cause of death being broadcast across the globe as naturally caused.

I would have pissed on his grave if his sudden growth of a heart hadn't saved my baby sister's life.

His unusual show of leniency makes me even more curious about his chosen inheritors. Today's meeting is an invitation-only event. Emerson wouldn't have known about it unless she had been named as a benefactor of my grandfather's estate.

I look up when the lawyer repeats my name.

It is finally showtime.

"Mikhail, you will inherit your grandfather's country mansion, Zelenolsk Manor, his primary suite in Moscow, and all funds left in his estate after settling any debts owed to your fellow inheritor." Paperwork ruffles before a sum almost knocks me on my ass. "Calculation of your inheritance if all tasks are achieved exceeds five hundred million dollars."

What. The. Fuck?

The lawyer's sum hangs in the air, heavy and suffocating. I have money. Plenty for an average schmuck. But five hundred million? That's a fuck ton of coins.

I glance at Andrik, whose suspicious eyes are bouncing between the lawyer and the paperwork he just recited. He knows the man still playing mind games from the grave better than me, so his suspicions of his motive formulate quicker than mine.

"What are the terms of the inheritance?"

The lawyer clears his throat before scanning the documents. Since my inheritance was the last on a long ledger, the once-brimming room is almost empty. Only Andrik, Zoya, the lawyer, and I remain.

Andrik is an impatient man. "You said the settlement will be calculated after debts owed to his fellow inheritor have been settled. Who is his fellow inheritor?"

It can't be Andrik. Despite already amassing billions, his family was awarded a fifty-million-dollar property portfolio and a similar value in cash assets.

The lawyer clears his throat again, agitating me further. "Your grandfather has some terms he requested be included in his will. If the terms aren't met, the inheritance will be forfeited."

"And that term is?" Andrik continues, beating me.

"Terms," the lawyer corrects. "There is more than one." His hand shakes when he passes me a thick wad of papers, his eyes unmoving from my face. "But the main thing is that you are to marry Emerson Morozov by the end of the week."

"What?" The word leaves my mouth before I can stop it, and I almost tear the terms of my inheritance out of the lawyer's hand when my heart demands answers before my head can register a single thought.

The lawyer didn't lie. The list of terms for Andrik Sr.'s last wish is extensive. It covers everything. Our marriage. The location of our first home. Events and traditions that all husbands and wives make during their first year of marriage are documented, and every milestone attracts a hefty supplementary bonus to the payout we will be rewarded if we survive one year of marriage.

I glance up at Andrik, who is watching me intently, when he says, "You should take the deal, Mikhail."

He knows the history between Emerson and me, the heartache that still lingers. He knows it well because he experienced it only months ago. However, this differs from what he went through with Zoya.

Emerson left me at the altar.

She broke my heart.

She can't come back from that.

I mutter to Andrik to get the fuck out of my head when he says, "The heartache will be worth it."

Again, I shake my head. My heart races, but my mind is blank. "I don't need the money. I'm fine how I am. I've built my own life, my own success. I don't need *this*." I dump the terms onto the conference room table at the end of my sentence.

Andrik tilts nearer, his voice a mix of empathetic and stern. "What about Emerson? Have you considered what she would want and what this could mean to her?"

I bounce my eyes between his, confused. Before he met Zoya, he didn't give a fuck about anyone but himself. It will take me more than a few months to become accustomed to his new empathetic side.

Upon spotting my confusion, Andrik attempts to ease it. He doesn't use words. He exploits my grandfather's terms and reminds me I won't be the only one who will benefit from our quickie marriage.

If Emerson follows my grandfather's rule, she will be an extremely wealthy woman in less than thirteen months.

My grandfather's lawyers have set aside a fifty-million-dollar check for her.

I try to pretend I still know the woman who broke my heart.

It is far from the truth.

"She would say the same as me. She can make her own waves."

"I'm sure she can, Mikhail. But there's a big difference between riding the waves you create and being pummeled by them."

Andrik steals my chance to reply to Zoya's statement by dumping a thick medical file onto paperwork I'm pretending doesn't exist. The name on the front is instantly familiar, and I reach for it before I can talk myself out of it.

My heart twists in pain when I read about Emerson's mother's diagnosis. Inga is the apple of her daughter's eye. She was the first to support my relationship with Emerson, and the one I wanted to seek advice from the most when it abruptly tumbled.

I made it to the end of her street before I chickened out. Emerson's family is full of opinionated women. I might not have made it out of the wreckage unscathed, so I put it on the back burner until I was confident I would survive the carnage.

One hour turned into a week.

A week shifted into a year.

Before I knew it, ten years had flown by.

No wonder Emerson ran before we made it official.

"Inga has weeks, Mikhail. Months, if she is lucky." Andrik forces eye contact before he takes the decision out of my hands. "She could have years, possibly even decades, if you let the past stay in the past. The treatment is expensive, but it is *extremely* effective. It could give her more time with her family."

I look away, the burden of my decision crushing me. The money, the marriage, and the memories Emerson could miss out on if her mother were to pass swirl together in a chaotic storm. It opens old wounds and has me torn on how to respond.

Emerson hates me. She must; otherwise why would she leave me on the day she was meant to become mine permanently?

But will she hate me more if I let this opportunity slip from her grasp? I want to say no and that I wouldn't care either way, but that's a cop-out.

I hate the thought of her hating me. So, against the better judgment of my head and my heart, I lock eyes with the lawyer and say, "When and where?"

Chapter 5

Emerson

Behind a bar that's seen better days, I wipe down a sticky counter. My family's once-thriving business is now run down, but every creak of the worn floorboards initiates memories of laughter, love, and heartache.

As I glance around at the faded photos on the walls, the chipped paint, and an old, barely working jukebox, warmth spreads across my chest.

Despite its condition, this bar is my home. It is my family's legacy.

My first paid position was peeling the potatoes for the meals we served by the hundreds every Friday and Saturday night. I pulled my first pint of beer here just shy of my sixteenth birthday, and this is where I met the man I thought would be the love of my life when he selected the corniest song on the jukebox and asked me to dance.

Mikhail spent as much time here as I did during our late teens and early twenties. We fucked on almost every solid surface and are wholly responsible for the jukebox's first lot of hiccups.

God, that feels like a lifetime ago.

What I wouldn't give to go back ten years. My time-traveler wish isn't solely to stop my heart from being smashed into smithereens, but also to educate my mother on early intervention and how passive smoking is worse than smoking itself.

When the entry door of the bar creaks open, now an unusual sound for this time of night, I look up. A wave of anger washes over me when I recognize the devilishly handsome face and icy gaze of the man entering.

He has no right to be here, not after everything he's done, and I'm too angry to pretend otherwise.

"You're not welcome here," I say to Mikhail, my voice cold and unwelcoming.

I hook my thumb to the wall of banned patrons behind my left shoulder. Most are abusive drunks, but I reserve the space front and center for the man who broke my heart.

"The wall of shame says so."

"Damn." Mikhail's smile makes me want to forget all the horrid things he has done. "I was quite the looker back in the day."

He speaks as if he already has two feet in the grave. He will if he doesn't adhere to my silent warning to leave now or peer down the wrong end of the barrel of a shotgun as per the warning above the banned patrons' mugshots.

"Though still shocked you said yes." He flashes me a wink that almost buckles my knees. "Do you remember—"

"No, I don't." I shake my head, my grip on the dishcloth tightening. "Nothing overly memorable has *ever* occurred here."

Grinning, he moseys to the counter and plops his backside on a barstool. I hope his jeans are thin. The cracked leather on the stools is famous three towns over for its skin-shredding capabilities.

"I can think of a time or two that were *extremely* memorable."

When Mikhail's eyes lower to a section of the bar that will forever conjure wicked thoughts, I throw my dishcloth in his face before twisting to face the only bartender we've managed to keep on the books.

Abram is hopeless but loyal.

"I'm heading out. Close early if no one comes in within the hour."

When Abram jerks up his chin, I gather my coat from the rack and head for the exit.

I barely make it halfway to the lot when the clomp of a heavy-footed man echoes in the quiet. Mikhail is tall and athletically built, but his feet slap the ground like the floorboards insulted his deceased mother.

"Go home, Mikhail." I twist to face him, stupidly desperate to see his eyes before finalizing my reply. "Go back to your wife and unborn child."

He recoils as if I sucker punched him, and then the most panty-wetting grin crosses his face. "Do you mean my sister and unborn niece?"

He homes in closer, like he's forgotten about the shotgun we keep behind the bar and how I can't absorb anything when his cologne lingers in my nostrils.

Did he say sister and unborn niece?

"Stands about yay high"—he fans his hand across his nipple—"blonde hair, blue eyes?"

I'm tired. I get snappy when tired. "Are you still describing your *apparent* sister?" I air quote apparent because Mikhail has no sisters. His brothers are endless, but there's been no mention of a living sister, much less one old enough to have boobs bigger than mine. "Or one of the *many* women you've been photographed with over the past ten years?"

He smirks, and I grunt, hating that he can still make me jealous after all this time.

Refusing to let him see that he's upset me, I recommence walking. "Go home, Mikhail. I don't care who it is to, as long as it's far from here."

"I'll leave..."—he delays long enough for my stomach to gurgle—"when you agree to come with me."

I wiggle my finger in my ear, certain I am going deaf. When it rewards me with nothing but a sore ear, I crank my neck back. Mikhail is standing in a kitchen that hasn't been used in years, smirking like he has the entire world at his feet.

I have news for him.

"And why would I do that?" I steal his chance to reply. "I have a life here. Family. My husband might also be opposed to the idea of me going home with an old flame."

Liar, liar, pants on fire!

The last guy I went home with still lived with his ex-wife *and* drove her minivan.

That was a shameful three years ago.

Upon spotting my disgusted expression, Mikhail laughs, grating my last nerve.

"Why is it so hard for you to believe that I've moved on?"

His eyes flash, pleased that he forced me to react. "It isn't that I don't believe you, Emmy—"

"Don't call me that."

He acts as if I never interrupted him. "It is the fact his"—he nudges his head to Abram—"eyes haven't been gouged that calls you out as a liar." Again, he steps closer, killing both my sinuses and my senses. "It doesn't matter how fancy the packaging is. If it is taken, you'd never look or let them look." A flare of jealousy darts through his eyes as he mutters, "He's been ogling your ass all night. If you were married, which I sure as fuck know you're not, he'd be bleeding from his sockets, because when Emerson Morozov's goods are claimed, only the man she let claim them is permitted to gawk."

Every word he speaks is true, but I act ignorant. "Abram is—"

"A douche." His smile... Kill. Me. Now. "I know."

Mikhail's expressions are simple to decipher. It is merely the chaos associated with them I struggle to understand. He looks like he hates me and loves me at the same time—like I'm the one who broke his heart.

My pulse throbs for an entirely different reason when Mikhail says, "He's also a thief."

He sinks back enough to expose Abram slipping a wad of cash out of his pocket and placing it into a backpack under the bar. It isn't the one we use to do a once-a-day bank deposit. It is the backpack he arrives with for each shift.

The puzzle pieces are already slotting together, but Mikhail gives them a gentle nudge. "Let me guess, you're not making enough to cover expenses on the nights he's rostered on?"

I nod, too shocked to speak.

Mikhail smiles, appreciative of my temporary wave of the white flag. "Because he's taking a fifty percent cut on all takings *and* a paycheck. Watch."

Seconds later, a regular walks in, orders a bourbon, and slaps down a twenty. He's given his change with his drink, but the twenty never makes it into the cash register. It falls into Abram's pocket before he replaces it with a lower denomination. His cut is far more than the tips some patrons leave, and it doesn't get close to the tip jar.

I usually avoid confrontations, but this thief needs to be taught a lesson.

"You're a thieving piece of shit!"

Abram's eyes twinkle with amusement when I march back to his side and demand that he empty his pockets. He follows my order. I doubt that would be the case if Mikhail hadn't traced my stomps.

Fury erupts on my face when he pulls out the twenty I watched him pocket. "Oops. How did that get in there?" He flattens out the crinkled twenty and places it into the cash register like that is the only money he stole today.

I fold my arms under my chest and arch a brow. "What about the rest?"

Abram peers at me in daftness, his expression hardening when I snatch his backpack from under the bar and rip open the zipper.

His cheeks twitch and his nostrils flare as he shouts, "Hey! That's my property. You have no right to search my property without a warrant."

He tries to rip his backpack from my grasp, but a stern rumble stops him. "If you fluff up a single strand of her hair, I will end you where you stand."

Mikhail's protectiveness isn't surprising, especially considering our location. He was the self-appointed unpaid bouncer here for almost three years. The staff respected him, the patrons feared him, and I loved him with every fiber of my being.

But he doesn't get to play that role now. He walked from the role he never applied for and the one he signed up for when he asked me to be his girl. Enough said.

After removing enough takings to pay the electric bill and our alcohol supplier's abhorrent delivery fee, I shove Abram's backpack into his chest and then give him his marching orders.

"I better not see you back here. Ever!"

He scoffs, but since Mikhail's narrowed gaze is burning a hole in his temple, he snatches his now-flat bag out of my hand and storms through the front exit doors.

"No, please," I beg when the regular follows his departure. "Your next drink is on the house."

He continues walking because he'd rather follow Abram to another drinking hole than receive a free drink. Abram can be overly generous with his servings since he doesn't have to pay for the alcohol he wastes.

With my humiliation as high as my anger, I slam shut the door our sole patron since 8 p.m. exited through, lower the bar that will keep our limited supplies safe, and then barge past Mikhail, standing frozen near books that haven't left the red for years.

"Emmy..."

I couldn't feel more embarrassed than I do at this moment, and it flattens my tone. "Don't. Just don't. This isn't your responsibility. It never has been."

My tears are close to spilling, so I double the length of my strides.

They nearly topple when I trip over my feet from Mikhail calling me out as a liar for the umpteenth time tonight. "That isn't true. I purchased half of this bar from your mother as a wedding present for you. Since we never got married, it is still in my name." He waits for me to face him before continuing. "I didn't know it had gotten this bad."

The disgust in his eyes when he drags them across the paint-peeled walls and warped floorboards guts me. We once treated this bar as if it were ours. Keeping it alive and thriving was one of the many promises he broke when he walked.

"If I had, I would have..." His words trail off to silence.

I refuse to let him off so easily. "You would have...?"

He doesn't answer me. He can't. Because that would require him to admit that he wouldn't have done shit. He would have still left, and I still would have put too much concentration on my heartache instead of the business that once kept my family's stomachs full.

"Go home, Mikhail," I repeat for the third time tonight while breaking through the back exit door. "And never come back."

Chapter 6

Mikhail

In less than twelve hours, I watch Emerson walk away from me for the third time. It stings, but this, her family's legacy appearing more like a shanty than an establishment that once attracted a thousand patrons a night, fucking burns.

Inga's pride and joy was once Lidny's hotspot. It catered to all walks of life. The rich, the poor, and everyone in between. It was so popular that I emulated its success in numerous bars and nightclubs across the country.

Its business plan made me rich.

What the fuck happened?

As disappointment smacks into me, I fight to hear both the pleas of my heart and my head. I should walk away as per Emerson's many requests, but I wasn't lying when I said I bought half this bar from her mother as a wedding present for Emerson.

My share of the once-thriving establishment gave me the capital to purchase my first watering hole. I've added two a year to my portfolio ever since.

My eyes fall to the ledgers Emerson was going over when I watched her from afar for the past hour. I only interrupted her when the gleam her eyes got at the last call for drinks sparked through her tired gaze for the quickest second.

The last call signaled that we were only an hour away from the rest of the night being solely about us. No drunk patrons, no wandering hands. It was just two teens in an empty bar that inaugurated my obsession with the retail industry that serves alcoholic beverages.

I had no clue what I wanted to be when I grew up until I walked into this bar, locked eyes with the pretty girl behind the counter, and grew an obsession with anything she had an interest in.

I didn't even have a favorite color until I took in Emerson's sea-moss-green eyes for the first time.

With my reputation on the line and my name still on the deed, I ignore the niggle in my gut warning me that this is a bad idea. I snatch up the books months overdue to be balanced and a bottle of whiskey from the shelf before I kick open the door of the only space that offered Emerson and me an ounce of privacy from a world determined to tear us apart.

———

I don't know how much time passes before I detect that I'm being watched. My ass is dead, the whiskey is half-empty, and I'm reasonably sure the wetness in the corner of my mouth is drool. It isn't thick enough to announce I've been asleep for hours, but it indicates that I slept sometime between Emerson's departure and her return.

Emerson's eyes, just as puffy as mine, shoot down to the books I've balanced before they return to my face.

"Before you say anything," I blurt out before she can speak.

My head is thumping and I drank on an empty stomach, but none of that matters right now. This—*she*—is far more important.

"Your supplier is overcharging. The price list he gave you is the retail price of the goods, not the wholesale cost." I hold my finger in the air when she attempts to interrupt me. "When you cut deliveries from three deliveries a week to one, he didn't remove the extra two charges from your monthly statements. He's also charging import fees on products made right fucking here in our own country."

Emerson's expression matches mine when I unearthed the error. "That dirty rotten scoundrel."

I nod, agreeing with her. "I contacted Darris on your behalf last night. He wasn't happy about my midnight call, but he shut the fuck up when I reminded him whose name is also on the deed of this business."

Her brows are tightly knitted, but they don't match the relief shooting through her eyes.

Her angry expression switches entirely to thankful when I say, "Your account will be credited with the missing funds before the bar opens this afternoon. The amount isn't life-changing, but it will cover most of *those*."

I wave my hand at the overdue bills tacked to the noticeboard next to her desk before standing to my feet and stretching. My body is all twisted up, and I'm sure I'll be dodging bullets soon, so it's better to stretch now than after I'm shot.

Emerson surprises me. She doesn't come out lock, stock, and barrel for me interfering in a business I will never see as mine. She takes in the updated books with the eagle eye of a first-year accountant before she strays her eyes to the bottle of whiskey that kept me awake long enough to unearth the numerous injustices.

This is the one part of my business I hate. The larcenous pricks who think they can take you for a row because you're young, and in Emerson's case, female. I'd be nowhere near as successful if I had tits instead of balls, and the knowledge pisses me off.

When Emerson's eyes, now narrowed, return to my face, and she cocks a manicured brow, I reach for my wallet. "Do you take Amex?"

As her teeth get friendly with her bottom lip, she nods. "We do, but..."

I'm not a fan of delayed gratification—for anything. But it is worse with this woman.

"You don't need to pay." I mistake the sincerity in her tone when she snaps out, "I will remove its purchase from the funds I'll transfer to you when you tell me how much I owe for the gift you *allegedly* purchased for me."

I stare at her in shock, stunned by the harshness of her tone.

Is she joking? She can't be mad. She has no right. I went on a limb to buy *her* a gift I knew she would love. The only reason I didn't hand it over was because she left me. Yet she's pissed at me?

Fuck that.

If she wants to be petty, I'll show her petty.

"*My* share of this business is not for sale."

She looks ready to blow her top. Her cheeks are red, her neck is flushed, and her nostrils are flaring.

She could only look more ravishing if she was moaning beneath me.

I give myself a stern talking-to before getting this train back on track. "But I am open to compromise."

Emerson's dazzling eyes sparkle as they dance between mine. "For what? I have nothing of value to offer you. Except perhaps..." Her words trail off as the heat on her neck stretches to her chest—her barely concealed chest since she's wearing an extremely fitted and low-neck-line shirt.

It's fucking winter. Did she miss the memo?

Her tits didn't. Her nipples are standing to attention, begging to be touched. Goose bumps dot her areolas, and I stare as if I have every right, as if I paid for the privilege.

Her game plan smacks into me as hard and fast as I once took her on the very desk wedged between us.

Emerson knows her appeal, and a long time ago, I folded every time she used it against me.

I'm older now.

Wiser.

And seconds from drooling on my fucking shoes.

Emerson's breasts are centerfold worthy. They were the second thing I noticed about her, only cheated out of the top prize by a face too beautiful for any painter to replicate.

Emerson stops fighting the urge to lower her eyes to my crotch to assess if her plan is working when I say, "Marry me."

Her eyes rocket to my face so fast that she makes me dizzy. "Huh?"

"Marry me," I repeat. "Then, if you survive a year, I'll sign over my share of the deed to you."

Spit flies from her mouth when she *pffts* me. "I'd rather rot in hell." She saunters around the desk, barges me aside, and then takes charge of the captain's chair. "It's no skin off my nose if you keep your share of *my* business. It isn't like I'll have to send you a small fortune every month." She peers up at me, her eyes glistening with impudence. "At this rate, you'll have to pay me to keep this place open."

She acts as if that line didn't hurt her to deliver as much as it did me to hear it.

She's full of shit, and I know it.

That doesn't mean I won't partially fold, though.

"The deed... and a cash settlement."

"Not interested," she responds, not bothering to look up.

I make her interested in a deal I know she won't be able to deny. "A cash settlement in advance, hefty enough to allow your mother to undertake a treatment option she hasn't told you about because she knows how far you'd go to lasso the moon for her."

Now I have her—hook, line, and fucking sinker.

I play it cool—just.

"You were willing to sell a piece of your body to the devil to save this"—I wave my hand around the office before guiding it down her scarcely covered body—"so how far are you willing to go to save your mother's life?"

"I'd sell my soul to the devil," she answers without pause for thought, her scorn announcing who she believes is the evil half of our duo.

For some fucked-up reason, she's lumped the title with me.

"But not just the part *he* chewed up and spat out a decade ago. I'd give him *every* piece of me."

I fight the urge to tell her I'm not the bad guy. I only harness the desire because our combined stubbornness will shunt us back to the start of our game.

Neither of us has time for that, and Inga's schedule is even tighter.

"Then accept my proposal." I dump our marriage agreement onto the desk, minus the page that announces how wealthy she will be at the end of our exchange, before collecting my suit jacket. "The priest agreed to set aside thirty minutes for us today."

"Today?"

I continue as if not interrupted. "Our allotted time is an hour away. If you make it down the aisle *this time*"—she snarls with me during my last two words—"I'll wire the money for your mother's cancer treatment the instant we say I do. If you fail to arrive..." I *tsk* like the money hasn't already left my account. "I wish you well in finding another way to fund her *vitally necessary* medical treatment."

It kills me, but I walk away like she means nothing to me.

Chapter 7

Emerson

My eyes stray from the excessive figure stated next to the first item on the agenda of my proposed marriage contract with Mikhail to my mother in the doorway of my room when I notice her presence.

The number cited is enough to pay my mother's mortgage arrears and bring her payments two months ahead, and all I have to do is stand across from Mikhail and act like I didn't rehearse saying "I do" in front of a mirror a million times to that exact man.

It is easy money.

I hope.

Curiosity echoes in my mother's tone when she finally announces the cause of her arrival. "Aunt Marcelle said you inherited one of Mikhail's businesses?"

"No," I reply, nervously gushing while hoping she won't recognize the lace peeking out of the bottom of my oversized trench coat.

I only wore this dress once, a long time ago, for not even an hour, but its design is highly telling. It is the wedding dress I asked my mother to make when Mikhail and I had planned to marry with an intimate ceremony for two.

"That isn't what I meant. I didn't inherit Mikhail's business. I was... given... a share of his businesses."

That was the worst lie I've ever told, but my mother acts oblivious. "So you're going away with him to work it out?"

I half nod, half grimace. "Since Mikhail used the equity in the bar to purchase his first business, we kind of own a share of all of his businesses." I take back my earlier confession. This lie is far worse than the latter. "To have everything transferred back to the correct names, I have to meet with his acquisition lawyer and sign a heap of paperwork. It should only take a week or two." I quickly scan the top terms noted in the contract before saying, "Three at the most."

I don't need to stay for the twelve months of the schedule. I'll have enough funds to get the bar out of the red and back on track by the end of the first week of our marriage. The following two to three weeks are purely cushioning for if Darris tries to renege on his agreement with Mikhail this morning.

"Do you have to leave right away?" my mother asks, her tone devastated as she takes in the bag I'm packing in a hurry.

"Yes. Ah... Mikhail said something about the jet being double-booked, so if we don't leave by noon, we won't be able to fly out for another week."

I receive more one-way tickets to hell at the end of my sentence. I deserve them. This is what happens when you try to seduce your arch-nemesis instead of using morally upstanding methods.

It isn't my fault. I forgot a decade had passed since Mikhail had fallen for the needy-bunny ruse I used anytime I found him sleeping behind my desk.

His head was flopped, his mouth was slightly ajar, and his thick arms were folded in front of his chest. He looked like he did multiple times when we dated. Back then, his exhaustion was more sexually based than from brain fatigue, though.

"That wouldn't be so bad," my aunt chimes in, joining us in my childhood bedroom.

Don't look at me like that. I moved out of my mother's home years ago. I only returned when my mother's cancer diagnosis meant she struggled to shower and perform other daily tasks.

"We've missed Mikhail. Haven't we, Inga? We would have happily accommodated him for a week."

I'm saved from an embarrassing conversation by an unlikely source. "Who's Mikhail?"

I glance past my mother's shoulder, my mouth falling open when I spot the innocent face of my baby sister. "Two missed school days in a row? You should buy a lottery ticket. I've never been so lucky. I broke my foot, and I still had to attend classes the same afternoon."

"Because you don't need functioning feet to write," my mother and aunt say at the same time.

Wynne laughs, then coughs, bringing up my defenses.

"Is she okay?"

My mother pats her back while replying, "Yes. She is a little under the weather. That's why she's home from school." She hands me another reason why I must accept Mikhail's offer. "She has a doctor's appointment this afternoon."

Doctor visits are expensive, and we now no longer have health insurance.

I ponder pushing Mikhail's leniencies out by an hour or two until I recall how he left my office without looking back. He doesn't seem the type to offer compassion anymore. He once cared for my mother, but he negotiated with her health like her soul was his for trading.

I'd never speak to him again if I had any other option. The treatment stated in the contract is over two hundred thousand dollars. I could never come up with the funds in enough time, so I have no choice. I must marry the man I'm growing to hate or bury my mother.

Tears burst in my eyes just considering the latter, and it fortifies my decision.

"Will you ring me after Wynne's consultation?"

"Of course," my mother replies, instantly appeasing my worry. "But I'm sure it is nothing."

"Still, please keep me updated. Not just on Wynne's appointment, but also on your upcoming ones."

"Of course, darling," she repeats, eyeing me suspiciously. "I hope you will do the same."

"With?" I say with a laugh, stupidly nervous.

"On your getaway with Mikhail. I'm sure the time you'll spend together will inevitably stir up some old feelings. When they arrive, I'm happy to listen."

I *pfft* like she didn't hit the nail on the head. "I highly doubt I will see him. Furthermore, we were young and dumb back then. We've both moved on."

When did lying become as easy as breathing to me?

Mikhail moved on with a bevy of big-breasted blondes, but the one from the will reading isn't on the long list of many that the media has kept the public abreast with. She's married to his brother, who now has a different surname.

During my lackluster sleep last night, I tried to make sense of the deceptive web currently weaved around the Dokovics. All the endless news articles rewarded me with was a headache.

"Emmy..."

I hate the concern in my mother's voice, and for the umpteenth time this morning, it fills me with worry that I'm making a horrible mistake.

"I'll stay in touch. If *anything* pops up, you'll be the first to know."

My aunt Marcelle's eyes bulge out of her head. "*Anything*, anything... or just any old thing?"

I'm reminded how much I love being raised by strong, independent women when I reply without the slightest hesitation. "*Anything*."

I laugh when Aunt Marcelle fans her overheated cheeks. "Oh dear. I think I'm having a hot flush."

Chapter 8

Mikhail

As I stand at the end of a long line of church pews, my heart beats fitfully. The priest is waiting at the end of the altar, peering at me curiously. I can't bring myself to stand next to him. I've been there, done that. It ended in heartbreak.

The thought of Emerson not showing up again makes me want to fold in two. I don't know why I'm worried. Our arrangement will benefit Emerson more than it ever will me. I have enough money to live off, plenty to survive without inheriting a penny of my grandfather's dirty money.

I must be a sucker for pain. What other reason would I be here with palms drenched in sweat and a wave of anger I'll never fully suffocate overwhelming me?

Definitely a sucker for pain.

As I stray my eyes across the church, memories of the last time I was here fill my head. We booked this church and priest the last time we decided to get married.

Emerson is a girlie girl, so I thought she'd want a big white wedding with all her family and friends in attendance. Her suggestion that we elope shocked me.

I assumed her decision was to save her mother from offering to pay for her only daughter's wedding.

How fucking dumb was I?

My sigh echoes throughout the empty church. There are no attendees to witness our union, and there is no fanfare. It is a replica of the empty church I stood in for over three hours a decade ago, waiting for Emerson to show up.

Back then, we were marrying for love, not money.

Or so I thought.

I'm still in the dark about Emerson's decision to end things. There's no guarantee she will turn up today, either. The lengths she will go to for her family are undeniable, but is her hatred for me stronger?

Ten years ago, I would have cockily declared she'd most likely arrive at the church before me. Now, I scan the face of every motorist who drives past Emerson's old family church, confident none of them will ever be her.

Sighing, I glance at my watch before peering at the priest. It is past the time I told Emerson to meet me, and I'm done pretending it isn't.

After a farewell chin dip to Father Loroza, I turn to leave. The embarrassment that Emerson fooled me twice is bombarding me enough to last a lifetime.

I break through double doors keeping the cool air from whipping between the church pews, and that's when I see her. Emerson is at the entrance of the church, looking as ruffled as I feel.

Our eyes meet, and her fretful expression softens before she reminds me that she's not accustomed to the high life I've lived for the past ten years.

"I forgot how much of a bitch it is to get through town in the middle of the day. It is like everyone goes out for lunch at the same time." Her eyes flick to the priest, and she grimaces about her potty mouth. "Sorry, Father."

He bows his head in acceptance of her apology before he asks if we're ready to begin.

I look at Emerson and then bite back a smile. She's eagerly nodding while undoing the buttons of a faded trench coat. Her expression is effortless, and her smile is genuine.

My lungs refuse to take in air as she removes her winter jacket, revealing a dress that demands the attention of every man in the room, despite its simplicity. The delicate fabric of a white lace dress flows gracefully down her body, hugging her curves and cascading to the floor in soft waves. Her hair is loose, framing her gorgeous face, and her makeup is a soft palette that hides her uncomposed demeanor.

Her eyes, still my favorite shade of green, hold a mixture of emotions. The most obvious are apprehension and determination, but that isn't all they display. She is also nervous.

As she walks toward me, I notice the subtle details that make her unique—the delicate arch of her reddish brows, the teasing curve of her plump lips, and the faintest rouge of color on her cheeks that has nothing to do with the makeup she applied in a hurry.

She carries herself with confidence, and each step she takes is measured and purposeful.

Her fingers brush mine when she accepts the bouquet of daises I purchased at the last minute from a florist two doors up from the church. Her smile, though small, is genuine when she whispers her thanks. It lights up her face, momentarily dispelling the tension plaguing our gathering.

"Are you ready?" I ask, my voice barely above a whisper.

The feeling of dread I couldn't shake earlier shifts when she dips her chin without pause for thought.

We walk down the aisle side by side, my nerves calming more with each step. Being with Emerson once felt as natural as breathing. It is similar now, just more tense.

When we reach the priest, we face each other and recite our vows as per the priest's instructions.

"I, Mikhail, take you, Emerson, as my lawfully wedded wife. I promise to support you, honor you, and stand by your side through all the challenges life may bring. I vow to respect you and to fulfill the commitments we have made to each other today until death do us part."

Emerson's focus is steadfast now, and I find strength in her determination when she returns my vow. "I, Emerson, take you, Mikhail, as my lawfully wedded husband. I promise to support you, honor you, and stand by your side through all the challenges life may bring. I vow to respect you and to fulfill the commitments we have made to each other today until death do us part."

Her eyes flare with mischievousness at the end of her vow, piquing my curiosity. However, the priest continues the ceremony before I can wordlessly grill her about it. "These rings are a symbol of marriage, a tangible reminder of the promises you've made today."

Father Loroza hands us the rings I will go to my grave pretending I purchased only seconds before we wed, before he gestures for us to gift them to each other.

Emerson's hand trembles slightly when I slide the ring onto her finger, the metal cool against her skin.

She takes a big breath before doing the same to me.

The priest's voice is as smooth as chocolate as he speaks the final words of the ceremony. "In the sight of God and the power vested in me, I now pronounce you husband and wife." He flicks his kind eyes to me. "You may kiss your bride."

Emerson leans in first, her eagerness catching me off guard.

I learn why when she draws in closer. A familiar scent wafts into my nose. It is nutty and buttery and announces that Emerson clung to one part of our vows while reciting them. The last five words. *Until death do us part.*

My back molars grind together as a mix of emotions envelops me. Emerson knows about my severe nut allergy. During our three-year relationship, she always carried an EpiPen with her, aware one stray nut could kill me.

Like a glutton for punishment, I lean in closer and flare my nostrils. The scent emanating from her mouth is unmistakable. Enough peanut butter to kill me coats her tongue, and a droplet of grease smears one corner of her full mouth.

As I inch back, a smile plays on my lips. I had hoped the woman I'd fallen in love with was still there, hidden beneath the years of dishonesty weighing her down.

This is more than I expected.

I conceal my smile while searching her eyes, seeking an explanation.

Emerson's expression remains unreadable, and it frustrates me more than her wish to kill me. Not that long ago, I could read her like a book.

I also hate that I'm losing a battle I had no clue I wanted to win until now, and I am done playing fairly.

Despite the pleas of my head, I band my arm around Emerson's waist and tug her in close. Her chest flattens against mine, and our crotches align, but the hiss she releases when she learns the response my body had to her cock-thickening dress is what I pay the most attention to.

She doesn't want me dead.

She wants me at her mercy and on my fucking knees.

The swift resurrection of her gall already has me halfway there.

As I press my lips to the shell of her ear, the scent of peanut butter lingers between us. It is a bitter reminder of the complexities of our union and the fuel needed to even the field of our coupling.

"Deny me again, and I'll show Father Loroza, on this very fucking altar, that a mouth isn't the only place a man can kiss *his* wife."

When she involuntarily tremors, I kiss the edge of her mouth, my embrace brief and mechanical, before I stomp down the aisle as I did ten years ago—without my bride at my side.

Chapter 9

Emerson

As I scan my eyes over a private jet gleaming in the late afternoon sun, I stuff the EpiPen I hid in my bra into the bottom of my knapsack. My pettiness is pressing heavily on my chest, but the confusion swirling in my mind is even more overwhelming.

I'm so confused. From what I've read, Mikhail is wealthy in his own right. He doesn't need his grandfather's money. So why did he marry me as if he's desperate for some coin?

I guess someone who's never had money can explain its allure. Before my mother got sick, my family lived comfortably, but it was never at this level of wealth. The private jet idling next to us is flashy, as sparkling as the diamonds now caressing my ring finger.

The taste of peanut butter lingers in my mouth as a shadow casts over half my torso. Mikhail is standing at my door, preparing to open it. I can see the hurt in his eyes, the confusion, but since those emotions are barely visible behind the arrogance of a man who left his wife standing at the altar for the second time in his life, I pretend not to notice them.

I refuse to let him blindside me like he did when he threatened to defile me on the altar of my family's long-serving church.

It pains me to admit, but I swallowed the bait he threw out without chewing it. My head was so airy from his closeness that the only thought that crossed it when he walked away was how I could deny him again and force him to make true on his threat.

The lightbulb only switched back on when the priest coughed, announcing I'd been dumped again—*after* our vows this time.

Mikhail's walkout told me everything I needed to know.

Our marriage is a sham. It is a ploy for payment.

Only a fool would act as if it were anything else.

So, instead of waiting for my husband to open my door and lift me into his arms like a groom would to a bride, I throw it open so fast that it skims past his crotch, almost castrating him.

"Jesus fucking Christ, Emmy! You almost took out my cock."

"Only almost? *Boohoo.*" I glare at him, warning him what will happen if he calls me Emmy again, before I march toward the jet.

"Where are you going, Emmy?" Mikhail's shout cuts my stomps in half before he quickly recovers. "Emerson? Our ride is that way."

He hooks his thumb to the left, and my heart falls to my shoes.

The deathtrap he's pointing to isn't a jet.

It's a sardine can.

I talk through the lump in my throat. "I'm not getting in... whatever the hell that is."

"That"—Mikhail smirks, loving my uncomfortable squirms—"is a Cessna 152." Since I'm still lost, he adds, "It's a plane. It just has two seats instead of dozens."

"One." I point to him. "Two." Now it's my chest's turn to be jabbed. "Three." I draw his focus to a random pilot, hoping he knows what the hell he's doing, even in a baby plane. "You're one seat short. I guess I better stay here."

I'd sit on my suitcase if I had one. Mikhail's one-hour demand left hardly any wriggle room. It takes twenty-eight minutes to travel from the bar to my mother's house and another twenty-eight minutes from my house to the church. I spent the remaining four minutes assuring my family that my departure wasn't forever.

From the hardness of Mikhail's cock when he flattened our bodies together, I believe his tight schedule was on purpose.

If he's hopeful a lack of luggage will have me prancing butt-naked around his fancy-schmancy new mansion he inherited when we tied the knot, he's shit out of luck.

I'll wear a potato sack if that's all on offer. Mikhail knows this better than anyone.

My eyes snap to him when he says, "There are only two seats because there are only two travelers."

I glare at him like he's grown a second head when he accepts a flight manifest from a man in a pilot's uniform before he slips into the cockpit of the baby plane.

"He can't be serious," I murmur to anyone listening when he fiddles with buttons and instruments like he's about to take this bird into the air. "He doesn't know how to fly a plane, does he?" My curiosity is too high to discount, so I tilt to the side and shout, "Do you know what you're doing? I swear there are laws where you must disclose that you're a trainer pilot to intended passengers before luring them into a deathtrap."

Mikhail laughs, and it does crazy things to my insides. "Come on, Emmy. Don't act like this will be the first time I've made you float between the clouds."

I snarl at him, but that is the beginning and end of my reply.

I'm too busy struggling not to squeeze my thighs together from how sexy he looks in his broke man's plane. The headset has pulled his messy locks away from his face, showcasing his panty-wetting bone structure; the microphone sits intimately close to his plump, meaty lips, and he's rolled the sleeves of his business shirt to his elbows, exposing his cut arms.

He also didn't lie.

45

Some days, it took hours for me to float back to earth.

Mikhail's orgasms don't float stars in front of your eyes.

They send you into space.

Since I'm struggling to keep a rational head with several feet between us, I make an excuse to leave. "I'm scared of—"

My phone pings, interrupting me.

Tears form in my eyes when I read the message.

MOM:

> You're probably still in the air, so you won't get this until you land, but I needed you to know first.

The document attached to her message announces her inclusion into the program that could save her life has been approved.

My fingers move over my phone screen at a million miles an hour.

ME:

> This is amazing.

I try to hold back, but it isn't in my nature.

ME:

> But why is this the first I've heard about this program?

Her message pops up instantly, which makes me suspicious she had it pre-typed.

MOM:

> Because acceptance wasn't guaranteed, I kept my application quiet until I was sure they would accept me. I have some trial medication to take now before an in-house consultation in four weeks. You should be back in time, but if not, no bother. Aunt Marcelle has offered to hold down the fort.

I wipe at a rogue tear clinging to my cheek. It smears across my phone screen when I reply.

ME:

I'll be back in time. But...

I stare at the last word I typed for eternity before I delete it and then stab the send button.

It takes my mother a lot longer to reply this time.

MOM:

Okay. I will call you later to tell you more.

I assume she's rushing off because she still believes aircrafts crash if anyone dares to switch on their phones midflight, but my assumption changes when I receive another message.

MOM:

Wynne is being called in by Doctor Clestonv.

My fingers fly even faster than before, yet my good luck message sits unread while I watch my phone, hoping for a notification.

Defeated and somewhat nauseous, I stow my phone away before focusing back on the task at hand. My face still shows my wish to flee. I just can't bring myself to do it now. The very man I'm endeavoring to run from paid for the trial program that could save my mother's life.

The reminder has me shouting, "Are you sure you know what you're doing?"

"Are we talking about flying a plane or making you come?" I roll my eyes, and Mikhail laughs. "I've got you for both if you'll get your damn ass in the plane."

When he nudges his head, soundlessly demanding me into his toy plane, I accept the hand being held out by a tarmac crew member before endeavoring to slot into the seat next to Mikhail.

I enter tits first, and then legs.

My ass is the last body part stripped from view.

Yes, it is as awkward as you're imagining, but I felt the heat of the crew member's watch, and the only time I refuse to not make Mikhail realize what he threw away is when I'm six feet under.

"I'll get it," Mikhail snaps out when the crewman attempts to fasten my harness, beginning the task at my chest.

Mikhail rips the straps out of the crewman's hands while narrowing his eyes at him. His response starts a point tally system that was reset over a decade ago.

Point one, Emmy.

Furious heat teems through me when Mikhail tugs hard on the restraints a second after latching my harness. It paints my dress to my skin and exposes my body's response to his closeness.

My nipples are erect and begging to be touched, and although enough lace covers my sticky panties, the scent lingering in the air announces my aroused state.

Mikhail flicks his eyes to my breasts for the quickest second before he returns them to the many instruments and buttons in front of him.

His effortless expression and ease with preparing the plane for takeoff announce this wasn't a last-minute decision to stain my underwear. He knows what he's doing and loves my panicked squirms as much as I do his jealous glares.

After requesting permission from the control tower to approach the runway, the plane jerks toward the landing strip. Partway there, Mikhail nudges his head to something behind my left shoulder. "If you want to talk during the flight, you'll need to put on your headset."

He says *your* like they're exactly that. Mine.

My throat grows scratchy when I tug on the strap holding the headset in place, and it tumbles into my lap. The headband has a name etched on its side.

Emmy.

While fighting back a sob that he customized my headset, I free it from its cables before placing the speakers over my ears.

48

I can't hear anything but the raging beat of my heart. I discover why when I peer down at my lap. The jack remains unplugged.

Mikhail and I reach for the port simultaneously. Despite my solemn vow to hate this man until the end of time, sparks jolt up my arm when our fingers brush.

It is so electrifying that I remain frozen while Mikhail mics me up.

Seconds later, his heavy breaths sound out of the speakers, dotting my skin with goose bumps, before his deep, commanding voice dampens my panties. "Can you hear me?"

I nod, untrusting of my voice not to betray the excitement of my body.

"If you want to speak, just hit this button." He points to an unilluminated microphone button in a panel in front of me. "I won't be able to hear you unless you push the button. Understood?"

Again, I nod.

I want to ask a million questions, like when was my name engraved on my headset, but I lose the chance to say anything when an air traffic controller gives takeoff instructions to Mikhail.

I listen with interest, suddenly fascinated.

Fear should be gripping me. I've never been on a plane, much less one this small, but fright is the last thing on my mind. I've barely lived the past ten years, so the thudding of my pulse in my ears is extremely cherished and missed.

After a handful of instructions and a brief weather update, Mikhail looks at me. He smiles as if he can feel the thrumming of my veins before asking, "Ready to take this bird in the air?"

His smile augments when I nod. It is embarrassingly eager but the most honest I've been for an extremely long time.

The faster the plane races down the runway, the more my pulse quickens. It is thrilling and scary at the same time, like a rollercoaster ride or an orgasm after prolonged foreplay.

As the plane lifts into the sky, my hands seek something to clutch. There are no door handles, no bracings. There's nothing but Mikhail's thigh that I sink my nails into the instant a weird stomach-dropping sensation hits my midsection.

"That's normal," Mikhail announces, bringing my breaths down a notch but doing little to save his thigh from being shredded. "As is that," he adds when a second weird screech fills my ears. "That's the wheels tucking in."

I stab the mic button, my hand shaky, before saying, "Don't we need them?"

He winks at me, increasing both my giddiness and my clutch. "Not while we're in the air. I'll bring them back down before we land."

"Which is how long away?"

I'm not scared. I am merely wondering how long the best foreplay of my life will last. This is exhilarating, but for all I know, it could be over as fast as our quickie marriage ceremony.

I only skimmed the contract terms. I have no clue where we're going or how long it will take us to get there.

I stop drinking in endless miles of snow-battered countryside when Mikhail says, "Depends."

Eagerness and another emotion I can't quite describe highlight my tone when I jab the mic button again. "On what?"

There's a radio crackle, and then, "On how long we want to stay up here."

I'm lost. Completely and wholly lost.

Mikhail laughs as if my daftness is cute. I'd whack him for his misconception if I knew how to fly and land a plane. Mikhail once said my chin jabs could take down a world champ. He was most likely lying, but I'm unwilling to test the theory while thousands of feet in the air.

"I thought we were going to the estate you inherited?" I almost said *our marital home,* but changed things up when the thought alone had me choking up.

Our plan was to go house hunting after our elopement and honeymoon. I unpacked boxes alone in a new sublet apartment six weeks later.

That was the first time it sank in to me that he wasn't coming back.

"We are." Mikhail waits a beat before saying, "But that's only a three-hour drive away, and it doesn't have an airstrip."

My brows furrow, sprouting lines across my forehead. "Then why are we in a plane?"

"Because I spent a fuck ton of money on her and didn't get to take her out once. So I thought, what the hell, why not do it now?" A flash of anger he's too slow to shut down says the words his mouth refuses to speak.

This was another wedding gift. That's why my name is engraved on the headset.

Mikhail didn't have a dime to his name when we met. Well, he did, but it was swallowed by the jukebox at my family's bar seconds before he asked me to dance.

During our courtship, I knew his family was rich and ruled all aspects of his life with an iron fist, but I didn't know the full extent of their influential power and wealth until the month before we broke up.

Mikhail had recently turned twenty-one, so the trust fund he had no clue about paid out. He was a little flashy with some things he purchased, like a service for the jukebox, some newer, updated records for us to groove to, and an engagement ring for me. But for the most part, he was responsible with his money.

Or so I thought.

Emmy isn't engraved on just my headset. It is on Mikhail's as well, and it is the name he gives the air traffic control officer when he announces that we've reached our desired elevation. "Lidny Traffic, Emmy 152, seven thousand feet."

As the control tower replies, I remove my hand from Mikhail's thigh and stray my eyes to the scenery, needing time to think.

I don't understand Mikhail's game plan. Honestly, I don't. Why would he buy a plane and name it after me and purchase half of my mother's bar, then throw away our relationship as if it were worthless?

Did the gaudy purchases make him realize he deserved better than me?

They must have, because that's the only explanation I can come up with as to the cause of his motive to end everything, and it pisses me off.

"We should go back. I don't like this. You..."

I stop talking when my shaky hand causes me to flick the mic button on and off during my last two sentences. The break in transmission and the crackle of our connection make it seem as if I said *I don't like you* instead of I don't like this, and the misconception ensures I'm not the only one now angry and confused.

Chapter 10

Mikhail

Taking Emerson to the private airstrip was a mistake. I wasn't thinking with my head when I made my decision. I also wasn't thinking with my heart. My dick took center stage like it did anytime Emerson negotiated with her body to get her way.

I thought maybe if she saw how hard I had been trying to give her the best life before she dumped me, she'd stop treating me like the enemy and, instead, give me the respect of a man she tore to fucking shreds.

I should have known better.

One of Emerson's best traits is her spitfire stubbornness. I love that she won't take shit from anyone. I just never anticipated I'd be her target one day instead of her spotter.

My phone rings as our chauffeur-driven car glides down a long driveway. I smile when I see the name flashing across the screen. Emerson snarls.

Our opposite responses remind me of the tit-for-tat game we kept a tally of our entire relationship, and it has me mentally calculating ways to even the score.

Shandi Boyes

After sliding my thumb across the screen, I squash my phone to my ear. "Hey, sunshine. Miss me already?"

Andrik, in a muffled voice, threatens to kill me unless I choose a new nickname for his wife. He believes I only give pet names to the girls I want to fuck. Since he is on the money, I screw up my nose before fighting the urge to gag. I didn't know Zoya was my sister when I gave her my digits and a nickname.

The rueful churns of my stomach weaken when Zoya asks, "Konstantine is tracking your movements. He said you've arrived at Zelenolsk Manor, but the tint on your SUV is too dark to infiltrate with a drone, so he's clueless if you're with company or riding solo. Please tell me she said yes."

I take a moment to digest all the secrets she spilled before I fling my eyes to Emerson.

She is trying to act unaffected by both my conversation and the nickname I gave.

She's a shit actor.

Jealousy has never looked better.

It has me pushing on the brakes earlier than planned. "I'm with company."

A snippet of conceitedness prickles goose bumps on Emerson's nape.

I squash them like a bug after recalling the last words she spoke to me.

I don't like you.

"But I can lose her for a few hours if you have something in mind."

Zoya gasps before talking at a million miles an hour. "Mikhail Marshmallow Man Dokovic, you're playing with fire."

"So?"

I'm not worried. Emerson looks set to crush my nuts with her teeth, but for some fucked-up reason, I am more excited by the prospect than scared.

Emerson isn't just good in bed.

She's fucking dynamite.

I've not met a woman with her level of stamina, and I never will.

Zoya continues to push. "Do you know what happens when a marshmallow gets too close to a fire?" She doesn't wait for me to answer. She squeals in my ear, "*He* turns into a soft, gooey mess."

Red-hot heat races across Emerson's face when I reply, "As I've told you previously, my heart is the only soft and gooey thing about me, sweetheart. The rest is hard and thumping."

I'm dead in all meanings of the word. Not just from the death stare Emerson hits me with, but also from the growl of my brother, who would kill, and has killed, a man with allergies for sniffing too close to his wife.

I just scribbled my name at the top of Andrik's hit list.

"Say goodbye to Mikhail, *милая*." Andrik's tone is controlled, almost reserved—until he adds, "Permanently."

I laugh like I'm not a dead man before trying to save face. It is two seconds after Emerson throws open the SUV's door and hightails it to the entrance full of employees I have no clue what to do with. I've lived alone since the day Emerson left me high and dry. I hate sleeping in a house full of bodies, especially when I don't know any of them.

After watching Emerson enter our marital home at the speed of a rocket, I say, "Give me until tomorrow afternoon before showing up at my door. I'm sure there will be something left to pick from my carcass."

Andrik growls, but that is the start and end of his reprimand.

Zoya isn't as eager to let bygones be bygones. "This would be a lot easier if you told her you're doing this for her instead of yourself, Marshmallow Man."

I *pfft* her as if she is stupid.

It couldn't be further from the truth. Her smarts are undeniable when she says, "You still love her, Mikhail. The sooner you accept that, the easier it will be for all involved."

"She left me, not the other way around. My feelings don't matter."

"Are you sure about that?" Zoya snaps out just as fast, her emotions just as heavy.

I lose the chance to clarify which response she's seeking clarification on when Andrik repeats his earlier request. "Say goodbye to Mikhail, *милая*."

He adds a handful more words to the end of his reply. But since I want to sleep at some stage tonight, I'll keep them out of my mouth.

Sometimes the worst nightmares form from words.

Mine started with three.

She isn't coming.

After tossing my cell onto the console in front of me, I rake my fingers through my hair. I'm tired as fuck, frustrated, and hard enough to drill for gold.

I didn't lie when I said fighting was foreplay for Emerson and me. We fought as often as we fucked, which was a record-high tally for two teens with no privacy.

But it's different now.

The pain is real.

The feeling of betrayal is real.

The way she looks at me like she hates me is real.

I fucking hate the latter more than anything.

With my lungs replenished and my mind forced into lockdown mode, I slip out the back of the SUV and head in the direction Emerson fled. I've been to this estate before. It was a long time ago. You lose interest in returning to the place that caused enough abuse to fill a family album with pictures of your numerous hospital stays once you reach your formative years.

This estate was one of my grandfather's favorites. The reminder has me again lost as to why he would gift it to me. I wasn't his favorite grandson. He hated us all the same.

If he thinks this is his free pass to heaven, I have news for him.

Soulless men only travel one way when they die.

Straight to hell.

"No. Thank you. I'm fine." I repeat my three short sentences multiple times while moving through the many bodies lined up outside the palatial mansion.

They stare at me as if I'm royalty and they're here to obey my every whim.

If the lusty gleams of the barely clothed women at the side of the den are anything to go by, that's the sole task of their job description.

Prostitution is as rife in politics as it is in bratva entities. The titles of the women selling their bodies are just altered to make them seem less dubious.

After shrugging out of my jacket, I scan the numerous bodies throughout the mansion, seeking a familiar face. Kolya will be here somewhere. He was my grandfather's chief of staff, and even after his boss's death, he remains his number one right-hand man.

Haunting me appears to have been my grandfather's dying wish, and Kolya is the best man to help him achieve that. He's been a thorn in my ass for over two decades, and I can't wait to see the back of him. I just need to wait until the end of Inga's treatment since that term added new provisions to the inheritance terms.

I find Kolya near the west entrance, drinking a pricy bourbon. Although my first thoughts should be on the multiple business objectives I set aside today, I let my heart speak for the first time in years. "Emerson?"

It might have been different if I hadn't received a text from Kolya minutes before taking Emmy, the plane, up for the first time.

Igna's inclusion into the immunotherapy trial is the sole reason Emerson entered the plane I'd purchased for her. But at the time, I wanted to pretend it was more than that.

For an hour, I wanted to pretend she didn't break my heart.

Our truce didn't even last ten minutes.

As I *pfft*, Kolya places down his whiskey before spinning to face me. "I had Loretta show Mrs. Dokovic to her room."

"Which is?" I ask, straying my eyes across the numerous doors on the second level.

This mansion has over thirty sleeping quarters, and there are too many bodies for me to detect one.

Well, that's what my head is telling my cock.

I stop looking in the direction I sense Emerson is in when Kolya answers, "The primary suite, of course." His pitch peaks during his following sentence. "This is your home now, so the owner's wing was prepared for your arrival." He attempts to catch me in a lie in front of an audience. "Unless you'd like me to arrange alternative accommodations for you? The east wing has a beautiful vista of the—"

I lose the utmost devotion of many eyes when I interrupt. "The owner's wing is fine."

If anyone not involved in the disbursement of my grandfather's estate discovers my marriage is fraudulent, the entire inheritance will be forfeited, including any payments already made.

I can handle bounced checks. I am wealthy in my own right. But Inga's inclusion in the trial treatment wasn't solely about money. The name on her admissions paperwork and the fact that only the elite get access to healthcare that should be available to all are the real issues.

In layman's terms, if a Dokovic hadn't supported Inga's application, the head research professor wouldn't have received it.

With a submissive dip of his chin, Kolya says, "I've made reservations at Cortots, the number one steak restaurant in the country. It has—"

"Cancel any reservations for this evening before asking Chef to prepare something. Have his selections brought to our room." With my lips still tingling in the aftermath of Emerson's stance, I add, "Make sure he is aware of my nut allergy."

Again, Kolya's head bobs. "Of course."

When unease flares through his eyes, I ask, "What is it?"

"It's nothing," he brushes off, waving his hand.

Over his theatrics and not having the strength to warn him to steer clear of them if he wishes to remain employed, I walk away.

He halves the length of my strides by asking, "Shall I organize for the doctor to arrive earlier than planned?"

I tilt back and arch a brow, seeking answers without words.

Kolya falls into line remarkably fast. "For the proof they'll require before payment."

Since I'm still lost and incapable of hiding it, he tugs me into an alcove, away from prying eyes, before leaning in close.

"Each supplementary bonus requires proof. A marriage certificate, media approval, the public's reaction to a charity event or gala." He stops, swallows, then starts again. "Proof of the consummation of the marriage."

It takes a moment, but when the truth smacks into me, my knuckles pop as my hands ball into firm fists. "If you touch my wife, I will kill you."

I've always been overprotective of Emerson, and my response proves it is as potent today as it was the day she left me.

Though if I were honest, I'd admit it isn't solely protection burning me alive right now. I'm jealous as fuck as well. Not once in three years did I witness Emerson flirt with anyone but me. Her response to the flight crew's bug-eyed expressions announces she isn't taking the rules of our vows seriously, which means she is wasting both of our time.

Kolya's pupils dilate as his Adam's apple bobs when I add a glare to my worded threat. "Not me personally. We have a doctor on standby. We scheduled his arrival for an hour after your restaurant reservation expired." Again, he leans in. "From the stories I've heard, eating in may require his attendance sooner than planned."

I can barely hear him over the grinding of my molars. My frustration isn't solely about what he says next, but also that stories are being shared.

I don't kiss and tell—ever. But associating Emerson's name with what I assure you is highly fabricated gossip strengthens my resolve.

59

Kolya keeps unknowingly digging his grave. "To process your bonus payment for that term, you must provide documented proof that you finished inside her."

I don't know what angers me more: that Emerson will be paid for sleeping with me or his belief that I'd let someone examine my wife.

When my fury spikes, I settle on the latter.

I've fucked around and fooled around for years, but this is different. As far as anyone is concerned, Emerson is my wife. That should instantly make her untouchable. Yet here they are, acting like a pelvic examination is a perfectly acceptable term of a marriage contract.

The tightness of my jaw shortens my words. "We don't need a doctor."

Lines sprout across Kolya's head. "Is your wife aware of that? She didn't veer straight to the marital room for no reason."

Needing to walk away before I forget Kolya isn't the playwright of a lonely and cruel old man's dying wish, I head for the stairwell that leads to the owner's wing while repeating my statement. "We don't need a doctor."

Kolya looks desperate to continue our conversation but keeps his mouth shut, his begging portrayed solely by his eyes.

He's smarter than I've given him credit for.

With my mood circling the drain, I enter the owner's suite without knocking. Emerson ditched the head maid as fast as I did Kolya, but from what my eyes land on, it was for an entirely different reason.

She removed her hideous trench coat and her cock-thickening lace dress, leaving only mismatched boyleg panties and a semi-padded bra.

She's practically naked, and I'm seconds from humping the air like a dog in heat.

Against the screaming protests of my head, I drag my eyes down her body in a slow and dedicated sweep. As I drink in a body too worthy for any man, my dick thickens so fast it is painful, the crown leaking pre-cum.

From the tiny bow at the top of her panties to the loose thread in her bra, everything about her makes my body convulse. She's a fucking masterpiece, and since I didn't stumble into a skit not prepared for me, I'm granted minutes to marvel at every perfect stroke.

My prolonged gawk makes my instant obsession with this woman worse. It also reminds me of the first time we locked eyes.

I wanted to fuck her hard back then, and I wanted it to be filthy.

The same is true now.

Angry sex is almost on par with jealousy sex.

Both are out of this world good.

But that's all it would be. Rough, angry, I-fucking-hate-that-I-still-love-you sex. Then she'd be gone. Never to be seen. *Again.*

The circled monetary amount on the contract dumped on our marital bed announces this, not to mention Emerson's let's-get-it-over-with expression.

This is worse than angry sex. Desperation sex is the lowest on the scale, and the one thing I refuse to do with anyone, much less with a woman I once cared about.

A woman I still care about.

So, after forcing my eyes to the floor, I deliver two words I never thought I'd speak in front of the equivalent of a walking wet dream. "Get dressed."

Chapter 11

Emerson

"What?"

I stare at Mikhail, confident my hearing is acting up. My ears haven't popped since our faster-than-humanely-possible landing, so my hearing could be at fault. But then why did I hear every snarled word he spoke when he organized a hookup in front of me? And the gurgles of my stomach when I pushed aside my pain for what I hope will be the greater good?

I don't want to whore myself out to a man I once loved, but consummating our vows is the biggest payout figure on our marriage contract and the only way I will leave this arrangement with my heart intact.

It's barely holding on, and we're still on day one. It won't survive weeks in this man's presence, and the knowledge leaves me with only one option.

Do the deed, get it signed off, then leave.

A divorcee tag won't be as bad as the jilted bride title I was lumped with ten years ago.

I'll get over it—eventually.

This, though, being rejected by the man who made me feel beautiful no matter the frumpiness of my outfit, hurts.

I've aged—obviously—but I have also kept in good shape. My tits are where they're meant to be, my stomach is flatter than my curvy hips and ass, and I religiously shave even with having no one to admire my gleaming skin.

I'm goddamn hot—just apparently not scalding enough for Mikhail.

"Get dressed," he repeats, pinching the last of my confidence.

He tries to smooth my hurt with a lie. "Chef is bringing dinner to our room, and Kolya will arrive shortly after him with an updated schedule of our appearances over the next month. He's old. I don't want you to give him a heart attack."

Kolya is in his forties, fifties at the most. He is far from ancient.

A tinge of modesty hits me hard, and it is foreign.

I've never lacked confidence, so I try to push past it.

"I'm not hungry. Well... not for food."

My flirting skills could use a polish, but Mikhail shoots them down like they'll give him the clap. "You need food. You haven't eaten since last night."

"I ate breakfast—"

His eyes floating up from the floor steal the rest of my lie. I haven't eaten breakfast since my preteens, and Mikhail knows that. We had many arguments about it because it gave us plenty of excuses for makeup sex.

I can see his fight not to lower his eyes to my breasts, and smell the torment on his skin, but he does it. He maintains eye contact while instructing me to get dressed again.

Victory flares through his eyes when I give in.

As I stomp to the closet to fetch my coat, he says, "Let's eat. Then we will discuss the terms of our contract."

"I don't need to discuss the contract. I've read it." I come across as a whiny brat. That's expected. That is precisely what I am.

I sling my eyes to Mikhail when he forces his next question through a tight, stern jaw. "Did you read *all* of it? Or just the parts that included a cash payout?"

I nod during his first question, preferring to lie without words. But my nod switches to a snarl during his last question. I skimmed the parts that lacked a monetary figure in front of them, opting for the bread and butter that will keep my family afloat. For good reason, of course. Time is not in my favor.

With Mikhail's cocked brow demanding a worded response, my chest sinks with a sigh before I add words into the mix. "Getting married rewarded us a ten-thousand-dollar bonus. If we fuck—like we have done a million times already, so what's another one added to the list?—the figure jumps to one hundred thousand. Attending a pompous gala with your father's favorite benefactors will add only five thousand to the tally. The rest of the terms have a similar value to the gala." I roll my eyes, praying the burn of their roll will stop stupid moisture from forming in them. "Except birthing an heir, and we'd have to have sex to do that. I also know your thoughts on procreation with someone you don't know. Considering you haven't stopped looking at me as if you have no clue who I am since you arrived at Lidny, I set that dot point aside for a much, *much* later date."

As I suck in some big breaths to calm my climbing anger, I go over the contract terms in my head. Although extensive, they're pretty basic. I'm clueless about why Mikhail is making a big deal out of them. I know his thoughts on having children out of wedlock and his dislike of schmoozing his father's backers, so I went for a term that should have been easy for us to cross off.

Or so I thought.

When Mikhail's nostrils flare as if he's disappointed in me for my nonchalant and somewhat arrogant reply, anger burns me alive.

He has no right to judge me.

None whatsoever.

"I know what I've gotten myself into, Mikhail."

"I disagree," he immediately fires back, his narrowed eyes straying to the contract. "So pick something else on the list for us to cross off first, and maybe, if you ever get your head out of your fucking ass long enough to scrub the money signs from your eyes, we will come back to *that* one later."

The way he says "that" ensures I can't mistake what marital privilege tasks he's referencing, and when paired with the arrogance of his tone, it sends my blood pressure rising.

Too angry to see through the madness swamping me, I shake my head so fast that my hair slaps my cheeks.

"No. *This*"—I jab the sole term left on our contract I'm willing to cross off since sex can be seen as an emotionless transaction when it is done with a man who no longer has a heart—"is what I've chosen. *This* is what I want to do."

This is about far more than stubbornness. The monetary amount of every other item on our list is a pittance compared to the payout I will get for this. They'll also take weeks and months to achieve.

I won't survive being in Mikhail's presence that long. My heart is already in tatters. It can't sustain more damage.

With Mikhail seemingly unwilling to budge on his terms, I fold my arms under my chest, soundlessly announcing his strip of my confidence did little to my stubbornness before saying, "It is *this* or nothing."

Mikhail doesn't fold.

Not in the slightest.

"Then I guess I will end this by saying it was nice seeing you again."

His words are like a punch to the stomach. They wound and devastate me.

I've never felt more betrayed.

I'm so angry that I rip my trench coat when I yank it from a coat hanger and stuff my arms into the openings. The sash remains untied around my waist. I'm too hot to consider the icy conditions outside and desperate to leave.

Because I dress in such a hurry, I fail to notice that I've reverted to the childish crazy person Mikhail always made me when he gave an ounce of attention to anyone who wasn't me.

I'm behaving foolishly, but I shouldn't be so hard on myself. No one had ever evoked such a fierce "mine" mentality from me before Mikhail landed in my life, and no one has since.

I race for the door, seconds from escaping, when Mikhail gives me no choice but to recant my threat. "If you read the *entire* contract, you'd know that leaving within the first month of marriage will see all gifts, payments, and agreements voided without prejudice."

Scarcely breathing, I peer back at him. He looks hurt, but I can't get the notion that he turned me down while I was vulnerable and exposed out of my head. "Like you care what will happen to me or my family."

His back straightens in an instant. "Then why am I here, Emmy? If I don't care, why am I here, torturing myself?"

Torturing himself?

Spending time with me is torturous to him?

Ouch.

That hurts more than any rejection could and has me acting like a brat.

My words hiss from my mouth like a snake about to strike. "Our contract says I have to consummate my vows. It doesn't say it must occur with my husband."

After a final snarl, I race for the door.

Mikhail beats me to it.

He slaps it shut and then crowds me against it.

He's so fuming mad that his breaths bead my neck with condensation.

I refuse to tell you the reaction of the rest of my body, or you'll think I'm insane.

It should be impossible to be furious and horny at the same time, but Mikhail makes it easy.

It's a fight not to melt when he presses his lips to my ear and growls, "You are *my* wife." He touches my chin, lifting and twisting my face until our eyes meet. "My. Fucking. *Wife*. I will not share you with *anyone.*"

The sheer possessiveness in his eyes ignites a blaze deep inside me. Everything ramps up at once—my heart rate, my pulse, the needy throb of my clit. Even my anger. I can't breathe for the fear that the expansion of my lungs will place unnecessary space between us. I can't concentrate on anything but the brilliance of his icy-blue eyes and the thickness rapidly growing against my backside.

He's hard enough to conclusively refute his claim that he doesn't want me. His fat cock digging into my ass cheek surges my confidence back to the record high it held when he called me his and has me wanting to act recklessly.

I won't, though. Too many years have passed, and too much hurt.

"You don't own me, Mikhail. No one does."

He smiles, and despite the mess it causes my panties, I want to smack it off his face.

I would if I could move. He's standing too close and leaning in deep. There isn't an ounce of air between us, and my body is ecstatic about his closeness.

The friction is driving me insane. I'm fighting with everything I have not to grind against him, and I almost lose the battle when he whispers, "I may not own you, Emmy. But legally..."—he waits until my internal temperature turns excruciating before finalizing his reply— "you're mine."

A moan escapes me when the gravelly delivery of his statement causes me to grind down. I feel every fantastic ridge of his cock, and I shudder at the thought of getting lost in them again.

I'm not the only one feeding off the tension. Mikhail's teeth graze my earlobe before his tongue soothes the sting of his bite. It is the most basic of touches, but it sends a wildfire blazing through my veins.

He teased me all the time, but I'm too worked up to remember this is meant to be a game.

I want him. *Desperately.*

And I'm too intoxicated by lust to act cautious.

Mikhail groans when I spin too fast for him to respond, propel myself onto my tippy-toes, and then collide our mouths together like I did anytime I was crowned the loser of our argument.

I don't swipe my tongue across his mouth or force it between his lips as my heart is begging. My kiss is as innocent as my baby sister's face, the sting of rejection still clinging to my skin too densely to ignore.

You wouldn't know that from the hardness of Mikhail's cock, though. It stretches halfway up my stomach and instigates another stint of reckless yearning.

I want to kiss him again—tongue, teeth, and lips this time—but the quickest swivel of my tongue in my mouth to wet it for our embrace announces I can't.

Although faint, there's still enough peanut butter lingering in my mouth to cause an anaphylactic response in someone with a severe peanut allergy.

Mercifully, Mikhail's commentary at the end of our vows announces his mouth isn't the only place I can kiss him, and he is as aware as I am that the worst reactions occur when the residue comes in contact with the mucous membrane, like the eyes, nose, and mouth.

His cock is safe—somewhat.

That doesn't mean he'll act on his desires, though.

He's too stubborn for that.

Or should I say, he once was. I don't know the man standing before me. We're practically strangers—who have an insane sexual attraction that won't adjourn for anything.

As Mikhail's hooded gaze burns me at the stake, reading my soul with only a glance, the hand on my chin lowers to my throat to compress my windpipe ever so slightly.

He pins me to the door with a firm yet erotic grip on my throat, sending my senses haywire before he rakes his eyes up my body.

They linger at the apex of my thighs and at my breasts before they eventually land on my face. He stares at me with lusty, fiery eyes while pressing into me deeper, flattening me to the door.

While fighting the urge not to grind against him, nervous energy leaves my body, replaced with need.

I can't look away. I don't want to miss a single emotion in his entrancing blue eyes. His hurt. His pain. His fury. They're displayed for me to see. But there's also admiration, attraction, and a chemistry no amount of disdain will ever be able to disregard.

My breasts grow heavy as I return his stare, and my clit pulsates.

Mikhail is an ace at poker, so I lay my cards on the table without a word being spoken.

He feels my hurt, my betrayal. *My rejection.* But instead of offering sympathies for them, he acts as if I don't deserve a single apology.

He treats me like a whore, and I'm too bound by lust to pretend I don't love his arrogance. "Since you seem to be having a hard time understanding what being a wife means, perhaps I should remind you."

The roots of my hair sting when the hand on my neck skates behind my head, and he makes a fist. He waits for me to protest, to knee him in the balls. When neither occurs, he uses his grip on my hair to lower me to my knees.

Everything happens so fast. I fall to my knees as Mikhail's belt slides through his belt loops; the hiss of his unzipping pants echoes the sound I make when his cock springs free.

A gasp leaves me during the latter. I forgot how big he is. His cock is throbbing with want and way too large for me to handle with one hand.

My pupils dilate to the size of saucers as I drink him all in. The piercings, the veins, the droplet of goodness pooling at the top. I take them all in as if it is the first time I've seen them before I lose the fight to hold back for a second longer.

I lunge for him, desperate to taste him again.

Air whistles between Mikhail's teeth when I track my tongue over the slit at the top of his cut penis, but that is as far as his praise goes.

He's trying to fake disinterest like he did earlier, but he can't fool me. The veins in his impressive manhood throb too much to misrepresent his interests, and although faint, his hips rock forward enough to pierce the head of his cock between my lips with every timed thrust.

Determined to bring him to heel and resolute to replace the disdain in his eyes with attraction, I circle my hand around the root of his girthy shaft and then jack it up and down several times in a row.

He's heavy in my hand, and each calculated pump encourages more pre-cum to pool at the tip.

I flutter my tongue over his cut crown, moaning when my licks lure more salty goodness.

While pumping him at the base of his thick cock, I pay dedicated attention to the vein feeding his magnificent manhood. I lick his shaft from the tip to the base multiple times, bunching his thighs and coating my cheek with his manly scent when I rub it against his balls resting on his thighs.

I hear Mikhail's back molars smash together when I draw him into my mouth with needy sucks, but other than that, he gives nothing away.

He's cool, calm, and collected... until I peer up at him.

The instant our eyes lock, his thigh muscles twitch, and more of his delicious pre-cum swamps my taste buds.

While maintaining eye contact, I pump him harder, suck him faster, and double-fist his cock. I work him so hard and fast that you'd swear he paid for the privilege.

In a way, I guess that's true.

I wouldn't be here if he weren't seeking a big payday and my mother wasn't sick.

Not wanting to ruin the moment, I take him to the back of my throat before flattening my tongue, accepting him in further. We fooled around like this thousands of times before I knew of Mikhail's family's political influences, so perhaps this isn't solely about one thing. Maybe other factors have contributed to our reunion.

Mikhail's grip on my hair tightens so much that it is painful. I love the sting of his touch. It drives me wild with desire and has me giving him the performance of my life.

The more I work him, the harder he struggles to hold back his needy, desperate gasps.

In minutes, his breathing deepens to an unmissable level, and he grips my hair with deadly force.

As he returns my lusty watch, he feeds his cock in and out of my mouth, grunting and moaning with every frantic thrust.

My jaw aches, but I refuse to give in. I go wild with desire, and my confidence flourishes with every desperate moan Mikhail can't hold back.

He's burning up everywhere, and I'm right there with him.

My clit throbs as salty droplet after salty droplet pumps onto my tongue.

I milk him with my mouth, hand, and tongue until I'm finally granted the ultimate prize for my dedication.

A moan unlike any I've heard erupts from my throat when Mikhail's hips still a second before streams of cum pump from his cock. They flood my tongue with his delicious taste and send my head into a tailspin.

As he stuffs his still-throbbing cock deep into my mouth, ensuring I don't miss a single drop of his release, anticipation builds in my chest.

I hold so much power right now. Although I'm on my knees, sucking his cock, I've taken control. The odds are now in my favor. That's how it has always been with Mikhail and me.

Excitement has already drenched my panties, but another truth wets them further.

Mikhail is at my complete mercy, which can only mean one thing.

I am mere hours from saving my family's bar.

Well, I was.

I stupidly forget to alter my expression before realigning my eyes with Mikhail's. He always could read me like a book. A decade-long hiatus appears to have not weakened his skills in the slightest.

"No," I plead when he pulls back, freeing his somehow still-firm cock from my mouth with a pop.

The manic throbs of his girthy dick when he tucks it into his black boxer shorts set my blood on fire, but no number of silent pleas work.

The game is over, forfeited by the person who would have won by a mile if he didn't have morals.

After a grumble about needing to inform Chef of his allergies, Mikhail heads for a secondary exit that I had no clue existed until now.

I assume he will leave without a backward glance, so you can picture my shock when he cranks his neck back just before he exits.

He takes in my kneeling stance and drenched panties my open trench coat can't hide before he lifts his eyes to my face.

The pain in his hooded gaze exposes how badly he's hurting, and I fucking hate myself for it.

This was not my intention when I allowed him to lower me to my knees. I don't want to hurt him. I'm merely trying to protect my heart so he can't smash it into smithereens for the second time.

Mikhail's voice is hoarse when he says, "Once you've dressed, join me downstairs for something to eat."

Despite being drenched with his cum, my throat's rawness makes my voice come out scratchy. "I thought we were eating in our room?"

His lips twitch to hike into a smirk, but he fights it. His mouth remains as hard-lined as his words that hack my already frail heart. "We would have if I trusted you. Since I don't, we will eat downstairs."

Chapter 12

Mikhail

Heaven has no rage like love turned to hatred.

Emerson's glare as she crosses the formal dining room gives that quote meaning. She's dressed in more clothing than she wore hours ago—if you class a mini skirt, dangerously high stilettoes, and a fitted sleeveless lace shirt as clothing. Her makeup is light, and she has released and brushed her hair, removing the knots my tight grip caused.

She's undeniably beautiful... and scowling furiously enough for me to keep that to myself.

I'm a fucking soft cock.

I was when I walked away like I hadn't recently flooded her throat with my sperm, and I am now when I pretend to peruse the menu the chef prepares each morning instead of admiring how smoking hot my wife looks in her little red outfit.

Emerson has a decade more on the clock than the women I had Kolya remove from the premises, rejecting their offers to take care of the bulge that refused to settle even after I learned I was being led by my dick, but she is a trillion times more stunning.

I know that.

73

Emerson knows that.

And so the fuck does every pair of male eyes stalking her arrival.

I stop collecting names when a deep voice on my right says, "Please, allow me."

A server dressed in black slacks and a white button-up shirt rushes over to pull out Emerson's chair. He blushes when she rewards his chivalry with a smile, like he's unaccustomed to praise.

That isn't surprising. My grandfather was a tyrant. He never gave praise, not even to the people who shared his blood.

The reminder would usually see me pulling on the reins, but the server's reaction to Emerson's racy little number is as readable as the flight deck crew member's interest at the airstrip.

He wants to fuck her.

He wants to bed my wife.

Over my dead body, fuckface.

With my menu dumped, I scald the server with a glare hot enough to deviate his focus off Emerson's tits and warn a handful of others surrounding us that I will tolerate most mistakes, but this, blatantly disrespecting me in my home by fawning over my wife, is the quickest way to get fired.

I was a jealous, neurotic fuck when we dated. I can only see it worsening now that Emerson finally has my last name, and I showcase my assumption in the nastiest way possible.

"While you were getting ready—"

"Ready?" Emerson interrupts, her brow cocked. "Do you mean when I had to take care of business myself because you left me hanging like you're no longer capable of pleasing a woman?"

The snickers from our staff taper to silence when my narrowed gaze shoots around the room.

They don't know me, so they have no clue I'm the cruisy, playful Dokovic heir. As far as they know, I'm as ruthless as Andrik and as heartless as my father.

There's only one person who knows differently. It is the same person attempting to goad me into making another mistake because she knows there's no possibility I will walk away twice.

Getting my dick sucked was satisfying as fuck, but it is the bottom of the barrel compared to Emerson's many other skills.

Bedding her is the equivalent of bedding a goddess—incomparable.

With the dining room silent, I try again. "While you were getting ready, I made some adjustments to our marriage contract."

Emerson tries to interrupt me again, so I speak faster, foiling both her attempt and Kolya's huffed admission that he has caught me in a lie with words.

I've done nothing in the past three hours but fight the urge to return to Emerson's room and finish what she started. She doesn't know that, though, and I'm too pissed she tried to play me for a fool—*again*—to act otherwise.

"All skirts or dresses you wear *must* have knee length or longer hems. Choose flats instead of stilettos. If you can't abide by that term because of budget constraints, go back to term one and scratch out knee length. Chiffon, lace, or any other material incapable of keeping your tits concealed are now banned."

Emerson's mouth falls open more the longer I speak.

I get off on her shocked silence.

I'm the first to admit that Emerson ruled the roost during our tumultuous three years. What she said went. No questions asked.

The change-up is addictive, and I get lost in the power trip as I am sure she did when I handed her the keys to the kingdom the first time she raked her teeth over my knob.

"If you flirt with another man in my presence, I will permanently remove him from your life."

I flick my eyes to Kolya before slowly shifting them to the server, who looks suddenly nervous.

"You're insane," Emerson snarls as Kolya removes the server from the dining room with two clicks of his fingers. "He was doing his job!"

Her reply reminds me of how fast my trust dwindled when she left me at the altar looking like a fool, and when she peered up at me after swallowing my release like she was hungry for my cum.

My "spare" title didn't shunt me from the family as much as my "inability to control my woman." My father and grandfather treated me like a leper for years after Emerson dumped me.

I refuse to step into those shoes again.

"Speaking of jobs..." I wait for Emerson's eyes to return to my face before saying, "You no longer have one. If I can't trust you not to flirt with members of our staff in front of me, I don't trust—"

"You don't trust me at all. Right? That's pretty much what you insinuated earlier."

When I nod, stupidly putting my head on the guillotine block, Emerson's cheeks redden so fast that her face competes with the coloring of the wine a female waiter fills her glass with.

"And if I don't agree with your new terms?"

She stares at me like she hates me when I nudge my head to the door she walked through only hours ago.

If she walks this time, she will lose far more than her heart.

Emerson's lips twitch in preparation to speak, but before she can, the chef announces our meals are ready to be served.

After ten seconds of flicking her eyes between the menu and the chef, Emerson settles them on me. They're still full of contempt and somewhat wet. "I haven't ordered yet, so how could my meal be ready?"

"I ordered for you," I reply while accepting the napkin a female waiter is attempting to place across my lap, happy to abide by the rules of our marriage, even after announcing them as if they're solely for Emerson.

The waitress has been giving me gaga eyes all evening. She's the type I'd usually go for. Blonde, big-breasted, and submissive. But with the tenderloin of all meats sitting across from me, it's hard to pay attention to anything.

I walk straight into Emerson's trap. "Then why were you eyeballing the menu when I arrived?" She doesn't hide her smirk like the dozen staff around her do. She frees it as viciously as her mocking expression. "Is the Big Bad Wolf scared of Little Red Riding Hood?"

I bring her confidence down a smidge. "I was perusing the menu because I didn't want anything to taint the image of you on your knees, gagging on my cock. Not even that pretty Little Red Riding Hood outfit that will only look better when it is sitting in tatters at the foot of my bed."

Since my reply is honest, she can't deny it.

Instead, she shifts her eyes to Chef and says, "To ensure there is no chance of that *mistake* occurring again, I would like to change my order, please."

Chef mumbles and groans before he seeks permission from me to humor her suggestion. Women have no say in the Dokovic world. Well, they didn't. The tides have been shifting since Zoya entered the realm. They just haven't stretched this far inland yet.

When I jerk up my chin, agreeing to Chef's silent question, Emerson waves him to her side of the dining room. I can't hear what she orders. My heart is thudding too loudly for that. But it doubles the devilish gleam in her eyes and wipes my schedule clean for the evening.

Hell has been vacated since a newer, more evil playground has been established.

With my meal selections returned to the kitchen to await the preparation of Emerson's dish, I settle in for a long wait. I doubt it will be as long as the three hours Emerson took to leave our suite, but I'm so fucking hungry that it will seem like a lifetime.

If only food could fulfill all my cravings.

A thick pane of glass forms the dining table, which could easily seat twenty. The only other setting excluding mine is directly across from me, meaning I can see the skin the dangerous split of Emerson's skirt exposes. It only needs to travel an inch higher, and I'd be able to see her panties.

Needing to take my focus off how damp her panties were when I raked my eyes over her body seconds after spilling my load down her throat, I attempt to spark a conversation. "Have you spoken with your mother tonight?"

Emerson scoffs but remains quiet.

So fucking stubborn.

"I read reports about her treatment earlier. The trial stats are impressive."

Why the fuck am I waving a white flag like I detonated the first bomb?

She kissed me.

She removed my cock from my trousers before trekking her tongue across the tip.

She broke my heart, not the other way around.

So it shouldn't be *my* responsibility to patch up *her* mistakes.

I'm saved from searching for answers I'll never get from myself when Chef returns to the dining room and says, "Dinner is served."

My brows furrow as my curiosity rises. Emerson must have ordered something basic, because it takes Chef almost twenty minutes to make a grilled cheese sandwich. That's how pedantic he is with his ingredient selections.

Anyone who prepares meals for the head of our country receives the same anal-pleasing chip implant.

A server removes the silver dome from my plate. It shows a medium-rare steak, mini jacket potatoes, and an assortment of vegetables, drizzled in Chef's secret garlic and herb sauce.

My stomach grumbles while taking in my meal, but I remember you don't have to be raised with manners to use them before digging in.

I stray my eyes to Emerson's side of the table in just enough time to see her dome lifted, exposing her dinner selection. She picked a peanut butter sandwich with a generous side serving of... You guessed it! Peanut butter.

As her teeth stab a sandwich filled with so much ghastly nuttiness that it oozes from the side, her eyes flare with victory. She wipes an enormous chunk of peanut butter from the corner of her mouth before pouting when it flops onto the exposed skin high on her thigh, completely missing the napkin she refused to place in her lap.

I banish the fantasy of licking the sheen her panties couldn't conceal in the owner's suite as Emerson mentally adjusts the score of our tit-for-tat game.

The fact she sucked my dick keeps the score even on my board, though I may need to change things up to keep it that way.

You can't win if you're unwilling to play out of the fear of losing, and Emerson hasn't feared anything in her life.

Not even losing me.

Chapter 13

Emerson

My stomach grumbles in disgust about a lack of nutrients when I flop onto the king-size bed in my room before switching my phone call to a FaceTime chat. Adding her face to the video call doesn't interrupt my mother's conversation, but it does change her expression.

"Are you okay, Emmy? You're looking a little pale."

I slide my thumb over the microphone at the bottom of my phone so she won't hear the angry grumbles of my hungry tummy before jerking up my chin.

"I think I ate too much..." I leave off my last two words—peanut butter—mindful she is very much a don't-kill-your-friends-by-being-selfish-and-bringing-peanut-butter-sandwiches-to-school parent. She even removed the satay chicken skewers from the pub's menu upon learning of Mikhail's allergy. "I've been a little gluttonous with my diet today."

Her laugh warms up my dead, cold heart. "You've always been a woman who gorges on her feelings. I'm just grateful you're eating regularly."

Someone please give her the Mother of the Year award already. It is long overdue.

"Is there anything you want to talk about?" I smile when she adds with a laugh, "With Aunt Marcelle at the bar, my ears aren't sure what's happening. They're not used to so much silence."

A million questions race through my head, but I ignore them all and shake my head instead. I don't know what the hell I'm thinking, so how can I explain it to anyone else?

"I was just calling to see how Wynne's appointment went." When a flare of worry darkens my mother's eyes, I sit up, and my stomach's gurgles double. "Is something wrong?"

"No, of course not."

Lies, all lies!

"But the doctor requested some further testing."

I nod but keep quiet, unsure I can speak without sobbing. My baby sister is my world. I'd lasso the moon for her as eagerly as I would for our mother... and perhaps Mikhail.

Don't look at me like that. Feelings don't vanish. They just get buried beneath a heap of ugliness not even the world's best long-range diver is prepared to wade through to free.

"Did you book the tests today?"

Her solemn headshake reveals the cause of her earlier flare. "They're very expensive. A clinic two hundred miles away is taking patients without insurance, but they're booked out for the next three months."

"Three months?"

She nods, breaking my heart further.

"We'll rustle up the money. Things seemed... steady at the bar this afternoon when I dropped Aunt Marcelle off for her shift. We might reach our goal by the time they have an appointment available."

I hate the word *might* as much as I hate the word *maybe*.

They're both so indecisive.

I shake my head, ridding it of the thoughts of a dark-haired man and his devastatingly roguish blue eyes, before asking, "If we can pull together the money faster, could you secure an appointment closer to home and sooner?"

My mother nods, her ability to talk when she's on the verge of crying as lackluster as mine. "But I don't think that's a possibility. Things are tight."

"But they don't have to be."

I draw in a big breath before straying my eyes to the window of my room. Things quietened quickly after I stuffed my peanut butter–loaded sandwich into my mouth, ensuring it smeared my lips, fingers, and thighs with enough nutty goodness to make Mikhail sweat. The only noise that has been crackling the past three hours is the outdoor fireplace—Mikhail's favored spot.

"I have a way to come up with some funds quickly. I just need a couple of days to instigate them."

My clit throbs in anticipation, mistaking my plans. It is as hopelessly devoted to the worthless cause of seducing Mikhail as my heart is.

Honestly, I wouldn't even care if he didn't touch me again. I enjoyed sucking his cock so much it was pleasurable even without orgasming. The taste of his velvety warm skin, his unique manly scent, and how the veins feeding his magnificent manhood throbbed harder with every greedy suck has me more than eager for round two.

And don't get me started on his moans when his cock jerked in my mouth, or how the tingles I'm attempting to douse will never subside.

I swallow to soothe the burn in my throat when my mother reminds me of the seriousness of our phone call. "The earliest appointment I could find isn't until next week, so you have time." The eagerness on her face slips away, replaced with worry. "But are you sure this is something you want to do, Emmy?" You'd swear she knows about my agreement with Mikhail. That's how motherly her statement is. "I don't want you putting yourself out. You've already done so much."

"It's fine. I'm happy to help." My last words are just for me. *And what's the harm? It isn't like he hasn't already smashed my heart to pieces.*

My mother smiles before she peers at someone over her iPad.

After a brisk nod, she returns her focus to me. "Darling, I have to go. Can I call you later?"

I nod. "But can you save it until tomorrow? I'm zonked."

She smiles like my tiredness isn't from my own vindictiveness before telling me she will speak to me tomorrow.

I reply with a similar sentiment before disconnecting our chat, tossing my phone onto a side table, and then slouching back. My head is thumping, I'm thirsty as hell, and if my calculations are correct, I'm close to my ovulation date.

That part of my cycle always makes me a little crazy.

As I age, my body becomes increasingly fussier about what it is being deprived of. It knows what it wants and doesn't hold back its desires for anyone. So you can picture how tightly coiled I am after being an inch from the finish line, then having it stripped back three miles.

I'm horny as fuck and desperate enough to do something about it.

After drifting my eyes to the open window of my room and noticing the healthy flicker of a raging fire dancing across it, I slacken my breaths before slowly gliding my hand under the waistband of the sleeping pants I tossed on after dinner.

Air whizzes from my nose when I roll my fingertip over my clit. It is still firm and buzzing with anticipation, even after replacing Mikhail's cum dancing on my taste buds with peanut butter.

My clit aches as I lower my fingers to the opening of my pussy. I keep the excitement high by pressing the pad of my palm against the nervy bud and piercing two fingertips through the lines of my pussy.

I'm wet—unashamedly. And the situation worsens when my hand explores myself with feverish eagerness.

A gasp parts my lips when I push my fingers inside deep enough to breach past the opening of my vagina, and then I moan when I remember how Mikhail used to milk my G-spot.

He is the only man who has ever found it, and the remembrance brings a smile to my face for the first time in a long time.

As I recall lazy mornings curled up on a mattress on the office floor at the pub, I pump my fingers in and out of myself. Sunday mornings were my favorite. Mikhail and I had spent the prior two nights wrapped up in the hype of Lidny's nightlife, but since our patrons reserved Sunday mornings for church and families, we had nothing to do but sleep in, fondle, kiss, and make love.

I learned all of Mikhail's best traits on Sundays. How his touch was both torturous and delicious, that he loves giving head as much as he enjoys receiving it, and that one orgasm is never enough for him.

He rocketed me to the outer galaxies a minimum of three times every Sunday morning and even more on the days we skipped church.

While recalling dark, full brows, icy-blue eyes, and a face capable of bringing a nun to climax without self-stimulation, I finger fuck myself faster. My pumps are desperate but controlled. They move rhythmically to the wild beat of my heart as sounds of pleasure fill the room.

Moaning, I move my spare hand to my breast to fondle my nipple. I tweak the hardened bud and scrape it with my nails, mirroring the sensation of teeth grazing over it.

"Oh," I moan when the quickest swipe of my tongue across my lips replaces some of the nutty goodness on my taste buds with the saltiness of Mikhail's cum.

I thought I'd washed it all away.

When the tingling of an orgasm forms low in my stomach, I blink through a blurry haze. I'm not solely excited to have found my G-spot. I am also relishing the taste of Mikhail's cum and naughtily plotting how to secure more.

He can pretend he hates me, but I know he doesn't. In a jealous, neurotic way, the terms he added to our contract recite this without fault.

Mikhail only gets jealous and protective about the people he cares about.

If he's not worried about you being stolen or hurt, you mean nothing to him.

His silence over the past ten years should slow my roll. It should have me pulling my hand out of my panties and scrubbing my fingers clean. But for some reason, it does the opposite.

I relax into the mattress before pushing my fingers in deeper, vainly trying to mimic the length of Mikhail's cock when he fed it into my mouth.

Hard breaths soon fill the air as the finish line I am seeking appears on the horizon.

It has never been this easy in the past ten years. I've tried to self-pleasure multiple times, but it always ended with a heap of frustration and a ton of angry words.

I directed most of them at Mikhail because I blamed him for my faulty womanhood.

You can't be bedded by a god and then expect to go back to faking it till you make it. But this time, I'm so close to the brink after only a handful of pumps that it's scary.

After pressing my body deeper into the mattress, I move my thumb to my clit and augment the unladylike sweep of my thighs. As I finger fuck myself, I close my eyes and let my mind wander. I whimper when the last face I should want to see increases the tingles racing across my core.

Mikhail's face is so crystal clear that I can smell his cologne lingering in the air and the unique scent his heated skin gets when he's about to come. They double the height of the wave about to crest in my stomach and have my spare hand searching for something to clutch.

As I fist the sheets in a white-knuckle hold, my entire body convulses.

My breath catches in my throat as fiery embers ignite my skin.

I'm about to come, and then, horrifyingly, I realize I'm not alone.

With my throat burning from the number of screams I've held back the past fifteen minutes, my demand for my intruder to leave my room immediately is a pathetic squeak.

My inability to talk leaves me no choice but to yank my hand from my panties like my mother busted me masturbating and stray my eyes to the person trampling my privacy.

A new fire blazes through my stomach when my eyes land on a pair identical to the ones featured during my self-pleasuring exhibition. Mikhail stands in the doorway of our room. His fists are clenched, his brows are furrowed, and a large rock is bulging behind his zipper.

He knows what he's walked in on but tries to act oblivious. If he is anything like the man I once dated, he is trying to save face for me, not himself.

"I thought I should check that you found everything okay." A ghost-like grin etches his lips high on one side. "You appear right at home." His smile sags when he takes in the pajamas I found in one of the many drawers in the enormous walk-in closet. They have Snoopy on them, as in the Peanuts franchise. "Still not done torturing me?"

He pulls a face that announces the size of the lump he just lodged into his throat before he crosses the room, undressing on the way.

I glance at my hands, trying not to look. It is virtually impossible. The definition of a god is in front of me, and my veins are still blazing like I'm only seconds from climaxing.

I am not strong enough for this.

Now Mikhail's many references to our exchanges being torturous make sense.

This, *him*, is torture. Pure murderous I-want-to-kiss-the-stupid-grin-off-his-face torture.

And he makes it worse when he cranks his neck my way a second before he enters the bathroom. He catches my admiring stare and the gleam in my eyes that announces how badly I want to track my tongue

over the tip of his cock again. But instead of discouraging my recklessness, he doubles it.

"There's no shame in masturbating. Only the shame of knowing it
will *never* compare to the passion displayed when soulmates unite. Not
even sex is good compared to that. It is a mundane trailer of a love story
people rarely get right."

Chapter 14

Mikhail

I'm tempted to punch myself in the cock while exiting the shower. Not solely because the fucker won't go down no matter how often I remind him that he achieved release only hours ago, but also because of the sentimental schmuck it made me out to be only twenty minutes ago.

I accepted Emerson's heartbreak like a coward—by fucking any woman with a pulse.

Don't throw stones just yet. It took years for me to look at another woman, and not once were my glances directed at someone with fiery red hair and sea-moss-green eyes. For five years, I focused on business matters, assuming the delay would make things more enticing.

It didn't.

The first time was a fucking sham, an emotionless transaction with a minute slice of mutual attraction.

The second was more about need than enjoyment, and the others followed the same path.

I arrived, exerted some dominance without sharing feelings, and then left.

Sex is boring as fuck when you're up there, swinging the bat in an

88

empty stadium. Athletes don't show up just to record a win. They want the admiration and wonderment of their peers and to be challenged like they won't be anywhere else.

Sex isn't close to that for me anymore.

It's how I explained masturbation to Emerson—a mundane trailer to the erotic love story I once lived. There are no sparks, no fireworks, no false sense of security.

It reminds me time and time again that I peaked in my youth.

Yeah, we were young, but what we had was amazing. You can't replicate or replace it. It was the best I'll ever get, and the remembrance pisses me off more than it excites me.

I have no fucking clue why I'm torturing myself. Emerson said she read the contract in full. If she's willing to sell her soul for a hundred K, why the fuck am I acting like a man without a cock?

Because you don't want to believe she is here solely for the money.

While cursing my highly accurate inner monologue, I enter my room without the weightless steps I used forty minutes ago when I heard a heartbreaking sigh leave my room.

I knew that groan from studying them in depth in my late teens. I knew what it meant, and how it differed from the one minutes later that announced how close it placed Emerson to climax. But instead of walking away and issuing her the privacy she deserved, I steadied my breathing and made the last handful of steps in complete silence.

My snoop steered in a direction I'd never anticipated within minutes of Emerson ending her phone call.

I couldn't see anything. Despite Emerson's solo trek starting hours after the staff finished their shift, she remained fully clothed. I didn't need her to be naked to picture every swivel her thumb made, though, and how drenched her fingers were after a handful of pumps.

I saw them in precise detail, as bright as the numerous times she self-pleasured while forcing me to keep my hands to myself.

Her self-love expedition made me hard as stone, and it has me wishing I hadn't shamed her for masturbating.

I don't see anything capable of shrinking my monster dick. Not even freezing water has eased its throbs in the slightest, and the situation worsens when I enter my room.

Emerson dumped her panties in a hamper that a maid will collect first thing tomorrow morning. They're the pair she was wearing while masturbating. How do I know this? The material is visually damp, and they're the same color as the pair that peeked out the top of her sleeping pants as her eyes rolled into the back of her head.

Evidence of her near orgasm moistens my fingertips when I pick up her panties without thinking and then veer them toward my nose. I inhale deeply, not the slightest bit ashamed. The scent of Emerson's aroused state is addictive, and I'm like an addict after a prolonged stint of forced sobriety.

One hit is never enough.

As I ponder where Emerson went, and if she did so without underwear, splashing fills my ears. When I move to the window where I sensed her presence many times tonight, I see Emerson in the pool. She's clothed, just—and her graceful moves as she does laps in the heated water draw the attention of everyone around her.

Her body cuts through the water with ease. Although she's a talented swimmer, she rarely swims for enjoyment. Time in the water is how she reduces stress. I always knew when she was close to crumbling beneath the burden forced on her when I found her near or in the water.

For several long minutes, I watch how the moonlight catches the water droplets on her skin, making them glisten brighter than the diamonds now on her ring finger, my emotions a tangled mess.

Our marriage is a sham, but seeing her like this, knowing she is struggling, and believing I am not the best person to ground her, adds to the mixed feelings I've been experiencing over the past twenty-plus hours.

I loved being the one she turned to during a crisis, the one who anchored and sheltered her no matter how dangerous the storm was.

But now, I only get to watch from the sidelines, shunted from the game with no clue as to the cause of my sidelining.

Emerson and I used to argue relentlessly, but the past few spats have been different. Each one has left a scar deeper than the heartbreak I felt when she left me. She's meant to be happier than she was when she was with me. More successful. She isn't meant to be miserable.

I hate the pain she burdened me with ten years ago, but I hate this more.

The woman I promised to love and support no matter how dark the storm when I proposed has been dealt shitty hand after shitty hand, but instead of demanding a reshuffle, I'm clouting about the multiple royal flushes I've been handed without doing a damn thing to achieve them.

That's bullshit.

That isn't close to the man my mother would have raised if given the chance.

I am better than this.

As I take a deep breath, resolve builds within me. It's time for me to man up, to handle matters with the maturity my age demands. I'm no longer a teen fighting to prove to the world that he's worthy of his girl's affection. I am a grown-ass man, and it is time to act like one.

What's the harm? We don't get second chances to fix things, but to show we can be stronger after failure.

It also won't be my heart Emerson will destroy if she breaks it again.

It hasn't belonged to me since the day I burdened its care to Emerson.

Chapter 15

Emerson

As I glide through the water, I find a moment of tranquility amidst the chaos that has become my life of late. My measured strokes and the coolness of the midnight air on my shoulders offer a temporary escape from the overwhelming thoughts plaguing me.

Swimming centers me. It rewards me with the ability to gather my bases while also suffocating emotions that shouldn't be surfacing as fast as they are.

I shouldn't be so hard on myself. The past few months have been a heartbreaking whirlwind of compromises and tough decision-making. The weight of their burden would inevitably take a toll on me. I just wish my breakdown wasn't occurring in front of the person who only needs to smirk to make them seem inconsequential.

This marriage, though necessary more than I'll ever fully comprehend, has added layers of complexity to feelings I hadn't anticipated handling again anytime in the next five decades.

The pressure to uphold our agreement and the tension it is causing between Mikhail and me are draining.

In the water, I can let go of the facade I must maintain to protect my feelings.

Here, I can be vulnerable, even if only for a short while.

Swimming allows me to breathe while also reminding me that matters could be far worse. I could be married to an overweight Bratva boss with a hairless head and a like for underaged mistresses.

A memory of me saying that exact thing to Mikhail when he complained about his family lineage makes me smile—and has me taking in a mouthful of water.

I cough and splatter more than I breathe during my final lap.

When I reach the edge of the pool, I pull myself out. Warm water cascades off my body in shimmering droplets as I tiptoe across the freezing tiles to fetch a towel. I can't catch my breath while wrapping the soft cotton around myself. The air is nippy and has nothing to do with the icy stare from a second-story window above the pool.

I noticed Mikhail's watch several minutes ago, but I was too focused on managing my stress levels to determine whether his glare stemmed from admiration or concern.

It could be a combination of both. I have a hard time understanding my whiplash moods, so I can't expect anyone else to decipher them without being lumped with a heap of confusion.

Losing my first love left a gaping hole in my heart, and although I hate how heartless it has made me, not knowing the cause of its abrupt ending is more loathsome.

Everything seemed perfect. Our love was exciting and fresh, even after three years. We were inseparable, sharing dreams and plotting ways to make them happen, believing that nothing could ever come between us. Now, pain and confusion taint those memories.

There were no arguments, misunderstandings, or hurtful words.

We were in love, then nothing.

It was gone.

I hate how much power our memories have over me and how they consume my thoughts and fuel my wish for revenge, but no matter how much I try to distract myself, nothing works.

Every time I look at Mikhail, the anger is right there, simmering beneath the surface, ready to explode. But that isn't the sole emotion I feel.

Being here with him is like traveling back ten years.

The fear of losing him again and returning to a lonely existence overshadows the joy of finding my soulmate again.

Our separation has drastically altered me to the point I feel like a stranger. I've tried to move on from it several times, but the pain is too deep and the heartbreak is too devastating.

Bitterness and resentment trapped me in a cycle I couldn't escape. Then, the only man capable of making me feel whole again showed up out of nowhere with an outrageous plan and an even more devastatingly handsome face.

This pains me to admit, but I would have given up years ago if I didn't have so many people relying on me.

Alas, being wanted sometimes is a burden even more than being disregarded.

I need to find a way past the anger and relish the opportunities Andrik Sr.'s sick game will reward me with. It'll be difficult, but I can't continue to let my past define my future. I must rise above my misery and reclaim my happiness.

It's hard to imagine when the very essence of my happiness is within touching distance, yet so distant.

Even while giving each other the silent treatment, Mikhail and I exchanged more words back then than we have over the past twenty-four hours.

It could be worse.

He could have failed to show up for a second time.

While trying to seek positives from my predicament, I hang my towel on a hook near the changing room before returning to the principal residence of Zelenolsk Manor. I feel more grounded and focused after my swim. Not even the beady watch of the man who once shadowed Andrik Sr.'s every move tapers the length of my strides.

Kolya watches me enter the marital room, mindful that not even I have a clue about what may come next.

After entering the room that's bigger than the apartment Mikhail and I intended to share, I tiptoe toward the bathroom, careful not to make a sound.

With his eyes closed, Mikhail is sprawled across the bed, pretending to be asleep.

Gratitude washes over me for his unspoken gesture of peace.

It's been a long day. The recommencement of World War III can wait until tomorrow.

Quietly, I gather my belongings before entering the bathroom, hopeful that a long, hot shower will wash away the remnants of the day's tension my swim missed.

I take my time showering, easing my body into relaxation mode. Despite the late hour, I'll need more than a Xanax to doze off. Mikhail is shirtless, and his sleeping pants leave *nothing* to the imagination. He is the equivalent of a wet dream and a horrifying nightmare wrapped up in one dangerously attractive package.

Once I've washed my hair and shaved my underarms, I dry off before slipping into pajamas I packed from home. This pair is a little more risqué than the ones I donned earlier, consisting of booty shorts and a spaghetti strap shirt with an inbuilt bra.

When I return, the room is dimly lit, even with Mikhail not appearing to have budged an inch. I slide into the bed opposite him, sensitive to his feigned slumber. The sheets are warm and soft against my skin as I pull them to my chin, trying to find comfort in the unfamiliar surroundings.

I am zonked, but sleep eludes me.

My head is a whirlwind of thoughts. It replays the events of the past two days, the conversations held, and the emotions displayed on repeat for almost an hour.

I can't quieten my thoughts, and the nearly soundless snores of the man next to me amplify them to an ear-piercing level.

I roll onto my side and hug my pillow, willing myself to relax.

Nothing works.

As the night stretches on, I remain wide awake, caught in the grip of my regret.

I'm not surprised. I've been acting like a twit all day, so it is no surprise my gurgles of remorse could awaken the dead.

When I deeply exhale, endeavoring to loosen the unease sitting heavy on my chest, the mattress dips under the weight of a man whose body has more muscles than flab.

I feel Mikhail's eyes on me, floating over my cheeks and brows, before they settle on my lips. He doesn't say anything for several painful minutes, but when he finally breaks the ice, our conversation starts at the last place I expect.

"Was that your mother you were speaking with earlier?"

Air escapes my nose as I grapple to survive his unexpected sucker punch.

He's meant to hand me a life vest, not force my feet into concrete boots.

Does his question mean what I think it does?

Was he watching me the entire time I... fondled myself?

I should be furious at the thought alone.

I'm not. Don't ask me why. I am too tired to make sense of anything.

While licking my lips, desperate for some moisture, I sheepishly nod.

Mikhail smiles in gratitude for my honesty while scooting closer, boosting the goose bumps prickling my skin with a scent that is uniquely him.

"Is everything okay?"

The genuine concern in his tone announces that I could ask him to borrow the money to pay for Wynne's tests, but that isn't something I can do. He's already given so much, and I'm at a loss as to why, so asking him would only gray things between us more than necessary.

To survive the next month, I must treat our marriage as the black ink on the white pages demands. As if it is a business transaction.

I realize I lie to protect my heart when I say, "I was asking her advice on a last-minute frock."

I lift and lock my eyes with Mikhail's, scarcely breathing when I notice how much pain is in his hooded gaze. He looks hurt, and since I'm reasonably sure I am responsible for the darkening of his usually light eyes, it burrows a hole in the middle of my chest.

It is a struggle to keep emotions out of my voice while moving our conversation in the direction it needs to go. "Your father's benefactor gala is this weekend, and I have nothing suitable to wear."

He nods in silent understanding, but it takes an excruciatingly long thirty seconds before he adds words to his nonverbal reply. "Is the gala something you're interested in crossing off our list?"

He sucks in a surprised breath when the briskness of my nod ripples through the air, and then he smiles.

I'm hit with an unexpected bout of jealousy when he announces, "I have someone who could help you find a dress. She's—"

"She?" I blurt out before I can stop myself.

I know how to trigger Mikhail's jealousy because my own neuroses surface whenever he receives attention from women.

That was every damn minute we dated.

I was a pro at schooling my annoyance within months of our courtship, but even the most stringent skill set can malfunction after a prolonged absence of use.

Mikhail's teeth shine in the moonlight. "Yes, *she*..." Jealousy jabs him in the ass firm enough to steal his grin. "Though I will need to attend the appointment with you." His rake of my body this time isn't pronged with anger. It is lusty and sends my pulse racing. "You're Nesy's *exact* type." His eyes return to my face, exposing their honesty. "And I don't care about the gender. I don't share. *Ever*. Especially not you." His last three words are whispers, and they have me bowing out of this fight as I should have when he displayed contempt about our reunion being solely about money.

My surrender makes Mikhail so envious that he gives up without a fight. "I'll make some calls tomorrow morning and get you an appointment. You will have your dress for the ball, Cinderella."

For the first time in hours, the heaviness on my chest lifts enough for me to take a full breath. "Thank you." I try to hold back the rest of my reply, but I wouldn't be me without some stirring. "It's about time you used your magic wand for good, Fairy Godfather."

His laughter takes care of the nerves fluttering in my stomach, sending them lower. As do the words he speaks next. "I can think of far better things to use my magic wand on than a hideously pompous dress you'll only wear once."

I should stop this train now, end it before it gets out of control, but you're always more daring under the cloak of darkness. "Such as?"

Lust floods my veins as his teeth graze his bottom lip.

Once, a long time ago, a smirk like that would have seen my underwear ripped off my body with one firm tug.

Tonight, it sees me going to bed horny and unfulfilled. *Again.*

Mikhail's breath floats over my face as he says, "Night, Ember."

I take a moment to relish a nickname I haven't heard in years before I reply, "Night, Coal."

Even with the tension easing tenfold after a small stint of playfulness, a sleepful slumber isn't easy to come by. I eventually find it, but within an hour of its delayed arrival, I'm awoken by a gentle tug on my shoulder.

After I roll to face Mikhail, an arm digs between the mattress and my body while another prepares to perform a hook-like maneuver between my legs.

If the move wasn't familiar, I would startle at being craned across the mattress and positioned over a warm body.

This was a nightly event for Mikhail and me during our three years together.

I'll never forget it.

As a child, Mikhail was starved of affection and touch. Not only was he uncomfortable when I suggested a quick spoon as part of a marathon romp session aftercare routine, he was wholly opposed to it. He didn't understand how two people could doze comfortably cocooned together, and he was confident that we would sleep more refreshingly on opposite sides of the mattress.

As I did multiple times during our tumultuous three years, I pushed him out of his comfort zone.

He became an addict of spooning after only one night.

It doesn't matter the setting. Mikhail will always find a way to snuggle. I cherished his need for comfort while sleeping as much as I did my next orgasm, and the memories it instigates find me drawing into his embrace instead of withdrawing from it.

I rest my head on his naked pec and hook my leg around his waist, my body involuntarily shuddering when my knee brushes the girth between his legs. He's soft—even a sex fiend's dick deflates when they sleep—but he doesn't need to be erect to understand what he's packing.

When I shift slightly, Mikhail murmurs something incoherent in his sleep. A smile tugs at my lips as I recall the countless times he's done that previously. It reminds me of the bond we once shared and how our feelings didn't need to be vocalized to be felt.

We loved hard, and we loved deep.

I truly can't imagine having those feelings for anyone else. Mikhail was *it* for me. My fate was to be with him and only him.

We just lived in a world too cruel to let young love flourish without interference.

The reminder has me inching back toward my half of the mattress long before I've had my fill.

"Not yet," Mikhail murmurs, tightening his grip around my waist. "I've not slept this soundly in over a decade. I'm not ready to let go just yet."

With my heart in my throat, I peer up at him, desperate to gauge the truth of his reply. The room is still dark, but enough moonlight is creeping through the curtains for me to see his face. His eyes are closed, and the rhythmic movements of his chest could lull me back to sleep, but there's something off with his expression. He looks like he's fighting a smile, like he's not truly asleep.

"Your Adam's apple moved!" I shout after watching it bob for the fourth time. "That doesn't happen when you're asleep. Circadian rhythmicity diminishes saliva production during sleep."

I laugh like the alarm clock on the bedside table isn't stating it is 3 a.m. when Mikhail's groggy voice fills my ears with the beats of my heart. "I have no fucking clue what you just said, and it is too early for the dictionary in my head to contemplate turning on."

"Layman's terms won't alter their meaning. You're a big fat fake sleeperer." *Was that even English?*

Mikhail laughs when I jab my fingers in his ribs in response to his humorous gawk at my confused expression, but he doesn't uncocoon me from his hold.

If anything, his grip firms.

"I learned from the best."

My mouth falls open, but since I stayed awake after our brief non-sparring conversation purely to watch him sleep, a peep doesn't sound from my lips. I screw up my nose and stick out my tongue before I return my cheek to his pec to count the lazy beats of his heart like it is perfectly acceptable for enemies to spoon under the covers and in the safety of darkness.

It is nice. Comforting. It reminds me of everything I lost but also of everything I could have again if I could just let my anger go.

I know a good way to begin that.

"Have you really not snuggled with anyone since... you know?"

The only noise over the next minute is the faint sounds from outside. Then, eventually, Mikhail's reply. "Yeah. It didn't feel right doing it with anyone else." Stupid sentimental tears prick my eyes. "It was *our* thing. I wasn't interested in sharing it with someone else."

"If only you could say the same thing about your magic wand, eh?"

I hate myself the instant my sneered comment leaves my mouth. Since I haven't exactly remained celibate, why would I expect him to?

"I'm sorry. That was uncalled for. I just..." I stop talking when I struggle to explain why I'm still jealous after all this time. It should feel as foreign as a dip in confidence. It just doesn't.

Mikhail's voice sounds groggy when he says, "We will talk more in the morning, Em." He yawns into my hair before he loses his nose between the messy locks. "For now, let me relish my first good night's sleep in over ten years."

I scoot closer to hide my grin and then close my eyes, optimistic that the steady movements of his chest will lull me back to sleep in no time.

Despite the chaos I'm confident will ensue again tomorrow, this moment of peace is more intimate than the refuge I sought swimming miles. We will face whatever challenges lie ahead, but for now, in the cocoon of his embrace, I'm going to relish the peace his closeness offers.

Chapter 16

Mikhail

A moan wakes me. A faint grind closely follows it.

I'm about to repel, assuming I failed to kick out my latest bed companion, until the shuddering breath hitting my neck registers as familiar.

Emerson presses her cock-thickening body against mine—her clit grinding along my thigh. Her eyes are closed, but her flushed expression as her soft breaths ruffle my chest hairs is extremely telling.

The arrival of her long-awaited climax is imminent.

Jolts of pleasure thicken my cock when her thigh muscles tighten for half a second before she rocks her hips forward again. I stiffen all over, my thoughts wickedly corrupt when it dawns on me what is happening.

I interrupted Emerson's self-pleasing expedition before she could climax. This is her body's way of evening the score, and I'm stoked as fuck that it's deemed me worthy enough to assist with its cause this time around.

Before the rational side of my head can take hold, I flex my thigh muscle, giving her clit something firmer to grind against.

A noise escapes me during Emerson's next thrust. I can feel the wetness of her pussy through the thinness of my sleeping pants and her panties, and the stiff peaks of her nipples scratch my ribs as her excitement notches up.

Her chest rises, drawing in a needy breath, when the firmness of my thigh doubles the tremors wracking through her. Every rock and grind shift the unease on her face to pleasure, and her moans make me an inferno of need.

Pre-cum leaks from the crown of my cock as I drink in the lusty expression softening her adorable features. Emerson has always been a sexpot, but now, dry humping my leg, she is more cute than fierce.

I love how she can flip a coin on its head and still be undoubtedly attractive.

I've never met a woman with so many layers of sexiness.

"*Shh,*" I murmur when Emerson's next grind spurs enough excitement to interrupt the breathing pattern that announces she's asleep.

She is seconds from waking, but I can't allow that to happen yet. I need her to get off first, to return the confidence I stole when I made out I wasn't interested when she laid herself bare before me.

"Keep going," I encourage, my voice a husky whisper of lust and need. "Don't stop. You're so close to climax that I can taste it. You just need a little more."

My fingers dig into the meaty flesh on her hip as I wedge my leg deeper between her thighs. Then I encourage the natural roll of her hips.

Lust crackles in the air as she rides my thigh for several long minutes, the friction unbelievably satisfying.

Who knew dry humping like a teen without protection could be more enticing than a foursome with three eager female participants?

"Fuck," I murmur under my breath, breathing hard when Emerson adjusts her position.

When her knee squashes against my thickened crotch, I can't help but match her grinds rock for rock.

A mouthwatering moan rolls up my chest when we find a perfect rhythm. Our pace is somewhere between manic fucking and soulful lovemaking, and the tension is insane.

Within minutes, a familiar sensation draws my balls in close to my body, my release close. I'm going to come in my pants like a virgin at a whore house, but nothing could stop this.

Our sexual chemistry has always been explosive, but this, having the ability to make Emerson come with her clothes on, is exhilarating.

It ensures I will wear the title of Pants Jizzer with honor.

Pleasure bubbles inside me, gathering momentum like a wildfire. The vein in my shaft throbs as spurts of pre-ejaculation lubricate my grinds.

"Keep going, Emmy. You've got me so fucking horny that I'm going to nut in my pants. But I need you to come first." With honesty comes clarity. "I should never have placed my needs before yours. It won't happen again."

Her rocks double as she grinds against me unashamedly.

Her smell, her heated breaths, and those fucking moans I've masturbated to for a minimum of once a day for a decade are enough to set me off.

I could come right now.

I don't purely because Emerson's pleasure must come before mine.

Earlier, I acted selfishly. I refuse to display the ugliness of our separation for the second time in under twenty-four hours.

"Jesus, Emmy." I barely recognize my voice. It is husky and brimming with need. "You're going to make me come so hard... in my fucking pants... but I don't care... you feel so good." Desperate, lusty breaths separate each statement.

Electricity shoots through me, adding to the tingling sensation keeping my balls close to my body.

Emerson is as turned on as I am. Even through layers of clothes, I can confidently declare her pussy is hot and wet, and her moans... *fuck.* They have me on the cusp of release.

I hump her leg shamelessly, my focus on the fold at the side of her knee and how it sucks at my dick like her pussy would if I'd answer a single plea of the millions flooding my head.

We dry hump each other for the next several minutes, and then we surrender to a sensation greater than the lies attempting to pull us under.

Emerson comes with a moan, her entire body shuddering.

A few mewls escape her, but she tries to muffle them with pressed-together lips and furled brows.

Her efforts to act unaffected by the strength of the waves pummeling into her are stellar, but one name still seeps through the crack of her barely parted lips.

She whispers my name, and its husky delivery sets me off.

I come hard, the throbs of my cock as frantic as the grunts that flare my nostrils. Blood rushes to my ears as years of pent-up frustration expel me in thick, raring spurts.

My release takes forever to surrender its clutch on my senses, only ending when the throb of its aftershock matches the bobs of Emerson's throat as she struggles to pretend she is still asleep.

Chapter 17

Emerson

As the tingling of my orgasm fades, embarrassment surfaces. I can't believe I did that. I can't believe I rode Mikhail's thigh to climax, and now I am pretending to be asleep.

The start of our exchange and who made the first move are unclear to me, but I know who finished it.

Mikhail is a sex god. He knows exactly what to say and do to swoon you out of your panties, so to hear he was on the verge of coming in his pants from doing something as minute as a PG grind-up was addictive.

It brought me out of my slumbering state, where I was having the best dream of my life, and had me determined to make it a reality.

The results were better than I could have ever imagined, and it is taking everything I have not to pop my eyes open and marvel at the goodness of Mikhail's post-orgasmic expression.

Is sweat clinging to his top lip? Are the roots of his sex-mused hair damp? Or does he look like a train wreck like I did whenever we messed the sheets?

I'll never know because I'm not skilled enough to pretend I didn't love everything we just did if I were to open my eyes.

I can't let Mikhail know how fast he's skating back under my skin, or he'll eat me alive.

Just the way my body is responding to his leg still being wedged between my thighs announces this without prejudice. The coolness against my throbbing clit confirms a large wet patch has formed on the front of my sleeping shorts.

Still, shame doesn't encroach on me.

The soft material caressing my knee feels just as damp. It proves Mikhail crossed the finish line seconds after me, and the knowledge is thrilling.

"Let me get something to clean you up," Mikhail murmurs a second before the mattress springs creak, protesting to his shuffle as ruefully as my still-aching clit does.

Even with early-morning sunlight streaming through the window of the owner's suite, I imagine Mikhail's steps instead of tracing them.

I plan to work the "I was asleep" ruse to my grave.

Blaming a sleep-deprived head for my actions is better than acknowledging how much my body still craves this man. His smell alone is enough to trickle desire through my veins, so the flutter of his pulse against a sensitive region of my body will always instigate disaster.

When a faucet turning on sounds from the direction of the bathroom, I pop open my eyes. I'm alone, but the thundering of my pulse assures me it won't be for long.

My first thought is to run like I did last night when the tension became too much. I would if my legs were up for another hundred laps. They're too shaky for that. I doubt I could stand right now, let alone walk.

My climax wasn't the longest I've had, but it was the most powerful. I couldn't stop coming, and my throat is raw from the number of screams I had to hold back when Mikhail's grunts during his release doubled their strength.

As I wait for Mikhail to return from the bathroom, aftercare clearly still a priority for him, my racing heart slows. It beats in a similar rhythm to the throbs of my clit, and it has me confident I'll make a mistake I can't take back if I don't close my eyes right now.

It pains me, but I shut my eyes with barely a second to spare.

With one sense down, the sensitivity of its counterparts increases. I hear Mikhail moving around his room. His footsteps are faint but deliberate. The crack of an elastic waistband has me picturing him removing his stained sleeping pants and replacing them with a fresh pair, and then the sound of nails raking over a scalp instigates images of him dragging his fingers through his sweat-damp locks.

I imagine each precise movement he makes with ease, his after-sex routine second nature to him. He always took care of me like this, but it was compulsory back then because I was in an orgasmic coma and incapable of taking care of myself.

Memories flood my head, but I keep my breathing steady, not wanting to break the illusion that I am asleep.

After pressing a washcloth between my legs, mopping up some of the mess clinging my panties to my skin, Mikhail adjusts the blanket we kicked off when our snuggles became too heated to require outside assistance, tucking me in.

My heart thumps when a gentle touch caresses my forehead. He brushes back a stray lock of hair, his gesture tender. It speaks volumes about the man he has become and how pain can alter your perception but not wholly change you.

The gentleness of his embrace and his sigh when I fail to respond to it has me convinced I broke his heart, not the other way around.

I want to open my eyes, to force him to take the blame for our downfall, but I remain still, savoring the peace he offered when he didn't recoil from me grinding against his thigh.

I've learned the hard way in the past ten years that an orgasm is a gift. It is not a given. So, as much as I want to remind Mikhail that we're practically strangers because of the actions he took, I can't.

Instead, I roll away from him, stuff a pillow between my legs as if he hasn't satisfied my urges, and then count backward from a thousand.

Sexually depleted, I fall asleep somewhere in the low two hundreds.

By the time I wake again, the high-hanging sun is streaming through the cracks in the curtains, and the thump of my tired muscles relishes the coolness of an unslept-on pillow when I roll over to check the time. The sheets are cold where Mikhail slept, and the silence of the room feels heavy.

My throat grows scratchy when I learn it is almost noon. I've never slept in so late, and the bar was once open until 2 a.m. during its heydays.

After a quick stretch, I throw off the covers and slip out of bed. My stomach grumbles loudly, reminding me of the minuscule meal I consumed before burning off far more calories with a late-night swim.

As I rub my eyes, the events of last night flood back in. The spooning, the touching, the way my ignorance didn't stop Mikhail from pulling me back onto his half of the mattress when he returned to bed. They all flood back in and cause me to shiver like the heating isn't at a ghastly setting.

I don't regret what happened last night, but I need to confront Mikhail about it. Mikhail and I crossed a boundary, and though I'd like to ignore it, I can't.

As I make my way downstairs, the busy hum of the Zelenolsk estate gobbles up my footsteps. A hive of activity occurs around me, but none of them are occurring by the man I'm seeking.

My eyes don't land on Mikhail until I enter the kitchen. He is seated at the breakfast nook, scrolling through messages on his phone. He appears well-rested, as if an orgasm solves everything.

He came twice in a matter of hours. I guess his theory could be valid. I feel extremely light on my feet, and I only floated between the clouds once.

Needing caffeine before I wrestle the obvious elephant in the room,

I plaster a smile onto my face before making a beeline for the brimming coffee pot.

"Morning," I greet halfway there to anyone listening.

Several pairs of eyes shift to me, but only one offers a vocal greeting.

"Morning," Mikhail parrots, his voice strained as he drags his hooded gaze down my body.

I'm still wearing what I went to bed in last night—sticky underwear and all.

Mikhail's eyes, now narrowed, return to my face when I say, "Before you say anything... these are shorts." I point to the extremely indecent hem of my pajama shorts before hooking my thumb to my shirt. "This top is cotton. So, technically, I'm not breaking your highly irrational dress code."

He looks confused. Utterly and wholly confused.

Still desperate for caffeine, I fetch a mug from an overhead cupboard like I've lived here for years before helping myself to the coffee in a recently replenished pot, horrifying the staff paid to answer Mikhail's every whim.

I doubt they've ever seen a Dokovic make themselves a cup of coffee. My new surname may only be temporary, but my dislike of being fussed over would be foreign to them.

While nursing a murky black brew with two generous sugar clumps, I twist to face Mikhail. Even with the coffee scorching hot, I take a sip, needing to use the mug to hide my smile about his miffed expression.

Half my booty popped out the bottom of my shorts when I rose to my tippy-toes to gather a mug. The lusty gleam from the gardener trimming the hedges near the kitchen window announces this, not to mention how scalded my skin became when a heated glare projected from Mikhail's half of the enormous space during my stretch.

With mouthfuls of dark brew settled in my stomach, I attempt to relieve the confusion not even a rueful glare could budge. "You said any hems on the skirts and dresses I wear should be knee length and that shirts need to be made from non-see-through material." I highlight my shorts again. "Shorts." Next, I showcase my spaghetti-strap top, which is poorly concealing my erect nipples. "Cotton. Both Mikhail-approved attire."

He grins, and I fight like hell not to squeeze my thighs together.

Why does he have to be so damn handsome?

This would be so much easier if he were ugly.

"I'm glad you paid enough attention to my jealous rant to put thought into your outfit selection. It shows you're coming into this a little more open-minded than you were yesterday. I appreciate the effort."

What he really wants to say is that he's impressed by my submissiveness when possible future orgasms are on the table. He just took the less confronting route. It is a tactic all nice guys use.

Instead of handing me a completed puzzle to marvel at, Mikhail gives me a solo piece I'll have no chance of deciphering without his help. "But I think you should reconsider. It's as cold as a witch's tit outside, and they're forecasting snow."

I'm both excited and peeved. I hate the cold, but if I have to choose between staying indoors and trekking through miles of snow, I will always pick the latter.

Though I need to keep that a secret from Mikhail.

"We're going outside?" I try to say "we're" with no emotion whatsoever. I shouldn't have bothered. Possessiveness blazes through Mikhail's eyes half a second before he bobs his head.

"As in the backyard or...?" I leave my question open for him to answer as he sees fit.

He follows my plan nicely.

There's always a first time for anything.

"I thought we could go for a ride."

With my excitement too blistering to harness, I eagerly nod.

My head bobs up and down for barely a second before I freeze and purse my lips.

"Ride?" I don't give him a chance to speak. "You bought a motorcycle?" Again, he nods, and then I speak at a million miles an hour. "When? Is it custom like you wanted? Or did you buy it off the floor? What color did you get? I hope you didn't go for the burnt orange paintwork the dealer suggested. That was hideous."

I laugh, stupidly nervous. I want to pretend I'm clueless about why I am anxious, but that would be a lie.

When we discussed Mikhail getting a motorcycle license, our lengthy talks included a lot of naughty, we'll-be-in-our-graves-before-we-turn-thirty scenarios.

Two people who are meant to hate each other can't be hopeful about crossing those experiences off their bucket list, so I have no right to be nervous.

Mikhail's smile widens, shifting from jealous to hungry and wolfish. "You'll find out."

His reply seems unfinished.

I learn why when he nudges his head to the breakfast nook and says, "After you've had breakfast."

I snarl, baring my teeth. Even with the chef going all out, nothing stands out as appetizing—except perhaps the man seated behind the layers of calorie-laden food.

I'd happily eat him.

Heat burns through me when Mikhail angles his head before cocking a dark brow.

Anyone would swear he heard my private thoughts.

I try to save face. "There's nothing on offer I want to waste calories on."

With his gaze hooded, Mikhail leans back in his seat and then leisurely glides his eyes up my body. I'm not wearing a bra. I rarely do while sleeping. But instead of berating myself for being a prick tease when my braless state has his eyes lingering on my breasts longer than an acceptable glance, I mentally high-five myself.

His baby blues haze with lust as he drinks in my practically naked form. My pajamas cling to my body like a second skin, the thinness of their material sparser than a lace glove.

I nearly combust when he wets his lips while returning his eyes to my face. There's so much tension, so much chemistry, that my pussy grows wet.

Mikhail has charm by the mile and a face that could stop traffic.

I am under his spell in an instant.

"Emerson?" Just the way he says my name makes me whimper. It is virile and hot.

I swallow thickly before attempting a reply. "Yeah."

His smile ensures nothing but sex is on my mind. As do the words he speaks next. "Get your fine ass over here and eat something before I feed you the one thing I know won't screw up your calorie count." A needy whimper escapes me. "It will dip it into the negative."

We always joked that cum is a negative-calorie food because of how many calories you burn preparing the feast.

I hesitate, and it makes the tension roasting. Then I join him in the nook like I wouldn't give everything I have to pretend he didn't break my heart.

Chapter 18

Mikhail

A cocky smirk hikes one side of my mouth high when Emerson slips into the booth and then grabs a slice of toast from a rack on her right. I'm not smug because she followed a warning that I would have enforced. It's from the way her eyes bounce between the oversized catering tub of peanut butter and the freshly made jam, her nose screwed up in contemplation.

She settles for the jam, making me as happy as a pig in mud.

Her temporary wave of the white flag keeps the tension manageable and sees me enjoying more of the spread in front of us. I sample a little of each dish on offer. Emerson consumes one piece of toast, minus the crust.

"You can't keep skipping meals. It isn't healthy."

"Tell that to your cardiologist when he's squeezing the fat out of your arteries from eating that." She jerks her head to the strips of bacon laden with maple syrup. Never one to diss other people's eating habits, she shrugs before saying, "Breakfast has never been my thing."

"Since?"

Her eyes flare with an array of responses.

Since you made up that cum is a negative-calorie food.

114

Since it forced you to show you care by reminding me of its importance.

Since the arguments it instigated inspired the best makeup sex imaginable.

But she settles for a shrug instead.

"I can ask Chef to prepare you something different," I offer after dragging my eyes over the options.

Chef created this menu for a man in his late eighties with one foot already in the grave. The grease already feels sluggish in my stomach. I don't blame Emerson for finding the offerings unappealing.

A throb beats through my cock when she whispers, "I doubt Chef has what I want."

"What was that?" I heard what she said, every lusty syllable. I merely want to test if she's game enough to repeat her needy reply.

That woman last night, the one who pretended to be asleep after getting off on my thigh, isn't the Emerson Morozov I know. My girl had grit. She'd never fold after one punch.

My cock thickens when she locks eyes with me, and she states matter-of-factly, "I doubt Chef has what I want."

There she is.

I slouch back like I'm clueless that my new position will reward her with an outline of my cock before I say, "How will you know if you're unwilling to ask?"

Emerson removes a crumb that my tongue was fantasizing about devouring before she furrows her brows. "You make a good point. Communication is vital for *any* relationship... and it isn't like you're overly good at it, so I guess I better man up for the both of us."

I don't get to register how quickly she flicked the switch before she flings her head to the side of the room and waves Chef over.

He arrives at her side in an instant, my reprimand this morning that Emerson's gender doesn't make her less than in any of my households no doubt still ringing in his ears.

"What can I help you with, Ms. Dokovic?"

The reminder of Emerson's new surname and my hurt that she's accusing me of having bad communication skills and not being man enough sees me jumping headfirst into a fight I was hopeful to avoid.

She didn't even have the decency to break up with me via a text message, so how the fuck can she accuse me of having shit communication skills?

"Mrs. Dokovic will have two poached eggs on a thick slice of toasted rye, a side of steamed spinach and sautéed mushrooms, and freshly squeezed orange juice." Again, I adjust my position, stealing the outline of my cock from her view since she's no longer privileged to see it. "Oh, and a side of cum. If you have it." I return my eyes to Emerson's and struggle not to smirk when I spot the shock on her face. "If not, no bother. I'm sure I can rustle up some for *my wife*. It is the least I can do since she's forgotten that the validity of the argument corresponds with the strength of the orgasm its makeup sex will inspire."

Chef doesn't know where to look when Emerson attempts to back away with her hands held in the air, bowing out like a coward.

Words tumble from my mouth with the crack of a whip, furious at her swift surrender. "Sit down."

"I think—"

"Sit before I pin you to the booth with my hands *and* my cock."

Emerson's nostrils flare, vainly trying to portray false anger. I know better. She's not raring up for a fight. For different reasons this time, she's fighting to avoid surrendering again.

She's also struggling not to kiss me as if her "man up" comment didn't shatter my confidence.

For weeks, my grandfather and father ridiculed me for being dumped and shoved me down the totem pole of importance. It took years to earn back the respect her wedding day dumping stole.

I will not let anyone strip it from me again.

When Emerson plops back into her seat like her dizziness is from a lack of nutrients, I suck in a deep breath to cool my heated veins before shifting my eyes to Chef. The heat of his beady gaze is the only reason I threatened Emerson with words instead of actions.

Chef swallows before he makes an excuse to leave. "Poached eggs on rye. Coming right up."

He scatters away, his footing as unsteady as my breaths, when I slowly return my eyes to Emerson.

The rise and fall of her chest matches mine when I say, "Was that communicative enough for you?"

Her eyes dance between mine for several long seconds, her confusion growing the longer they bounce before she eventually jerks up her chin, once again bowing out without drawing blood.

Chapter 19

Emerson

I'm lost as to what just happened. We were flirting and getting along, and then Mikhail took my swipe at his inability to communicate with cold-heartedness.

I was trying to be playful, hoping some humor would stop me from acting like he's my personal sex slave.

It seems to have had the opposite effect.

Back is the moody, leave-me-the-fuck-alone man I only dealt with once. It was after we visited his father's palatial mansion to announce our upcoming nuptials.

Our plan to woo the heads of the Dokovic realm with a whirlwind yet stable romance story worthy of a romance novel was snuffed out in less than a minute.

Mikhail's father laughed when I told him how Mikhail had proposed in a field of my favorite flowers he had a farmer plant instead of wheat, and his grandfather shook his head.

"They'll never approve," his father said while eyeing me up and down. "You don't have the lineage for the Dokovic name."

"Nor the wealth," his grandfather added.

I won't lie. Their rejection stung like a thousand bee stings, but an hour later, the pain was minimal when Mikhail embraced my suggestion that we elope. He said, as plain as day, that it was me or no one, that I was the only woman he would *ever* marry.

I fell in love with him then more than I thought possible.

I've held on to those words for the past decade and secretly hoped that was why his grandfather picked me out of all the women in the world to marry his grandson.

He knew Mikhail was stubborn and that he wouldn't marry despite the heftiness of his inheritance, but I'm clueless as to why that would place me at the top of his ledger of approved wives.

My confusion is evident in my unusually lenient words.

"I'm sorry," I murmur, even with the words tasting bitter.

I'm not an apologetic person, but I am standing firm on the boundary I set last night. Wynne needs tests, and my mother needs treatment. I also haven't dismissed my theory that his grandfather chose me for this project for a reason.

Furthermore, our next goodbye could be permanent.

That hurts even to admit, and it isn't something I am ready to face just yet. Our banter isn't as playful as it was years ago, but I'd rather fight with Mikhail than not have him in my life for another ten years.

Remembrance of that has me adding more to my apology.

"My snarkiness was unwarranted. I just..." My words trail off when I struggle to explain myself.

My snappy attitude attracted Mikhail to me. I was shooting down the advances of a preppy trust-fund boy who struggled to take no for an answer, when Mikhail stepped forward to help. I told him I was fine before I popped my knee into the future rapist's groin and had him tossed out of the bar by a burly bouncer.

Mikhail didn't move his hands from his crotch once over the next three weeks. Not even when I finally accepted his invitation to dance.

You can imagine how awkward that made his dance moves.

The fact that he was up to the challenge of taming a wild woman who didn't need a man made him that much more endearing.

I guess we've done more than age during our time apart.

Mikhail's expression doesn't alter, but he lifts his chin before lowering his eyes to the spread of food in front of us.

Tension runs rife for the next ten minutes. I squirm more than I did the prior ten, and I'm not the only one noticing.

Mikhail watches me under hooded lids before he eventually murmurs, "Need something firmer to rock against, Ember?"

An I-have-no-clue-what-you're-talking-about lie sits on the tip of my tongue, but no matter how hard I try to fire it off, it refuses to relinquish it.

Fibs haven't gotten me anywhere fast, so I switch tactics.

Mikhail sucks in a quick breath when I dip my chin.

His shock makes me smile.

"That's why you called me Ember, wasn't it? I was forever sparked."

"That... and..." I die a thousand deaths waiting for him to answer. The near coronary is worthwhile when he murmurs, "Because you were the only thing capable of making me burn again."

My heart launches into my throat when I recall a famous Russian saying. To make the ember burn again is a metaphor for bringing someone back from near death.

Mikhail called me Ember the first time I told him I loved him. I jokingly referred to him as Coal because it takes longer to heat, but once it reaches its desired temperature, it can maintain it longer than anything else.

I assumed that was how our love was. Unfading.

I'd never been more wrong.

I take advantage of Chef's return to the kitchen by tilting my head back and peering at Mikhail. He watches me with so much heat in his eyes, and his gaze speaks words I don't expect to fall from his mouth anytime in the next century.

I'm still the ember capable of making him burn again. I just have to earn the right.

My last sentence leaves our conversation in limbo for several uncomfortable minutes. I can't deny the hurt I felt when he left me, but I also can't deny that it would hurt more to live without him.

As I stab at the eggs to ensure the runny yolk smothers the ghastly steamed spinach leaves, I try to shift my focus off my heartache and move it to something that matters. "Do you really have a sister?"

Mikhail meets my eyes and smirks before blasting my veins with envy. "Yeah."

I have no right to be jealous. He's speaking about his sister, for crying out loud. But I'd be a liar if I said jealousy wasn't obliterating my understanding.

I get a moment of reprieve when he confesses, "She was whom I was speaking with yesterday."

An ugly green head has me snapping out a reply before my brain can remind me that I've given my little sister many nicknames over the years, so how can I be so judgmental? "You call your sister sweetheart?"

Smirking, he shakes his head. "Not since she hooked up with Andrik."

His smirk slips as his cheeks whiten. I understand why. How the hell are Andrik and his sister hooking up? I thought inbreeding ended with Tsar Nicholas II's execution. Also, Andrik is in his late thirties and has not once shown an interest in pedophilia.

This storyline gets more intricate the more I consider it.

When Mikhail spots my bewilderment, his smirk shifts to a full-blown smile. "You look how I felt when I found out Zoya was my sister."

"Zoya, as in Andrik's wife?"

Damn, they really brought Tsar Nicholas II's practices into the modern world, didn't they?

My head won't stop swirling with information, so Mikhail sets out everything in bullet-point format. He tells me how Zoya is the sister his mother was pregnant with when she went missing twenty-eight years ago, and that she and Andrik aren't related because Andrik's mother

121

went outside of the marriage for fertility assistance, which resulted in her conceiving a child with her fertility doctor.

His brief rundown of events that only occurred months ago answers a lot of questions, but it also encourages more. "Your mother is alive?"

He looks torn about how to reply, equally gutted and relieved.

He briefly nods while saying, "Though she has a long way to go before she will ever feel that way." My sympathetic look keeps communication lines open. "They shipped her from one side of the globe to the next for decades, and she has birthed many children." His smile is back, though weak. "I have another full sibling I know of. The rest are half or no relation whatsoever."

I peer at him as if to say, *How can that be?*

Mercifully, he is still as skilled at reading me as he was last night when he made my dream a reality.

"They used in vitro fertilization to impregnate her." He scrubs at his jaw, the prickles filling my shocked silence with a rough, abrasive noise. "She was nothing but a fucking incubator for them."

I don't balk at his outburst. He's expressed similar views previously. Although they were only rumors, for months, people circulated the story that his mother's disappearance was staged because she had conceived a daughter instead of the preferred male heir the Dokovics desire.

Year after year, Mikhail's hope of finding her, though fervent, diminished as the likelihood of her being alive lessened.

Last I heard, he was preparing a plaque for the memorial wall of a local cemetery. It was a small token compared to how much love he displayed for his mother during his formative years, but it was better than the nothing she had.

Needing to be closer to him, even knowing it will inevitably hurt me, I scoot to his side of the booth. He watches me under heavy lids, but he doesn't sound a protest, freeing me from the panic that I'm making a mistake.

"Is there anything I can do to help?" My offer would seem worthless to anyone else, but to Mikhail, who was raised in a very bigamist, male-driven world, it is the equivalent of a pot of gold under the rainbow.

I'm highly skeptical he knew women had rights before he met my opinionated and extremely vocal family. My mother, like her mother before her, raised me alone, and my aunts speak of matrimony with disgust.

Mikhail considers my offer for three heart-throbbing seconds before he shakes his head. I'm disappointed until he adds words to the mix. "Though I'm sure my mother would love to meet you. Her face lights up every time I talk about you."

He talks about me?

Still.

Even after all these years.

The sob in the back of my throat chops up my words when I say, "I would love to meet her."

When I scoot to the unblocked side of the booth, a deep rumble courses through my body before settling between my thighs. "Not now." Mikhail's laughter dies. "She's in rehab... and will be for some time." He aligns his eyes with mine, the admiration for my eagerness still obvious even past the cloud of hurt. "But the instant she's given the all-clear, I'll take you to see her."

"Okay." I breathe out slowly, nodding.

I suck back in the air I just released when he mutters, "After you've eaten breakfast, of course."

Tingles return when I pout like a teenage girl while saying, "If skipping breakfast is the worst thing I achieve today, I'm not torturing you right."

Chapter 20

Mikhail

With my latest battle with Emerson sailing over with relatively minor damage, I call the hospital where they admitted my mother three months ago, hopeful for good news.

My luck appears to have run out.

The news isn't great. Her mental health is still extremely fragile, and she's struggling to make progress. My heart aches as I absorb the information, feeling a mix of helplessness and frustration. I wish there was more I could do, but right now, all I can do is fund her recovery.

Dr. Firenze thinks that seeing me could hinder her progress. I'm a reminder of what she lost, and since I look so much like my father, she takes the loss in the wrong manner.

She still thinks she is pregnant with Zoya, which is insane to contemplate.

Zoya turns twenty-nine in a couple of months.

As I disconnect our call, after a grumbled promise that I won't call again until next week for an update, I take a deep breath, trying to settle my anger.

This, my mother's diagnosis, is the exact reason I struggle to remain angry at Emerson for the way she left. Before they exposed Andrik's lineage as fraudulent, I was at the very bottom of the Dokovic totem pole. My father was one spot from the top, yet he still failed to protect my mother, so what chance did I have with Emerson?

They could have taken her from me permanently. That would have been far worse than an absence of choice, and the reminder takes care of the frustration bubbling in my gut.

The only woman I've ever loved is breathing in air no longer riddled with unfairness and inequality.

That's worth any amount of heartache.

As I glance around the room, my thoughts still lingering on my mother, I detect that I am being watched. My eyes shoot to the secondary entrance of my office, my body still capable of seeking out its mate even in a crowded room.

Emerson is standing in the entryway, her presence the fresh air my lungs were seeking moments ago. She's wearing a long-sleeved dark-red woolen sweater, its hem floating dangerously close to the waistband of her fitted jeans. Her skintight jeans flare out just above her ankle-high boots.

Her jeans aren't the only thing about her that makes me envious. The crisscross sweater design accentuates her breasts' natural swell, and her tight jeans display her body in cock-thickening detail.

The rich coloring of her sweater amplifies the red hue on her cheeks when she notices my prolonged watch. It isn't my fault my tongue is hanging out of my mouth. She is stunningly beautiful. Only a fool wouldn't gawk.

Furthermore, her beauty is a welcome distraction from the turmoil in my head, and I'm not the only one aware of this.

The excitement in Emerson's eyes is palpable, and both my ego and cock feed off their pulses.

After a quick swallow to lube her throat, she says, "Hey." Her plump lips lift into a soft smile. "How's your mom?"

I try to brush off her inquisitiveness how I do anytime Zoya and

Andrik try to stomp over my privacy, but my heart chooses another option. She's arrived to offer me comfort. It would be impolite to squash it like a bug.

"Not great. But I'm trying to stay positive."

She enters my office, further shifting my thoughts from morose to optimistic with two hip sways. "Do you want to talk about it?"

I consider her offer for half a second and then shake my head. Emerson's comfort rarely comes in the form of words, and as much as I want to get drunk off her body, our exchange this morning still has me wary that she'll flee the instant our contract frees her to do so.

Disappointment flares through her impressive eyes, but she hides it well. "If you change your mind, you know where to find me."

Her support means the world to me, and it surges my gratitude for the foolish game of a lonely old man. He finally saw what I had tried to show to him all those years ago—that the pursuit of wealth only ever leads down a path of emptiness—just a decade too late.

Or so I believed.

Bitter resentment tainted Emerson's return to my life, but it isn't the only emotion I've felt in the previous twenty-four hours. I had almost forgotten what it felt like to have someone care for me beyond the superficial layers of success. Money will never fill the void in my heart. True happiness comes from meaningful connections and love.

For years, I've been blinded by ambition. I thought extreme wealth and success were the keys to getting over my heartache.

Now, I see the truth.

Money is fleeting, but love can be eternal.

I just need to get the fuck over myself to give it a genuine chance.

Emerson's last line made it seem as if she was seconds from leaving my office, so you can picture my shock when she fiddles with a handful of knickknacks on a shelf before she spins to face me.

The thick woolen material of her sweater makes sense when she asks, "Are you still up for a ride?" Sentiment flares through her eyes. "I think it would be good... for both of us."

Since I agree with her and appreciate her offer to suffocate the tension between us with an adrenaline-spiking activity, I jerk up my chin.

Emerson's shuffle replicates a child busting to use the bathroom. "Now?"

I wait for the desperation in her eyes to reach a fever pitch before nodding again. My approval of her suggestion sees her boots lifting from the floor.

A jolt of electricity shoots up my arm when I place my hand on the small of her back to guide her out of my office. Each slight brush of my fingers sends a shiver down her spine and dots her nape with goose bumps, and I find myself making purposeful contact again and again.

The chemistry brewing between us as we walk through the bustling atmosphere is intense, as blistering as the smile of anticipation stretching across Emerson's beautiful face.

I remember the list we made and how hardly any of them involved clothing. We would have been dead within a month of me getting my motorcycle license if we had followed it to the wire.

The threat of death wouldn't have stopped us, though. We couldn't keep our hands off each other when we were a couple, and the remembrance is intoxicating.

Under the watchful eyes of Kolya and a handful of his minions, I guide Emerson to the garage at the side of the principal residence of Zelenolsk Manor. The anticipation of taking her for a ride on my custom Irbis lifts my spirits.

I've never anticipated a passenger when I placed an order for the bike of my dreams, or offered for someone to ride with me. However, I'm glad I reserved that privilege for Emerson.

When we arrive at the garage, I hand Emerson a helmet and a jacket. She puts them on, her grin stretched from ear to ear.

After donning my own jacket, I mount my bike, kick up the stand, and then hold out my hand in offering to Emerson. She slips onto the pillion seat as if it were custom designed for her before wrapping her arms around my waist.

The sensation of her body pressed against mine brings up memories of our grind-up last night, and if the lusty gleam reflecting in the side mirror of my custom ride is anything to go by, I'm not the only one taking a trip down memory lane.

I take a moment to savor Emerson's closeness before kicking over my bike. When the high-powered engine roars to life, Emerson releases a similar purr. The rumble of her excited catcall vibrates through my chest before it settles several inches lower.

"Ready?" I ask, my tone hinting at the thickening of the region below my belt.

Emerson nods, her eyes shining with excitement as they lock with mine in the side mirror. After a frisky wink, a subtle reminder of the wish list we created eleven years ago, I tuck her hands into my jacket pockets to keep them warm before I take off down a long and winding driveway.

The staff who exit the primary residence and the many others dotted around it watch our departure as if we are my grandfather in his bulletproof motorcade, their faces blurring as we race past.

Wind whistles through my hair, flattening it into a slicked-back design as I have no doubt Emerson's helmet is doing to her glossy red locks when we reach public roads, but I don't weaken my thrashing of the throttle. I keep the revs as high as Emerson's elated screams.

As the open road stretches out before us, any worries left lingering fade. Our ride is everything I had hoped it would be when I considered ways to knock down the massive barriers between us. The imposed freedom, the bond of our adrenaline-junky hearts, and the thrill of our dangerous speed ease the tension quicker than I ever thought possible.

The pressure on my chest is so light that before I consider the consequences of my actions, I take a left at the T intersection instead of a right.

I thrash the living shit out of my pride and joy, losing the security detail Kolya is adamant I need to protect Emerson. He's not a part of my inner circle, so he will never hear the story about the time I had to take on four guys at once when their drunken stupidness assured them that waiting for the sexy bartender in an unlit lot at the end of her shift was a good idea.

I won—obviously—and the victory sent whispers through the gallows that Emerson Morozov was untouchable.

Cold air bites my skin as we get closer to our implied destination, but anticipation builds like wildfire. For the first time in ten years, I'm following my heart's pleas instead of my head's. It could thrust me into the dark, fighting to find a way out. But in all honesty, when you've lived in the dark for ten-plus years, it isn't as daunting as it once was.

The further we travel, the more the scenery alters. It switches from an urban jungle of buildings and asphalt roads to lush greenery and loose-gravel roads in under twenty minutes.

Emerson's arms tighten around my waist when I veer down a road we traveled many years ago. Her excitement is as palpable as mine, her memories as vivid. This is where I took her on our first official date. It was summer back then, and we were in the comfort of her mother's car, but we made enough memories to last us a lifetime, which means this is only our second visit.

After weaving past a locked boom gate, I park at the side of an empty lot before helping Emerson off my bike. She removes her helmet and fluffs out her flattened hair, the excitement on her face as breath-taking as the sight we're about to take in.

In silence, we walk toward the sound of rushing water. I can tell the exact moment Emerson spots the waterfall that will never stop flowing no matter the temperature. Her breath catches in her throat as the most dazzling smile stretches across her face.

"It is..." She can't finish her sentence. The cascading water has rendered her speechless, and it makes me even more grateful that I set aside my earlier frustrations.

Seeing her like this, speechless and in awe, could only be better if she were naked beneath me, panting in ecstasy.

The waterfall is even more stunning than I remembered. The constant flow of water creates a mist that cools the air around us even more than my unrelenting speed, but its natural beauty makes it barely noticeable.

Emerson's nose is the color of beets, but she doesn't seem to mind. The water captivates her, her eyes sparkling with joy.

I linger back, certain the combined view of Emerson and the waterfall will far exceed a natural wonder centuries in the making.

Emerson steps close to the edge before dipping her fingers into the water. Despite the chill, when she twists to face me, her smile is capable of warming my chest more than any synthetic material.

We share an array of memories without a word being spoken between us, and it heals the cracks her equally silent departure caused.

Water could always calm Emerson's wildest storms. I now understand why. The atmosphere feels almost magical, so much so that I don't hesitate when Emerson asks if we can climb to the crest.

The last time we were here, the area had recently experienced a deluge of rain. It made the conditions unsafe, so instead of spiking Emerson's blood with adrenaline with a dangerous climb, I achieved a similar result in the back seat of her mother's beat-up Lada.

The path is steep and slippery, but the enthusiasm beaming out of Emerson is infectious. I match her eagerness, and in no time, the silence is filled with chatter and laughter. We talk the entire way, the sound of rushing water accompanying us.

The climb is challenging, but when we reach the top, the view makes it worthwhile. It is breathtaking. The landscape stretches from one side to the next, a mix of greenery and sparkling water so cold that it is the bluest of blues.

I twist to face Emerson when she murmurs, "As icy as your eyes." Her cheeks whiten when it dawns on her that she said her statement out loud, but she tries to play it off. "And as blue as your balls have never been." She grimaces, and it ends the tension in an instant.

She has always sucked at analogies.

"Careful," I murmur when she moves close to the edge, desperate to tear her embarrassed face from my view.

"Wow," she whispers, her chest stilling as if she is too afraid to breathe for the fear of a deep gasp pulling her out of her dream. "It is so beautiful."

With my eyes locked on her instead of the natural wonder before us, I reply, "It sure is."

Memories of our past linger in the back of my mind while I drink in the beautiful vista. I wonder if Emerson is thinking the same, but I don't dare to ask. World War III can take a moment of reprieve as well.

Emerson turns to face me, her eyes reflecting a myriad of colors. "Do you remember the first time we came here?"

I nod, a smile tugging at the corners of my lips. "How could I forget?"

It was the summer that changed everything.

It was the week she officially became mine.

Emerson sighs, a mixture of sadness and nostalgia in her expression. "We were so young back then and so full of hope." Her laugh echoes in the quiet. "I also thought we were so grown up."

Her eye roll stops halfway when I say, "We were."

She *pffts* me. "We were planning to marry at twenty-one."

Interested to see where she's going with this, but not wanting to dictate the course of our conversation, I keep my reply short. "And?"

She follows along with my plan nicely. "And your family had every right to be apprehensive." I huff, but she continues as if I didn't make a sound. "We were too young and too naïve to understand the complexities of marriage."

"What does age have to do with anything?" I talk faster when she tries to answer my rhetorical question. "Love is enough. It can overcome any obstacle."

Emerson once said my optimism was one thing she loved about me the most, but today, it seems as if my words hurt her as much as the three words my brother spoke to me that fateful day.

She isn't coming.

"But it didn't overcome any obstacle, Mikhail. We—"

I want to throw my phone over the cliff when it buzzes, cutting her off. This conversation will hurt, but it is inevitable. And, in all honesty, I'd rather it take place here than in front of witnesses who mean nothing to me.

My teeth grit when my phone buzzes again, my calendar as impatient as the man who set it.

"Sorry. I thought it was on silent."

I cuss while pulling my phone out to silence it. It isn't Kolya calling to berate me about losing the security detail, as suspected, or the alarms I set to remind me of the many appointments I made earlier today. It is an email from a company I contacted while waiting for Emerson at her family's church for the second time in my life.

"What is it?" Emerson asks, moving closer. I see the conflict in her eyes, the desire for us to continue with our conversation, but she picks the civil route, also wary about bringing up a subject that will cause conflict so soon after we've reached an amicable pack to be pleasant. "Is that the suggested meeting time for the dress fitting?"

"No," I answer before replying to the email and storing my phone. "It is far more important than that."

"More important than me not wearing a potato sack to an event that charges twenty-five thousand a plate?" She scoffs, and it makes me smile. The disappointment the interruption caused is gone faster than I can snap my fingers.

"Wouldn't be the first time you rocked the shit out of a potato sack. Doubt it'll be the last," I say before I can stop myself.

Emerson's family lived comfortably throughout her childhood, but when things are tight, you toss a potato sack on your five-year-old, scrub some dirt on her face, and call it a costume.

We replicated her outfit many moons later, but instead of writing potatoes in thick black ink on the hessian bag covering Emerson's delectable curves, we wrote onions. I attended the party as the Grinch. I'll let you guess why.

I stop recalling how badly we itched for days after that party when Emerson says, "I don't think a potato sack will cut it this time. If my outfit isn't perfect like the other attendees', people will ridicule me for months."

"Over my dead body."

I'd never let anyone ridicule her. Not back then, and not now. But I'd be a liar if I said I wasn't wary of us attending this event. The last time Emerson and my father were in the same room, he mocked both her and our relationship. We almost came to blows because that exchange was the first time I didn't immediately heel when barked at. I told him that either Emerson would become my wife or I would remain single for the rest of my life.

My bachelor status at the start of the week should clue you in on how that negotiation turned out.

Emerson smiles, grateful I still have her back, before she takes a final glance at the waterfall. When she pouts, disappointed the magic is over so soon, my smile augments. Her bottom lip lowered often when we dated. She isn't a sulker. It's because I threatened to bite her bottom lip anytime she did it.

Still moping, she repeats, "It is so beautiful."

"It sure is," I echo, still staring at her.

After twanging her protruded bottom lip, the only movement I can make that won't expose the hand I'm meant to be holding close to my chest, I lead our trek back to the lot. "I'll go first. That way, I can catch you if you fall."

Emerson's eye roll cuts off partway around when her wish to take the lead sees her non-hiking-approved shoes losing traction on a shiny rock.

Her mouth forms an O as she struggles to maintain her balance,

133

and my heart stops beating. She's close to the edge, teetering danger-ously toward a life-altering drop, and I care too much about her to pretend I'm not filled with fear.

Faster than I can blink, I snatch her wrist and tug her into my body, plucking her to safety.

The briskness of my snatch-and-grab routine causes me to also lose my footing. I stumble backward, colliding hard on the ground with a thud. Emerson lands on top of me, her unexpected ribbing knocking the wind out of me.

"Are you okay?" A range of emotions fills her voice. The most notable is relief. For me saving her? I don't know. I just know she is relieved.

While trying to replenish my lungs with air, breathless from the fear of her near-fatal fall, I nod. "You?"

After she nods, we lie still for a moment, stunned and thankful.

The torrent of the waterfall is nothing compared to the thumping of my pulse in my ears when our eyes meet. Emerson's eyes are wide with shock, but they quickly haze with lust when it dawns on her how closely our bodies are aligned.

The world fades away as I take in my favorite shade of green, leaving nothing but me and the woman I once declared I'd follow to the end of the earth.

Electricity courses between us as all the unease of our earlier exchanges disappears. I firm my grip around her waist, tugging her in closer, careless that she may hear the brutal pounds of my heart.

Emerson's gaze remains steadfast, the scent of her skin thickening my cock.

Lust flickers in her hooded gaze as the space between us narrows even more. I caress her cheek, sending surges of electricity rocketing up my arm. All doubts vanish when she leans into my embrace. Her eyes close for the briefest second, as if making sure she isn't dreaming, before they open again, fired with desire.

The urge to kiss her, to forgive and forget, grows stronger the brighter her eyes become. Her gaze is vulnerable but filled with the same hope flooding my veins. They offer a glimpse of how explosive we could be again if we stopped looking back and only peered forward.

Its silent promise is an aphrodisiac, and I'm dependent on its powers in under a nanosecond.

A desperate mewl vibrates against my lips when I roll my hips upward. I don't know if it came from Emerson or me. It could be the combination of our desperations.

"Please," Emerson begs, her breaths whistling between her teeth.

When I stabilize her hips, she rocks against me, stroking herself with the length of my thickened cock. My dick is hard and aching, so its rocks against her heated core cause the perfect amount of friction.

I want to fuck her, desperately. But it has nothing on how badly I want to kiss her.

Kissing is the one thing I've deprived myself of for the past ten years.

It is the sole thing I reserved for my wife.

As the ferocious need to fuck claws at me, I brush my nose down Emerson's cheek, drinking in a scent that is uniquely hers, before saying, "If we do this—"

Our faces are half an inch apart, the anticipation palpable when Emerson pushes past the barrier I am attempting to keep erect between us.

She squashes her lips against mine.

The world stops when my lips part at the request of her lashing tongue and she spears it into my mouth. Our kiss is soft and gentle, but it swiftly moves to passionate when I take charge of our exchange. I am desperate to taste her again, so within seconds of Emerson handing over the reins, my tongue strokes the roof of her mouth as my throat traps her husky moans.

The flavors that erupt on my taste buds make my chest ache. They're so familiar, so wanted. They remind me of the good times I thought I'd never have again and have me frantic to relish every second.

Our kiss overflows with the emotions we've suppressed, and within minutes, it consumes me.

I kiss her with everything I have, evolving her excitement while also claiming her as I struggled not to the moment I laid eyes on her again.

Emerson's fingers get lost in my hair as she pulls me closer, deepening our embrace. She returns my kiss with as much intensity—with as much ownership.

Our kiss feels as long as an eternity and as minute as a heartbeat at the same time. I'm raring for more and far from having my fill, but I also want it to end so we can take this to a more suitable location. This tourist spot isn't as popular in the winter months, but its beauty still attracts a handful of tourists each day.

Again, I rock my hips upward, needing her to feel how much I want her, before I attempt to pull back.

I say attempt because Emerson pounces again before a snippet of air can separate us. She kisses the column of my throat before nuzzling her cheek against the two-day stubble I've not had the chance to shave.

A shudder rolls through me when she confesses how much she has missed my smell, and then it shivers through her when I roll her over.

After looping my arm around her back and yanking her hips upward, I reunite our lips. I kiss her like I'm not out of practice with modern-day techniques, and Emerson can't get enough.

She moans my name and arches her back as sparks of pleasure rain over her skin. Then her breathing stills when I wedge a hand under her woolen sweater.

We rock in sync for the next several minutes while I tweak her nipples through her lacy bra. I'm so fucking hard, and my dick is leaking pre-cum so much that I'm certain there will be a wet patch in the front of my jeans by the time we finish, but I don't give a fuck.

I couldn't stop this now even if we suddenly received an audience.

Emerson is all fire and lust. She moans into my mouth while rubbing against me, grinding her sweet-scented pussy along the length of my shaft. My balls tighten as our grind-up offers a spicy prelude to how explosive the sex will be when we finally give in to the tension.

Last night, I slowed down our rhythm, not wanting our frantic thrusts to wake her.

I don't do that this time around.

I pin her to the soddy ground, squeezing, moaning, and tweaking. My hands don't stop moving. I play with her breasts, fondle her nipples, and grip her ass firmly enough to mark while returning a kiss hot enough to wear the Pants Jizzer title for the second time in twenty-four hours.

Emerson doesn't seem to mind. She matches my rocks grind for grind while licking my lips and telling me how close to the edge she is.

I fucking love being able to get her off with nothing but a PG grind-up, but I need more.

More tension.

More friction.

More her.

"Tell me what you need, and I'll give it to you."

"I need you inside me." Her words tumble from her mouth with a needy gasp.

"Where?" As one of my hands skates to the waistband of her jeans, the other tilts her hips high in preparation to drag her jeans to her knees the second she announces where she wants me. "Tell me where."

"Anywhere. I just need you." Her last sentence thickens my veins with exhilaration. My brain hazes with lust as we explore each other's mouths, touching, tasting, and devouring. "Please, Mikhail."

I trap her pretty little moans with my mouth while ruefully tugging at the fastener in her jeans. The button pops without too much coercion, but before I can lower the zipper, a giggle sounds from above us.

An alerted howl closely follows it.

I look back so fast that I almost give myself whiplash. A girl I suspect is around sixteen has her eyes covered by a woman I assume is her mother. The elder of the duo scowls at me so unrepentantly that wrinkles sprout from more than just the corners of her eyes.

She looks like she sucked on a lemon while scalding our highly inappropriate hookup spot. "This is a *public* area. You should be ashamed of yourselves."

I should be, but I'm not.

Kissing Emerson righted the axis of my world again. It is no longer tilted.

I won't let anyone take that from us, much less a woman who looks like she's never had a day of fun in her life. She's in her forties, not dead.

For the first time in the past twenty minutes, Emerson isn't on board with my plan. "You're right. I'm so sorry. It won't happen again."

"Like fucking hell it won't," I mutter under my breath when she rolls out from beneath me, buttoning up her jeans and righting her sweater on the way.

Begrudgingly, I follow suit, though my movements are slower since I don't want to be arrested for public indecency.

After wiping her muddy hands down her jeans, Emerson thrusts one out in offering. "You have my word."

When the lady huffs, rudely dismissing her wordless offer of a ceasefire, the teenager wrangles free. "Come on, Mom. You're acting like I was conceived by immaculate conception." After giggling at her mother's horrified expression, the blonde slips her hand in Emerson's, shakes it, then tilts in close. "The Gen Xs still think people come here solely for the view." Her disgusted expression brings her age bracket closer to seventeen than sixteen. "That may be the case during daylight hours, but once the sun goes down, all bets are off."

Emerson giggles, loving her free-spiritedness, and I move closer.

Big mistake.

The blonde's eyes widen to the size of saucers as her mouth falls open. Emerson's eyes rocket to my crotch, assuming the outline of my cock isn't hidden by the low hang of my shirt and jacket. She's not accustomed to my face being recognized by the younger generation. When we dated, the money-hungry gold diggers my grandfather dealt with during his entire political career fawned over my father and Andrik. I didn't get a look in until I created my own hype.

Regretfully, it isn't the type of exposure I want Emerson to learn about.

"Oh my god!" The teen's breaths whip out of her mouth along with her words. "You're Mikhail Dokovic!"

"Dokovic?" Her mother murmurs, her eyes raking over my face as a backpack is shoved into her chest. "As in, Ellis Dokovic's son?" Her eyes flicker as if she is recalling me sitting next to my father at my grandfather's televised wake. "Oh dear..."

Before I can assure her that she didn't insult the future president of our great country—Andrik's shoulders bore that burden from the day of his conception—the teen re-enters the conversation. "Mikhail Dokovic, as in Bachelor of the Year finalist three years straight. And..."—she pauses, building the suspense, only speaking when she wrangles a glossy magazine and an iPhone out of the backpack she shoved into her mother's chest—"Russia's most prolific fuckboy."

The mother scoffs again, adding to the shame heating my cheeks.

Emerson remains quiet.

With the magazine stuffed under her arm, the teen lifts her iPhone to document our exchange. No one believes anything these days unless you have proof, and although this isn't the shoot I was preparing to undertake today, I'd rather mollify the teen with a handful of snaps than see the details of my escapade splashed over the covers of magazines tomorrow morning.

A fan will defend its idol to the end of time—*if* the idol remembers they'd be nothing without their fans.

Emerson twists in enough time to miss the blinding flash of multiple images being snapped in quick succession, and then her hands shoot up to protect her eyes from further damage.

Well, that's what my heart is telling my head.

My head believes her motives are more sinister, like she's embarrassed to be photographed with me. And its beliefs worsen when she offers to be the photographer for the teenager.

The blonde eagerly nods before punching a hole in Emerson's plan. "You should get in a handful of images, too. We can take selfies."

"No, it's fine." Emerson brushes off her offer with a wave of her hand before she snatches the iPhone from her grasp and switches places with her.

She pretends she's not knowledgeable about how iPhones operate, her ruse long enough to remove any unwanted photos from the teen's album before she snaps a handful of images of us.

The teen's excitement is infectious. Even the mother gets in a handful of photographs toward the end of our mini shoot. Her sourpuss expression never alters, but she takes part—unlike Emerson. Not once does she accept their numerous offers to be photographed with me.

Her constant denials nosedive my mood and have me grimacing in the last handful of snaps instead of smiling.

Chapter 21

Emerson

Our kiss and grind-up was everything I could have hoped for, but as I lead our walk away from a gleaming teen and a middle-aged lady with a "Vote 1 Dokovic" pin fastened to her water bottle, I can't shake the feeling of sadness weaving between the lust still thickening my veins.

Mikhail has never been good at masking his feelings, though he tries his best now. The way his eyes never fully meet mine while instructing me to be careful while scaling over another grime-soaked boulder announces he is attempting to re-erect the walls our kiss lowered.

When he holds out his hand in offering at the opening of the trail, I try to convince myself that he's more concerned about me slipping again than other matters, but uncertainty about everything lingers during our trek back to his bike.

Unlike our climb, our descent is done in silence. We walk back to the semi-isolated lot, the sound of the waterfall cresting behind us fading as rapidly as my hope that I'll make it out of this arrangement in one piece.

Old feelings have been bubbling at the surface since the will reading, but they've reached the boiling point now. Our make-out session at the crest of the waterfall was too hot for them not to bubble over.

"Here. Put this on. I don't want you getting sick." Mikhail removes his leather jacket before draping it over my shoulders and pulling my hair out of the collar.

After stuffing my arms into the openings, I pull his coat in, loving that it smells like us, before asking, "What about you? Won't you be cold?"

He smiles like his eyes aren't gauging the honesty of my fretful tone before he murmurs, "I'll be fine."

After hooking his leg over his bike, he assists me onto the back. Since I'm wearing his coat, he can't warm my hands in its pockets this time, so he tucks them under his shirt instead. The bumps on his abs and a handful of felonious hairs tickle my fingertips when he kicks over his bike and revs the engine. It switches some of my worries back to lust, but only a smidge.

"Ready?" I feel Mikhail's question more than I hear it. That's how close our bodies are. It is like we're back at the crest of the waterfall, but Mikhail is the wrong way around.

Our eyes align in the side mirror when I jerk up my chin.

The roaring of Mikhail's engine fills the ride to the bustling metropolis with adrenaline. But my thoughts are elsewhere. I wonder if our make-out session meant as much to Mikhail as it did to me or if the memories were too potent for him to move past without trying to rehash them?

I'd like to think it is the former. Our contract encourages public displays of affection, but no one else was with us at the waterfall before we were interrupted. It was just us and memories I'm praying never become haunted.

The wind rushing past us ensures my cheeks are dry by the time Mikhail parks his custom bike in front of a fancy boutique. The town, a hundred miles from Zelenolsk Manor, is bustling and extremely high-end.

Only the wealthy live in this part of the country, and the locals' faces show it when Mikhail dismounts his bike to help me. His snatch-and-pluck maneuver saved me from a life-ending fall, but his jeans weren't so lucky to escape the carnage. They're stained in the back, as murky as he made the front of my jeans when he kissed me senselessly while fondling my breasts.

The reminder of the chemistry brewing between us during our make-out session assures me it wasn't an act. You can't manufacture electricity like that on a whim. It takes months to inspire and years to perfect.

With my heart not as heavy as it was moments ago, I shadow Mikhail into Wilfred Iwona's invitation-only boutique. The atmosphere is lively and welcoming. Staff greet us with warm smiles, and grungy music fills the air.

The boutique is overflowing with racks of beautiful clothes, each piece more stunning than the last. As I take in the impeccable stitch of a ballgown that costs more than my first car, I overhear the sales clerk telling Mikhail that Nesy had a family emergency, so Wilfred will assist us today.

I almost pee my pants. Wilfred is Russia's number-one designer. She distributes her garments globally and clothes many celebrities. But I try to play it cool. The one time I expressed bewilderment about someone's obvious wealth saw me shunted from Mikhail's family's life with a "you're not worthy" endorsement stamped on my forehead.

"Wilfred shall arrive shortly. Until then, you're welcome to peruse the garments on offer."

Nodding, Mikhail removes his wallet from his muddy jeans and then hands a fancy black Amex to the clerk before he joins me in the central hub of the boutique.

There's still a snippet of pain in his eyes, but I try to brush it aside when he asks, "See anything you like?"

"Um..." I scan the outfits, seeking one with a price tag under a thousand dollars. The closest I get is three thousand. It is hefty but well below its counterparts. "I like this one. With the right accessories, it could work for a benefactor event."

Mikhail screws up his nose, and it is a fight not to smile.

The dress is cheap because, unlike its fancy companions, it is hideously unflattering.

A potato sack would show off my curves more than that outfit.

"What about that one?" Mikhail nudges his head to the dress my eyes landed on the instant we entered. It is gorgeous. The dress features a detailed bust, a flared skirt, and a dangerously unique split. It is a dress you'd expect a movie star to wear during the premiere of her movie.

"It's lovely, but..." My reply trails off when Mikhail acts as if I only spoke two words.

He plucks the dress with a five-figure price tag off the solo rack designed to showcase its flawless design before he hotfoots it toward the dressing room.

"Mikhail—"

I'm cut off again, with words this time. "I can still taste you on my mouth. Now is not the time to argue with me, Ember." He twists to face me, his tongue stroking his lips as if seeking a morsel of our kiss on his mouth. "I also don't need another reason for people to rubberneck. Imagining you in this dress"—he waves around the dress he's mentioning—"is giving them more reasons to arrest me for public indecency."

I'm lost, but mercifully, he's quick to point out the reason for the bodies camped outside the boutique, gawking. He's hard. I'm not talking about an outline that might give my grandma a heart attack. I'm talking about a bulge not even the frumpy outfit I tried to convince him to purchase could conceal.

Is he hard because we're in a boutique that screams sex and sensuality, or because he is still as worked up as I am over our grind-up?

When his tongue delves out for the second time in the past minute, I steer toward the latter.

Warmth blooms between my legs, and because I am forever weak when it comes to this man, its heat has me walking toward Mikhail with my hips swinging and my eyes full of lust.

For just a moment, I relish the electricity crackling between us. I allow it to build my confidence to a point it will never topple before I snatch the dress out of his hand and enter the dressing room before him.

I didn't think my plan through. A curtain forms the changing room's door. There's no lock. I've not even hooked Mikhail's pick onto a hanger at the side of the ample space before his imposing aura pinches the last of the air in my lungs.

"What are you doing?" I ask, attempting to portray that I have some sort of morality when it comes to this man.

His predatory stalk flashes up images of his eagerness to remove my jeans only an hour ago, and they make me wet.

I'm not the only one feeding off the lust brewing in the air. Mikhail's reply almost crests the wave in my stomach. "With a sixteen-thousand-dollar purchase price, you can be assured that I'm going to make sure it is the perfect fit before handing over a penny."

I love his attempts to squash the last bit of tension between us with playfulness, but I can't help but tease him. "Isn't that Wilfred's job?"

He stares straight at me while replying, "Usually." His lips twist as he shakes his head. "But not when it comes to you." When his words freeze me, he tilts his head and hikes up one side of his chunky lips. "If you're shy, I can twist away—"

I shut him up by unbuttoning my jeans. The hiss of my zipper as I lower it matches the whistle that rustles through his teeth when I peel my jeans down my thighs while maintaining eye contact.

I'm not watching him solely to prove my confidence will only ever surge in his presence instead of wilting. I am also doing it so I don't miss a single expression that crosses his gorgeous face.

Mikhail's eyes speak a million words before his mouth articulates a single one.

Every nerve in my body ignites when a deep murmur sounds from his chest as he takes in my printed underwear.

"Sunflowers." He lifts his hooded eyes to mine. "Fitting." He rakes his teeth over his lower lip, augmenting the throbs hitting my clit. "Though I prefer daisies. They're delicate and sweet."

They're also the flowers he ordered to be grown across acres of land when he proposed.

The planning of his proposal proves it wasn't a quick-winded decision. It took months to implement and made me truly believe he asked for my hand in marriage because he wanted me to be his wife and the mother of his children.

Vying to ignore the heartache of our lost years, I toe off my shoes and shimmer out of my jeans. "They're my favorite print too, but they seem to have gone missing." His eyes flare, but his mouth remains tight-lipped. "You need to give them back. In my hurry to pack, I only packed five pairs of panties."

I struggle to keep up when he tosses out mixed signals. "That leaves four pairs too many."

I assumed his daisies reference was to maim my heart. Only now am I wondering if he is attempting to conjure happy memories like our trip to the waterfall instigated?

I pretend I'm not being swallowed by confusion. My skills are top-notch... until I bend over to gather my jeans from the floor.

I don't bend with my knees. With a flourish, I pop down in a way Elle Woods would be proud. I thrust my rear end out and cock my hip, giving Mikhail a bird's-eye view of the area he made moist during our grind-up.

It is an extremely unladylike poise that has Mikhail growling like he's a beast under attack. You'd need superhuman eye strength to see through the minute crack our entrance to the changing room caused, but Mikhail acts as if it is as gaping as the hole he left in my heart when he left.

He rushes forward to cover me with his body so fast that the briskness of his long strides cools my overheated skin.

I moan in appreciation, loving its relief.

Mikhail doesn't hear my moan in the way I intended. I understand why. I'm only good at lying when I am trying to convince myself it is for the greater good.

When Mikhail's heated breaths batter my earlobe, I know I should walk away, disappear into the disappointment that will inevitably surface like it did when our grind-up was busted, but for the life of me, I can't. My heart hasn't beaten at this rhythm for over a decade, and it was never as low as it is thudding now.

After checking that we're still alone, Mikhail steps us forward until I'm barricaded by the massive mirror and him before his hand skates around the front of my body. He splays his hand across my stomach before slowly lowering it. As he hooks his thumb into the top of my cotton panties, his eyes lock with mine in the mirror.

I panic I'm not expressing myself appropriately when the crack of elastic settling back into place sounds through my ears a nanosecond before the sting of my panties snapping back into place slaps my skin.

It doesn't linger for long.

"Give them to me."

"What?" I push out slowly, acting daft.

Mikhail would never let me follow the I'm-just-a-silly-girl ruse.

"Give them to me," he repeats, his tone neither stern nor demanding. It is more hopeful than anything.

"I..." I stop, swallow, then try again. "We..."

Out of excuses and honestly not strong enough to deny this man, I hook my fingers around the waistband of my panties and tug them down. My pace is slower this time, more teasing, and my eye contact is unbroken.

Heat burns through me when my arch to free the damp material from my ankles causes my ass to brush against Mikhail's groin.

He's the thickest he has ever been.

I grip my panties in my hand, almost wringing them of the wetness they would contain if they were still pressed against my vagina, before asking, "Now what?"

Mikhail licks his lips as his eyes slowly float up my body. "Now your bra."

"Why—"

The hand on my hip squeezes, and I lose all cognitive thoughts.

I pull down the straps of my bra, roll the hooks from the back to the front, then unlatch them. I usually remove my bras by unlatching them from the back, but since that would place unwanted distance between Mikhail and me, I changed things up.

Mikhail's hiss is silent this time. I don't need to hear it to know of its existence, though. It ruffles the hairs on my nape and brings the wave in my stomach close to cresting.

As my bra falls to the floor, Mikhail stares at me as if it is the first time he's seen me naked, and his hooded watch makes it seem as if I am worth millions of dollars.

"Like a fine wine," he murmurs, his voice barely a whisper.

He drinks me in for several long minutes before he plucks the dress from its hanger as if it is worthless and then carefully slides it over my head. The brushes of his hands as he guides the delicate material down my body doubles the tension firing between us.

I'm moments from being set ablaze when the back of his hand brushes past my aching pussy. It isn't solely his touch setting me on fire, but how he treats me as if I am worth far more than the pricy gown he's assisting me into.

He once told me that a man's wealth should never be calculated by the funds in his bank account. That true wealth can only be measured by the memories in his heart.

He is making true on his statement now.

Mikhail's eyes lift to mine when I whisper, "They're not selling dresses here. They are selling fantasies." A familiar glint sparks in his eyes. "Fantasies of what could happen in this dress. How someone puts it on and takes it off. The fantasy of being looked at like you are looking at me now. That alone makes the steep price tag seem worth it. But they've failed to realize you'd still look at me the same way even in a thrift store–purchased garment."

His lack of retort assures me of this, not to mention the thickness behind me.

The love in his eyes, the pure admiration, has me so desperate for answers I act impulsively, like my heart's fractures don't matter. "Why?"

Why did you leave?

Why give me enough to hook me for life with no desire to reel me in?

Why do you look at me as if I broke your heart when it was the opposite?

Mikhail's furrowed brows convince me that he heard the words my confused and broken heart refuse to express, but before he can answer me, we're interrupted by a likely source since this is her boutique.

"Wow. You are the exact picture I envisioned while designing that dress."

Chapter 22

Mikhail

Tension fills the ride back to Zelenolsk. It isn't all sexual this time. I'm confused as to why Emerson continues to seek answers from me for the decision *she* made. Her questions are rarely vocalized, but I feel them pumping out of her every time we lock eyes.

She is acting like she's as lost as I am as to why we broke up, and the confusion is muddling my mind more than my body's inability to act nonchalantly in her presence.

It wants her no matter the cost, and in all honesty, so does my heart. That's what my machoism at the boutique was about. I wanted her to rebel, mindful that sometimes the only time she is truly defenseless is when she's fighting no one but herself.

She didn't rebel. She submitted, and it has me the most confused I've ever been.

As we approach Zelenolsk, I remember a plan I made before I drank any caffeine. People are bustling around the manicured lawns and numerous sitting rooms, setting up equipment and arranging props.

Accepting a five-figure deal for a photo shoot with a world-renowned gossip magazine seems senseless when my establishments profit more than that per hour, but I knew it was the only way I could help Emerson without risking losing her for another ten years.

Her share will allow her to contribute to the funds her mother is seeking, but it will keep her at my side hopefully long enough to get some answers.

I park my bike at the side entrance of Zelenolsk Manor before assisting Emerson off. Crinkled brows and twisted lips show her confusion, and it makes me smile.

It is about time I handed her the confused baton.

I relish her bewilderment for a few seconds before attempting to ease it. "I thought a photo shoot would be a good way to announce our nuptials."

"Oh." Emerson nods, agreeing with my concept, but her eyes betray her nonchalant reply. I learn why when she twists to face me. "I didn't tell my family about this." Her hand flaps between us during the "this" part of her reply. "I made out I came here to endorse some business documents. That's why I deleted the images of us off the teen's phone. Our agreement shouldn't be revealed to my family by the media. I want to tell them myself."

With furrowed brows, I stare at her. I'd wondered what she had told her family about our agreement. Now I have my answer.

Although it hurts to acknowledge she told them our marriage contract is nothing more than a business transaction, I prefer it over believing she deleted the images from the teen's phone because she didn't want to be photographed with me.

Our relationship was already complicated before the ten-year break. Tossing a heap of unwanted opinions into the mix will worsen an already bumpy road.

I wet my lips before reducing the deepness of the groove between her reddish-brown brows. "They won't print the story until the end of the month, so you have time." I leave my reply short, unsure which direction to take. Time to tell her family? Or is it time to stop the publication of a highly fabricated story? I truly don't know.

Upon spotting the disappointment I cannot conceal, Emerson says, "I wanted to tell them, Mikhail. I was just..."—her chest sinks as she whispers—"worried you wouldn't show up again."

Again?

What does she mean *again*?

I was there the first time, at the end of the aisle, waiting for her.

She was the one who failed to show up.

I'm about to vocalize my confusion, when we're joined under the awning by the photographer. "Finally!" She greets us with a warm smile before guiding Emerson toward a studio-like setup in the den, pulling her away from me. "We've been shooting for thirty-four minutes of an hour-long pre-shoot, so whatever this is will have to wait until after we've captured it for eternity."

The photographer's assistant gestures for me to join them in the den, though several bodies remain between Emerson and me the entire time they stage us for the shoot.

The number of bodies separating us places our conversation on the back burner and has my focus shifting to the present instead of the past. Nothing said will change our past. We can either dwell on it or let it go like we did at the waterfall.

Over the next half hour, the photographer's voice is a constant stream of instructions.

"Mikhail, look this way."

"Emerson, tilt your head. Perfect. Just like that."

"Now, relax your shoulders."

She styles Emerson's hair as if its voluptuous look was intended for this photo shoot, her influence diminishing as my touch replaces hers. I return a stray lock of Emerson's hair to its shiny counterparts before rubbing at the groove between her brows.

I hate the sadness in her eyes, the uncertainty. It hurts more than heartache ever could, and the reminder has me speaking as if she didn't break my heart.

"Still my favorite color."

I don't need to elaborate on my reply. Emerson knows the origin of my favorite color. I told her a minimum of once a week for the three years we dated.

My fingers itch to trace her ghost-like grin, but further instructions from the photographer steal the chance.

"Hold still. Beautiful. That pose is perfect."

She moves closer, intruding on our space, before the clicking of her camera drowns out the thump of my pulse in my ears.

Emerson and I are standing so close that I can feel Emerson's pulse as easily as mine. It is a frantic, lively beat that proves ten years is barely a blip when it comes to a lifetime of memories.

I couldn't remember a single bad thing she did or said when she was moaning beneath me, begging for me to touch her. It was just us against the world.

"Almost done. Just a few more, then we're almost set for the real thing." The photographer's last sentence breaks the tangible string tethering us together.

"Real thing?" Emerson asks, her shock as high as my brows. "Is this not the actual shoot?"

With a giggle, the photographer lowers her camera. "This is the pre-shoot to check we have the lighting right. We don't want any pesky shadows hiding your beautiful face." She snaps another handful of photos I plan to purchase for my private collection. Emerson's confused face is adorable. It is one of my favorite features. "This is also a bridal shoot. We can't have you photographed in muddy jeans and a lint-pilled sweater. We have a range of gorgeous dresses ready for your approval."

Emerson's eyes stray to the rack the photographer points out before she returns them front and center. "I don't want a random dress."

"The dresses aren't random. Well-known designers crafted all of them. They're elegant and beautiful—"

"But they're not *my* dress. It isn't the dress I wore when we wed."

Emerson's eyes are on me, hot and wet. "It isn't the dress my mother made for me to marry you in."

My eyes bounce between hers for several long seconds. I didn't give her much time to agree to my proposal. I didn't want to give logic the chance to enter the equation. So there's no way her mother would have had enough time to whip together a basic dress, much less the intricately designed gown she wore yesterday.

That can only mean one thing. She wore the dress she was meant to wear ten years ago—the one her mother made when we decided to elope.

Not only does that reveal she held on to her wedding dress for over ten years, as I had our wedding rings, but it also shows she didn't go into this with a totally closed mind. She put thought into it, and feelings.

I turn to face Loretta, who is watching the shoot with a handful of staff. "Bring Emerson's dress to the den."

The photographer gasps. "We have a contract to endorse a designer for this feature. She can't wear a dress her mother made. That would be preposterous."

"Either my wife wears the dress she wore when we wed, or we cancel the shoot." My tone is the same snapped timbre I used when my grandfather, who at the time was the president of our great country, thought he could railroad me into marrying a stranger.

I was drunk, alcohol my only defense when fighting the urge to drive to Lidny and demand answers years too late, when he handed me a list of socialites to pick from.

I tossed their dossiers into the fireplace before I stormed out. My journey to Lidny ended abruptly when I crashed into a gulley, resulting in a drunk driving arrest.

My grandfather swept my criminal record under the rug, but it came at a cost. He relegated me to the lowest position I'd ever held and withheld the inheritance all Dokovic sons receive on their twenty-first birthday.

Fortunately for me, I already had a successful establishment under my belt, and my determination not to follow my grandfather's life plan saw it expanding into a multi-location establishment within the next twelve months.

The photographer sighs, shifting my focus back to the present before she glances at her team to gauge their response to my threat.

They all side in my favor. Even Kolya.

"It isn't ideal, but if it's that important to her—"

"It's important to me," I interrupt, stopping her from saying something that will see this shoot ending before it has truly begun.

"If it's that important to you," the photographer corrects, "we'll make it work." She flicks her eyes to Emerson, who is staring at me in awe. "Perhaps we can get a handful of shots of you in their garments that we can use in future promotional features?"

Emerson nods, happy with the compromise.

Her agreeing gesture slackens the worried lines scouring the photographer's forehead. "Okay. Great."

While she barks orders at her team, Emerson hands me everything I'd lost with two short words. "Thank you."

Chapter 23

Emerson

Studio lights cast a warm glow over Mikhail and me as we follow the directions of the photographer. She dictates the entire shoot from behind the lens, but my focus is more on Mikhail than her. His subtle touches, the excruciating pressure of his fingers on my waist, hips, and ass, and the electricity bristling between us have kept my focus gripped on nothing but him for the past three hours.

And lust... that has been in abundance as well.

It's been one nonstop chemistry pose after another. I doubt any of the photographer's suggested poses are suitable for public consumption. The brushing of our bodies is an intimate dance—one I would give anything to take behind closed doors. They grow more intimate the longer the shoot progresses, bordering on pornography.

Take our pose now, for example. I'm seated on a chair, and Mikhail is kneeling in front of me. They pulled the flare of my dress halfway up my thighs, and seconds later, Mikhail slipped his hands beneath the layers of lace.

We're meant to be replicating the removal of the garter I left on the desk in the corner of my room, but it feels far more salacious than a newly wedded couple would be in front of their family and friends. Desire is hanging heavily in the air, and I can smell my bubbling arousal.

"Deeper, Mikhail. I don't want to see a single thread of your dress shirt."

Mikhail slides his hand up my thigh as per the photographer's instructions, sending a shiver rolling down my spine. His fingertips tickle the skin high on my thigh, and my insides clench.

He never returned the underwear he forced me to remove at the boutique, and I've not had a minute to myself in hours to replace them.

Mikhail is only an inch away from discovering I am naked under the dress my mother made from my baptismal gown.

When my lust-crazed head forces a subtle arch in my back, I lower my gaze to Mikhail. The world fades away when our eyes connect. Once again, it is just the two of us lost in a moment, cherishing every touch, throb, and whispered moan.

"Yes. There. Perfect."

The camera clicks, capturing images I will never approve for print. They're too X-rated.

I'll never recover if my mother sees my expression. Hence another reason I deleted the teen's photos. I spun fast, but not fast enough for the eager snap of a fan.

The heat creeping across my cheeks descends to my chest when the photographer's assistant says, "Isn't the groom meant to remove the garter with his teeth?"

He flicks through a celebrity wedding bible the magazine's editor demanded they fill as a salacious smirk stretches across Mikhail's face. It tells me everything I need to know. He knows I am sans panties, and he has no intention of helping me out of the pickle he placed me in.

"Yes. Here it is."

The photographer peers at the folder that's so heavy it needs two hands to hold it up. "Oh... I love it." Her eyes flicker for a handful of seconds before she adds, "But I think we should do it in a black-and-white film. It will give it a regal edge."

She calls a ten-minute break so her assistant can fetch some old-style film from her van. The lighting crew, makeup artist, and stylist rush for the refreshments Chef placed out earlier.

In seconds, the den goes from a bustling hive of activity to almost isolated.

Only Mikhail and I remain.

Now is the perfect time for me to replace my undergarments. But for the life of me, I can't move. Mikhail's gaze is hooded, and his hands are still under my dress.

I'd be a fool if I were to walk now.

Mikhail *tsks* me. It sounds as playful as the glint firing through his icy eyes. "Emerson Morozov, what will your momma say when she finds out you did an entire shoot while not wearing any panties?"

I reply with as much sass as he's issuing. "She'd probably ask me who stole them and then demand an update on their removal."

Mikhail throws his head back and laughs. It does wild things to my insides. "I said what would your momma say, not your aunt Marcelle."

"Tomato, *tomato.*"

His laughter increases, but it does little to ease the tension. His hands are still on me. Not even a tsunami could put out the fire raging in my stomach. As his fingertips creep closer to the heat making my brain a hazy mess, he asks, "How would you answer her question?"

I take a moment to contemplate before choosing the honesty route, hopeful it will see me rewarded. "I removed them to save them from getting soddened, but someone interrupted me before I could reimagine my wildest dream."

Mikhail's deliriously handsome face and fingers inch closer while he murmurs, "Reimagined?"

I nod, the burning of my throat too incinerating to speak.

He will never let me off so easily. He angles his head, sending a dark lock falling across his eye before he arches a brow in silent questioning.

I wait until the tension becomes excruciating before whispering, "Because once magic is mastered, it can only be reimagined. Though sometimes it is pointless. There's only one version of *The Shawshank Redemption* for a reason. Why—"

"Fuck with perfection."

I nod, surprised by the heavy sentiment in his eyes when he speaks a statement he once regularly used.

For a moment, he doesn't say anything, but once he eventually speaks, it is better than I expected. "Does anything achieved in ten minutes qualify as perfection?"

"Depends."

His deep rumble rolls over my lips when he asks, "On?"

"On whom you've awarded the ten minutes to." I twist my lips to hide their painful furl. "A random stranger with no personal connection whatsoever would probably underestimate the significance of those ten minutes, but someone who clings to every single second would cherish every one of them."

I stop seeking something to focus on when Mikhail says, "What if she was the only one you've ever given those ten minutes to? What would she say?"

I can't tell if I'm angry or confused by my tone. "If you're trying to make out you've not been with anyone since me, you need to teach the photographer's assistant how to whisper. He—"

"I'm not talking about sex, Emmy. I'm talking about this. Us. Now." He brushes his hand down the cleft of my pussy, stealing my thoughts. "A man kneeling in front of *his* woman." The way he says "his" floods my veins with lust. "They say you only kneel to those above you, that it is degrading to do it for any old fool." The sentiment I mentioned earlier is nothing compared to the emotions flaring through his eyes now. "I kneeled in front of you every day, Emmy. You and *only* you. No one else has had my respect enough for me to kneel in front of them."

I want to sob but hold it back, needing answers. "Then why did you le—"

I want to scream when we're interrupted again.

"All right. Break's over! Let's get this shoot wrapped up."

Chapter 24

Mikhail

"What kind of shoot were you doing again?" Zoya pulls the phone in close as if it will make my face do the same. "I thought Playboy spreads were a solo adventure?" She snickers at my eye roll before laughing.

My words cut her chuckles short. "Stage lights are hot as fuck. What's your excuse for your inflamed cheeks?"

I gag when she purrs like a little kitty snuggling up to her owner.

The churns of my stomach chop up my reply. "I had wondered why Andrik hadn't shown up to kick my ass yet. Thanks for taking one for the team, Sis."

Bile burns my throat when she murmurs, "You're more than welcome. Andrik is—"

"Can we skip the deets? I just ate, and I'm not a fan of vomit." I shudder while recalling the one time I mistook vomit for porridge. My childhood went downhill from there.

After a silent apology for the greening of my gills, Zoya asks, "Seriously, how are things?"

I ponder a reply while straying my eyes to my office door. Today was different from what I was expecting. Don't take that in a bad way. We had a handful of hiccups, but for the most part, it was a good day.

My smile radiates when I say, "We took a ride out to the waterfall."

Zoya sits up, her adorable face filling the screen of my phone. "*The* waterfall or..."

"*The* waterfall." I adjust my position while recalling how our climb to the top progressed. "Emerson nearly slipped. Honestly, it scared me half to death."

Last night, I had decided to forgive and forget, but her near miss solidified my decision.

I'd never been more scared.

I laugh like Zoya didn't hit the nail on the head when she says, "And that's when you realized you still love her, so you hooked your leg over your white horse, galloped in to save her, and told her you'd never let her go ever again." She *pffts* me when I arch a brow and stare at her like I have no clue who she is. "Shut up. Hormones are weird. One minute, I'm horny as fuck. The next minute, I want to cry. I'd hate it if Andrik's response to my mood swings wasn't the same. Hot, raunchy—"

"We kissed."

That gains her utmost devotion and saves me from being sick. I hate vomit—from both me and others. "Tongue or no tongue?"

"Tongue," I answer, struggling not to smirk like a smug prick.

"Grinding?"

I nod. Eagerly.

Zoya's expression goes deadpan. "Did she moan?"

Again, I nod.

I also readjust my position again.

Even without the "big brother" title, Andrik's control over my life is apparent when Zoya questions, "Then why did Kolya inform Andrik that the consummation of the marriage has yet to occur?" I'm not rewarded with a chance to answer. "Because you're worried she'll leave the instant the deed is done?"

I *pfft* like her hammer missed the nail this time around.

She knows it is a lie. "You do know there are plenty of other things you can do to take care of that bulge in your pants that don't involve sex, right?"

She isn't the only one skilled in acting daft. "What the fuck are you talking about?"

"Even if you had your crotch hidden under layers of sugary goodness, Marshmallow Man, a nun wouldn't have missed the tent you were pitching during your photo shoot."

It takes a moment, but my back molars grind when the truth smacks into me. "I told Konstantine to turn off surveillance at Zelenolsk, not to use it to spy on me."

My jaw almost cracks when she whispers, "Would it make you less cranky if I said Konstantine only does as ordered?"

"Andrik—"

"Not him."

I stare at the screen, my mouth ajar. Andrik only hands the power baton to one other person. It isn't our father, as you'd believe. It is his wife.

"Sunshine—"

"You're my big brother," Zoya interrupts. "I'm just trying to keep an eye out for you."

She's called out as a liar by an accented voice. "And she's the biggest snoop I know." Dr. Nikita Ivanov's pretty face enters the frame. She's wearing a stethoscope, scrubs, and a friendly smile. "But we should probably give her some leeway. Bed rest isn't fun."

Worry echoes in my tone. "You're on bed rest?"

Zoya waves off my fret like only months ago the gender of her baby wouldn't have glued her missing person flyer to a milk carton. Birthing a son only awarded you five years in the Dokovic realm. A daughter is an instant dismissal. Or I should say *was* since that fascism died along with our grandfather.

"My lady bits aren't playing nice, so Dr. Anal placed me on two weeks of bed rest." Zoya's eye roll is immature but effective in lowering my worry. "How do you think I know you can still relieve tension without penetration?"

I shake my head to make sure the images her question triggered do not get burned into my memory.

Zoya laughs, mindful that a dirty mind is hereditary.

Her laughter is interrupted by my phone pinging, announcing I have a message.

> VTB BANK:
>
> You transferred $58,000 to an account ending in 8179.

I sit up straight, my heart thudding against my ribs.

What the fuck?

"What?" Zoya asked, adapted to my confused expression.

I scan the screen of my phone. "Someone just transferred fifty-eight K from my checking account."

My eyes widen when another message pings.

> VTB BANK:
>
> You paid $62,000 to Noestrdem Pty Ltd.

I clench my jaw when another message arrives.

> VTB BANK:
>
> You spent $15,800 at Moeses Online, bringing your spending to $135,800 today.

"Some fucker has hacked my bank account."

I slide my office chair under my desk and fire up my laptop.

After three failed login attempts, my bank sends another message.

> VTB:
>
> Your payment of 1,200,000 to Maserati Global Sales was successful.

"One point three million gone in the blink of an eye!" I mutter while typing my password in slower this time and still getting an error message. "And they seem to have locked me out of my account."

"Not a they," sounds a voice out of my phone, a highly recognized voice.

I stare at my phone as Zoya twists hers to face Konstantine, Andrik's hacker and my half-brother, sitting across from her. "It's a her."

"Her?"

My heart beats at an unnatural rhythm when a surveillance image pops up on my phone screen. It shows Emerson entering my office twenty minutes after our photo shoot ended. She's still wearing her wedding dress, and her dilated eyes would have you believing I'm a man who is happy to eat his wife's pussy in front of an audience.

I'm not, so the shoot ended not long after the photographer called the first break of the shoot.

After drinking in the way Emerson's dress hugs every one of her curves, my eyes land on a thick wad of papers in her hand. "What is she holding?"

A hum vibrates in Konstantine's chest as he zooms in on the footage playing on my laptop. "A checkbook." Seconds pass before he adds, "Her checkbook."

The pieces of the puzzle slot together the more the footage rolls. Emerson sits at my desk and fires up my laptop, her access immediate since I don't bother with a passcode. Finding anything of importance is difficult since Andrik buried it beneath a heap of red tape years ago.

"It looks like the magazine paid for the shoot by instant wire transfer."

"At my request," I reply to Zoya's mumble. "I told them I wouldn't accept their offer if they couldn't pay immediately." My tone lowers. "Emerson needed money, and she would have never accepted it from me."

"Emerson received the entire payment for the shoot," Konstantine says, his words as fast as his keystrokes. "She transferred fifty percent into your account and the rest into her mother's."

I realize this investigation is a group effort when Nikita says, "Why would she transfer your share to you, then spend far more only a few hours later?"

The answer hits us seconds later. In the footage Konstantine found, after transferring 22,500 dollars to me and 22,500 dollars to her mother, Emerson seeks a piece of paper to jot down a note that she used my laptop. She did the same anytime she borrowed my computer to order stock for the bar.

"What is that?" Nikita asks, the only one lost since she is unaware that my marriage is a sham.

"Our marriage contract," I answer, put off by the silence. "The real one that stated she would inherit far more than I made out when I presented her my grandfather's terms."

"Shit," Nikita murmurs, her cuss word almost regal sounding in her British accent. "She thinks you stiffed her, so she's spending her share." Her tone is piqued with interest. "How much does she have left to squander?"

"According to her calculations, a little under forty-nine million," I say with a laugh, shocked.

Konstantine's deep timbre breaks through Zoya's and Nikita's shocked huffs. "I'll place a hold on your accounts. It will slow down her spending."

"No," I answer too fast for my brain or heart to comprehend. "If my wife wants to have a tantrum, let her have a tantrum. It is her money she's wasting."

"Are you sure?" Konstantine checks. "She could wipe you out, Mikhail. Your accounts have no daily spending limit. It could all be gone in a matter of hours."

I nod. "I've handled worse than bankruptcy when facing Emerson's wrath." Money couldn't fix my broken heart.

Before Zoya or Nikita can vocalize the concern I see on their faces,

I instruct Konstantine to send me Emerson's location details. "Money attracts the worst kind of people, and I want to make sure she isn't taken advantage of."

Well, that's what my heart is telling my head. In reality, I don't want anything to come between Emerson and me—not even the possible loss of five hundred million dollars.

Chapter 25

Emerson

A pounding headache wakes me. My mouth is as dry as a desert, and my stomach is churning. The room spins, and warm bedding falls into my lap when I sit up. I groan while rubbing at the obvious signs of a hangover. My temples are throbbing, and my scaly skin shows signs of dehydration.

As I scan the owner's suite of Zelenolsk Manor, I prompt my sluggish head for an update on what occurred last night. Portions are a blur, alcohol forever a good cure for painful memories, but a handful are clear enough to recall.

I remember transferring Mikhail's half of the payment for the photo shoot to his bank account and the other half to my mother, and the paperwork I stumbled onto when attempting to tell Mikhail I had used his computer. But other than that, my night is a haze of short video montages.

The roiling of my stomach worsens when I glance at my phone, hopeful it will clear up some inconsistencies. Notifications from various shopping apps flood the screen. I didn't stick with Temu and Shein this time. I splurged on goods at high-end department stores, and there's even a purchase for a top-of-the-range sports vehicle.

The total amount on the screen makes me sick, and not even the remembrance that it is barely ten percent of the amount Mikhail tried to stiff me on eases my guilt.

I feel sick, not just from excessive drinking but from the realization of my actions when more memories flood in.

Last night, I didn't just throw Mikhail under the bus. I tossed a handful of Zelenolsk staff under the wheels with him.

Needing to make things right, I drag myself out of bed, my body protesting every movement. I need water, something to settle my stomach, and some aspirin before I can even contemplate how to fix my monumental fuckup.

As I make my way downstairs, I recall how my spending began with spoiling the staff at Zelenolsk Manor. With Mikhail's credit card details at the ready, I ordered a feast fit for kings and enough alcohol to make senseless mistakes seem logical.

I can't take back the purchases. They disappeared in a matter of hours. But I can ensure that my ill judgment doesn't affect the people who helped me forget the woes of my life for a couple of hours.

The unease of my stomach settles in my chest as I descend the spiral staircase. The silence is unsettling, and I can't shake the feeling that something is amiss.

As I cross the marble tiles, my footsteps echo in the quietness of Zelenolsk Manor. The hum of activity from yesterday is absent, and the emptiness of such a large space feels eerie.

As I approach the kitchen, I rake my eyes across the multiple living areas. As per the worst outcome I thought possible, all the staff are gone —including the maintenance crew, who ensured I vomited on a paved area so the lawns and gardens would maintain their pristine, non-stomach-bile-scorched appearance.

A manor that once housed hundreds of residents on its grounds is silent, and my anxiety grows with each passing second.

I fucked up.

I fucked up *bad*.

In the kitchen, I find Mikhail. Like yesterday morning, he sits at the breakfast nook, cradling a cup of coffee. His hunched shoulders and the dark circles under his eyes are noticeable. He looks tired, though he is still the most handsome man I have ever laid eyes on.

Worry spreads across my chest, but I try to play it off. "Morning. Where is everyone?"

Mikhail looks up, and that is when I realize he knows everything. The millions I squandered, the liquor I drank with his staff, and the loathsomeness I felt when I tried to flirt, only for it to be politely dismissed.

"Perhaps it is time to call it a night, *Mrs.* Dokovic?" rang on repeat last night.

"The economy is in a crisis, Mikhail. Your father won't get close to his competitor if his voters find out you let go of hundreds of employees because you were jealous." I hate myself for my last word, but when you're clutching at straws, you throw more than morals into a burning building. You take people undeserving into the flames with you. "You could lose your father the presidency, all because you don't trust me to let my hair down occasionally."

Last night was about more than letting my hair down, but arguments fizzle too fast when you start with the big hitters, and then nothing but lies are told instead of the truth.

Mikhail's lack of retort stings.

It burns like a thousand bee stings.

I know everything I need to know, but I can't help but push. "That's what this is about, isn't it?" I wave my hand around the empty kitchen, its flap deafening in the silence. "You don't trust me."

"It has nothing to do with that," he lies, breaking my heart.

He didn't deny that he doesn't trust me.

He denied that it was the motive of his foolhardiness this time around.

Too angry to think rationally, I roll my eyes before exiting the kitchen with more speed than I entered it. My throbbing temples move toward a blinding migraine, but I keep moving, confident no amount of coin is worth this level of heartache.

Mikhail is on my heels two seconds later. "Don't walk away from me, Emerson. You don't get to do that again."

Hair slaps my face when I whip around to face him, my footing unsteady but resolute. "Again? I didn't do it the first time, so how could I do it again?"

"Oh, that's right. You would have had to show up to walk away. I forget not showing up isn't the same as walking away." His snarky words are like knives to my chest, so it is only fair I hit him with the same level of aggression.

I storm up to him and bang my fists on his pecs while shouting, "You're the one who failed to show up!" I huff in his face. "And for what? The makeup sex was good, but it wasn't good enough to take it that far."

"Good?" He laughs a tormented chuckle that exposes he didn't sleep a wink last night. "The sex wasn't good, Emerson. It was so fucking unbelievable that it ruined every other sexual experience I've had."

Excitement blisters for half a second before it's stripped for jealousy. "I'm so sorry to have ruined your ability to stuff your dick into any trollop you meet without having a conscious thought. How dare I crave fireworks so blistering that I couldn't imagine doing it with anyone else, let alone being upset it could ruin future endeavors."

"Oh no, because you'd much rather pretend it didn't fucking happen at all. Wouldn't you? That and running seem to be your go-to coping mechanisms these days."

I go to slap him, but he catches my hand before I can, and then he uses the same hand to pull me into his body.

Every muscle in my body tenses when I smell my scent on his skin. Our combined smells expose why the minuscule hours I got last night were so restful, and it makes my insides feel like liquid instead of solid masses.

We slept in the same bed, and one whiff of his heated skin last night had me wanting to forget my anger as swiftly as it does now.

I'd like to blame alcohol for the actions that occurred shortly after I told him he smelled like home, but that isn't true. By the time Mikhail joined me in bed, I was already halfway sober.

Mikhail's heated words bound off my cheek when he snarls, "You got off on my leg but didn't have the decency to look at me after it... *again!*" His angry eyes bounce between mine. "Spent over a million dollars in under an hour and didn't buy me a single damn thing. But that is nothing compared to when you walked out of my life without so much as a goodbye after three fucking years, Emerson. Three. Years!" I'm not granted the chance to display my shock, much less articulate it. "What did I ever do to you to deserve that level of disrespect?"

I cringe at the morbid bitterness in his tone. He can't be serious, can he? He broke my heart. That deserves far more than a snippet of disrespect. I trusted him and believed in him, and when he left, he shattered our dreams and broke all the promises he'd made. He drowned our memories with turmoil and made them warp in my mind like a cruel joke.

He hurt me badly, and the fury of that cracks my tone when I say, "I'm not the bad guy in this situation, and I refuse to let you make out I am."

"And I am?"

"Yes!" I scream, the hurt of his betrayal too painful not to react. "You're to blame for everything!"

I thrash against him again, desperate to get free.

The memories are too painful, the hurt still real.

To my absolute horror, I whimper out a moan when my fight to get free of his hold has my leg brushing past his crotch—his *extended* crotch. It flashes up memories of last night and exposes how he didn't just watch over me after I stumbled into the owner's suite. He was in every frame, close enough to catch me if I were to fall but not close enough to intervene in my rebellious streak.

I try to remember my anger and the pain that hasn't subsided in over a decade while saying, "Let me go. *Please.*"

"No," Mikhail says sternly, his voice steady. "I'm not letting you walk away from this. From me. I shouldn't have let you do it ten years ago, and I won't let you do it now."

His shunting of the blame again fuels my anger. I continue to fight, to place necessary distance between us, but he holds on tight.

"You can't just decide to fight now," I snap out, my voice rising. "It's too late. *Years* too late."

Even as the words leave my mouth, a part of me is grateful, pleased that he's finally showing some fight and not letting me go without protest this time.

The memory of Mikhail leaving me at the altar is still fresh, a wound that refuses to heal, but his silence for the past ten years hurts more.

I honestly don't know if I can go through that again.

"It's not too late," Mikhail argues, his tone softer now but still resolute. "We can move past this. We can get over it. Fuck." His eyes are full of emotions and on me, hot and heavy. "I can't lose you again, Emmy. It will kill me."

A twisted mix of emotions hits me at once. Anger and gratitude are most prominent. But hope is there too, and it leaves me feeling conflicted. "It's too late. You should have fought for us sooner."

"I know," he admits, his voice cracking with emotions as his grip on my arm loosens. "I should have demanded answers a long time ago, but I..." His eyes bounce between mine. "I didn't want to know the truth. I didn't want to face the fact that we were over. I couldn't bear the thought of hearing that from you."

I stare into his eyes, fighting back the moisture looming in mine. As much as I hate to admit this, the hurt in his tired gaze suffocates some of my worry, replacing it with a glimmer of hope.

Maybe, just maybe, there's something still worth fighting for. We just need to heal the wounds we're both carrying and rebuild what we've lost, and my hungover head is confident it knows the perfect way for us to commence that.

Chapter 26

Mikhail

ir whizzes from my nose when Emerson uses the tactic she always does when she's losing.

She kisses me.

I could pull away. I don't because I don't have the strength.

I'm a human, not a fucking superhero.

This woman could stab me in the heart over and over again, and I still wouldn't deny her. That's how under my skin she is, how badly she drilled herself into my brain. Even when I am furious at her, she's forever on my mind, and I'm done pretending she isn't.

Even if it only awards me an hour of her time, I'll let her have every penny I own before I will ever stop this.

With my fingers weaved through Emerson's hair and our lips squashed together, I kiss her with everything I have.

Our embrace isn't close to sweet. It is angry and indulgent, and it makes my dick leak pre-cum. This was always our pattern: cruel and vindictive, but once the tension was released, the hurt faded, and mutual admiration and respect emerged.

I can only hope we will follow the same route now.

As our tongues dance an intricate routine, I back us up until the first step of the grand staircase of Zelenolsk Manor almost knocks Emerson off her feet, and my cock throbs halfway up her stomach.

She grips my hair, fisting it roughly, when a second after I lay her across the top three stairs of the stairwell, I lower my mouth to the region of her body that teasingly badgered me for hours on end last night.

My only task was to ensure her safe arrival home, but her regretful groan changed my plans. I slipped between the sheets and pulled her into my chest before a single thought crossed my mind, only escaping mere minutes before the fight I knew would inevitably occur began.

After pulling Emerson's sleeping shirt up to her chest, I curl my tongue around her erect nipple. I suck it into my mouth before gently grazing it with my teeth, doubling the harshness of her breaths. Her back arches as I feast on her delectable breasts.

When my fingers brace at the entrance of her pussy, her moans echo in the emptiness of my grandfather's most beloved estate. I press my thumb down ever so slightly on the nub at the apex of her almost bare mound, drawing out the moans I would go to the end of the world to hear time and time again.

The air dampens when I touch her through panties too scant to be classified as an article of clothing. I toy with her clit for several long minutes, making her panties and tiny sleeping shorts moist and pliable. They come away from her body with only the slightest tug, as fragile as the wire I am precariously balancing on.

I pocket her damp panties, hopeful they won't be the last pair I collect from her, but I do it so absentmindedly that it doesn't ruin the tension keeping the air sticky with humidity.

Emerson's shoulders join when I part her with my fingers before slamming two inside her. I finger fuck her roughly, almost cruelly, but she can't get enough. Her pussy grows even wetter as mewls for me to take her hard and fast spill from her lips.

I comply. I fuck her hard with my fingers while my thumb circles her clit with every brutal pound. In seconds, she's racing toward release, so I free her clit from my thumb and concentrate solely on her pussy.

"Mikhail, please," she begs, too rehearsed on my go-to coping mechanism when I'm spiraling. I take, take, take and only give once I'm on the cusp of exhaustion.

Curling my fingertips, I calm Emerson's panic slightly before saying, "If you want to come, stop holding back."

"I'm... not... holding... back." Her eyes roll into the back of her head as I increase the speed of my thrusts for every word spilling her lie.

When she bites her lip, stifling the screams I'm desperate to hear, I lose all sense of control. I replace my thumb with my tongue and stretch her wide with three fingers instead of two.

I nuzzle the cleft of her pussy first before allocating all the focus of my lips and tongue to her clit.

Emerson grips my hair tightly when I swivel my tongue around the nervy bud before sucking it into my mouth. Her moans are erotic, almost where I need them to be.

She's warm and wet and tastes as fucking sweet as I remember.

"I could eat nothing but your pussy for a year and not feel like I was missing out on a single fucking thing."

An indecipherable sentence falls from her mouth as she pushes me in closer to her pussy, wordlessly demanding I continue eating her for breakfast.

She's still angry at me but incapable of looking past the fireworks that forever erupt when we're in the same room.

Furthermore, consuming her like this, in this location, is much more intimate than fucking. I'm on my knees in the very place that almost cost me my life, and she is above me, on the pedestal I placed her on when she made my life seem worth living.

The memory of how she saved me makes me eat her more expertly.

Her moans fill the air as her taste erases years of painful memories. Hardly any of them belong to her, but I struggle to remember anything when my head is buried between her legs.

When you're angry, the closest target is the easiest.

I guess I could say that's why I stayed away so long.

It was easier to respect Emerson's wishes than admit she deserved better than me.

I entered our relationship with more baggage than an international flight.

Only one remained when she left me. It was the biggest, but that doesn't matter. She cleared off the conveyer belt for me and made the burden of my birthright less obvious.

The recollection has me sucking her clit into my mouth with so much force that her back bends as a ferocious orgasm scorches through her.

Her moans bounce off priceless paintings, mingled with my own. I'm the hardest I've ever been and fighting like fuck not to extend her orgasm to endless.

I wouldn't hesitate if I weren't desperate to be buried deep inside her.

After bringing her back from the clouds with more delicateness than I used to rocket her to an outer galaxy, I shoot my hand down to my pants and free my cock.

Emerson's moan when she takes in how angry and hard I am rolls through me like liquid ecstasy. I feel the same heat between her legs that I feel in my veins when I brace my cock at her pussy's entrance and pierce its head between her wet folds.

"Yes," Emerson whispers when I push in, stuffing inches of my rock-hard cock inside her with one thrust.

"Christ," I bite out. "You're so damn tight."

I clench my jaw, refusing to make a fool of myself like I have previously.

We have years to make up for. I want this to last as long as possible.

"Please, Mikhail," Emerson begs, withering beneath me. "I need you to move. I can't come after only one pump. It will make me starfish for the rest of our exchange." I almost laugh until she completes her reply. "I don't want to be remembered as a dud."

Remorse for her words blisters through her eyes, but it's too late.

The damage has been done.

The spell has been broken.

As her words ring through my head on repeat, I pull out faster than I entered, and then head for the closest exit, fiddling with my zipper on the way.

I hear Emerson call my name, but I keep moving, the fight not in me. I am furious, fucking enraged, but since I'm the only fool deserving of my wrath, I must keep moving.

The beep of a call ending sounds into my ears a second after I slide into an idling SUV in front of my grandfather's estate several long stomps later.

Kolya drifts his confused eyes over my flushed cheeks and sex-mused hair before his lips twitch in preparation to speak.

I beat him to the punch. "Transfer one hundred thousand into Emerson's account."

I'm at the end of my tether. It is *not* the time for Kolya to test me, but he pushes like he knows my reputation isn't as fierce as my siblings'. "They will require proof."

"Transfer her the money!" I demand again, my shout arriving with my fist landing on the headrest in front of me.

I hit it again and again, needing the thumps of my fists to drown out Emerson's underhanded comment that our romp was a once-only reimagining.

She did it for the money, not for the memories, and the knowledge is killing me.

"Okay," Kolya caves. "I will have it transferred immediately."

My nostrils flare as I suck in some big breaths, endeavoring to calm my anger before it spirals out of control.

I shouldn't have bothered. "Then organize for her things to be returned to her home before I return this evening."

Kolya mumbles his understanding of my request before the SUV door opens, and he exits without a glance in my direction.

Chapter 27

Emerson

"Mikhail?"

I jackknife into a half-seated position when the creak of floorboards draws my focus to the entryway of the owner's suite at Zelenolsk Manor. My stomach gurgles when the crispness of the cuff on the white shirt of my visitor registers as familiar.

All the staff at Zelenolsk wear the same uniform. Crisp white button-up shirts and either black trousers or pencil-pleated skirts.

"That is the final bag," Loretta announces to a man in his mid-fifties, her professional tone hiding her deceit.

I arrived with only a bag, so I will leave with one as well. Loretta is merely saving face for a woman undeserving of her grace.

As I watch them walk out my belongings, my fight with Mikhail echoes in my mind. I feel horrible for how our exchange ended, but anger is there too, simmering just beneath the surface.

I shouldn't have said what I said, but my head wasn't in the right frame at the time to evaluate every word. When snowed under, my mouth runs away on me, but it's far worse when lust clouds my judgment.

Mikhail could have stayed and spoken about it maturely, but again, he chose the cheat's route.

He walked, which frees me to do the same with my head held high.

I just need my heart to get the memo. Its devastation has my shoulders slumped like they know I lost, and no amount of reassurance from my brain can convince it otherwise.

As I follow my belongings, neatly arranged by the staff I thought Mikhail had gotten rid of, my heart slips to my feet.

Turns out, the staff was just given the morning off. Mikhail's prediction of how our fight would pan out was more accurate than even I could have imagined.

The realization he can still read me so easily adds another layer to my already bruised ego. If I were honest, I would admit that I don't want to go. The past forty-eight hours have been a rollercoaster of emotions, but they were still filled with that messy gooeyness I couldn't get enough of when Mikhail was mine.

Since I've not been honest with myself for a long time, I continue shadowing Loretta's steps, each stride an effort.

I could have left abruptly like Mikhail, but when you've been kept waiting for so long, there is a desperate need for closure.

I couldn't stop playing the words Mikhail spoke before I kissed him through my head, or the pain in his tone. It seemed as if our time apart was as torturous and confusing for him as it was for me.

There's also the matter of the massive transfer that my phone pinged with only minutes after I sulked to my room, feeling empty and confused. The "consummation of vows" payment was wired too soon after Mikhail's departure to announce it was done by anyone but him.

As much as that money could help my family, I can't accept it. It doesn't feel right because nothing I've done since gorging on a peanut butter sandwich has been done for a payout.

I kissed Mikhail because I couldn't take the tension a second longer, and I begged him to fuck me because there's no such thing as heartache when his hands and lips are on mine. There is no one in the world but us.

After announcing to Loretta that I won't be a minute, I head to Mikhail's office. My steps are nowhere near as flighty as they were yesterday afternoon when I breezed into his office as if I were weightless. Our afternoon had been magical. I thought nothing could bring it down. Then I saw the contract his grandfather had drafted in full.

I don't know why I was angry. I didn't earn a penny of the Dokovics' fortune, so I had no claim to it. I was simply hurt believing that my interactions with Mikhail were solely about money and that he had prioritized it over genuine feelings.

My refusal to accept payment for the consummation of our vows stems from the possibility of someone accusing me of doing the same.

When I push open Mikhail's office door, my breath hitches in my throat. A dark figure sits behind his bulky desk. Regretfully, when the figure turns to face me, I see the blue eyes I'm seeking, but they belong to the wrong man.

Andrik, Mikhail's older brother, lifts his eyes to mine. When they meet, for a moment, the world stands still.

Although he doesn't share the same blood as Mikhail, the impact of my loss smacks into me. I struggle not to fold in two, feeling more lost than ever, and the hollow emptiness overwhelming me almost takes me under when Andrik says, "Mikhail was inside the church, waiting for you. He only left hours after I told him you weren't coming."

Chapter 28

Emerson

My hand shakes when I'm handed a glass of water. At some point during Andrik's long confession about his contribution to his brother's heartbreak, I sat down—whether by choice or force, I'm not sure. My mind is spiraling so much that I'm struggling to remember which way is up.

For years, I believed Mikhail had left me at the altar. I had no clue he was standing next to the priest, awaiting my arrival, because his grandfather bombarded me before I could walk through the church doors.

Now the way he looks at me makes sense.

He truly believes I broke his heart.

My mind races back to that moment, the confrontation with Mikhail's grandfather, before I stammer out again in disbelief, "Mikhail was inside the church?"

Andrik nods, his unvoiced reply hitting me like a punch to the stomach.

Even hearing it multiple times hasn't lessened its impact.

Mikhail didn't leave me at the altar.

He was there, waiting for me.

Zoya moves closer when I involuntarily sway before she encourages me to take a sip of water. When I do, she smiles softly before squatting down in front of me, her swollen belly resting between her slim thighs.

The slightest groan sees Andrik at her side in an instant. "*милая*, you're meant to be resting."

"Shh." Zoya waves off her husband's worry as if it is unfounded before returning her focus to me. "What Andrik orchestrated was wrong. Your shock is valid. But at the time, he believed he was saving your life and the life of your unborn child."

A wave of confusion washes over me. "What are you talking about?" I ask, my voice barely a whisper. "What child?"

Andrik rejoins the conversation, willing to face the brunt of my anger if it will shield his wife from it. "I saw the pregnancy test, Emerson, and the ultrasound results. I thought they were yours." He looks down, his expression pained. "My advisor did, too. We remained unaware until our grandfather passed, and the lineage he had amassed over the years was sought for his estate." I'm sucker punched for the umpteenth time when he murmurs, "When you never came forward as claimant, I prompted his attorney to what I believed was another subsequent recipient of his fortune." He coughs, seemingly embarrassed. "It was then that we learned the pregnancy test and ultrasound images I had seen were not yours. They were—"

"My mother's," I interrupt, flabbergasted.

For the first time, his stern expression softens before he nods. "I was wrong, but I thought I was protecting you."

The room spins around me, and I feel like I can't breathe. "How? It doesn't make any sense. Even if I was pregnant, how could breaking us up protect me?"

Mikhail's confession about his mother being alive and how she was used as an incubator by a government institution meant to keep her safe answers my questions on his behalf.

"They took his mother because she had conceived a daughter." I lock my eyes with Zoya. "Because she had conceived you."

Zoya grimaces before nodding.

I take a deep breath, trying to process everything. The betrayal, the lies, the misguided attempt at protection. Then I think about how Mikhail would have felt standing at the end of the aisle, waiting for me, and for him to believe I never showed up.

A solemn tear rolls down my cheek as I murmur to myself, "I should have gone inside. I should have fought harder for us. I should have trusted him enough to know he would never hurt me like that."

"No, honey," Zoya denies, waddling closer like a duck. "You are not to blame. Mikhail is not to blame." Andrik drags in a needed breath when she murmurs, "Andrik isn't to blame, either. He did, at the time, what he thought was right, and when he learned otherwise, he endeavored to fix his mistake."

I bounce my wet eyes between hers, lost.

She smiles as if she finds my daftness cute before she relieves it. "This"—her hand floats around Mikhail's office as if she is highlighting the entirety of the Zelenolsk Manor—"was not Andrik Sr.'s doing." Her eyes shift to her husband, hot and heavy. "Just a man who is slowly learning he is a mere mortal, like the rest of us."

"So the five-hundred-million-dollar inheritance isn't true?" I don't care about the money. Truly, I don't. I'm just lost as to what is happening and how I am involved in the cruel ruse Andrik is playing on his brother. Hasn't Mikhail been through enough?

"The inheritance is valid," Andrik announces. "It is just coming from me instead of Andrik Sr."

His generosity is astonishing, but it doesn't alter the facts. "Paying Mikhail off won't fix this."

"I know," Andrik agrees, his head slightly bobbing. "That isn't what this is about. Mikhail is wealthy in his own right. He wouldn't have cared if he didn't receive a cent from our grandfather's estate." Zoya's cheeks flush when a glint passes through his eyes as he rakes them over her face a second before he shifts his focus back to me. "But you... he would do *anything* to help you. Especially if it would force you to become a part of his life again."

Confusion echoes in my tone. "Then why not just encourage him to do that? Why force him to take part in an elaborately designed skit?" I answer my own questions. "Because you made him believe I had left him, so this is the only way you could make him face his heartbreak headfirst?"

When he nods, I want to hate him. I want to place the blame for a decade of hurt solely on his shoulders. But I also understand why he did what he did.

Ten years of heartache has nothing on a lifetime, and that is what Mikhail and I would have faced if the federation that once ruled this country had made the same mistake Andrik did.

There would have been no second chances then.

"During the first year of your separation, Mikhail tried many times to see you, but *they* always found a way to detour his thoughts." The disdain in Andrik's voice announces who he is referencing.

My name never left his grandfather's "unworthy" list.

Shock rains down on me when my arrow veers toward the bullseye before it misses its target.

"The federation had used Mikhail to control me for years, but I had no clue they had gone that far." My fists clench along with Andrik's when he mutters, "They almost killed him when they forced him off the road on your birthday the first year you were apart, and although he didn't fear dying, he believed in fate." I can't breathe through my shock, and he worsens it. "I don't know if the numerous DUIs Mikhail collected over the years were poor judgment on Mikhail's part or the federation's doing, but I will find out. I promise you that."

His word should mean nothing to me, but his love and respect for Mikhail are undeniable, so I absentmindedly nod instead of responding how I really want to—with violence.

After a deliberation nowhere near long enough to lift my confusion,

I lock eyes with Andrik and say, "I understand why you did what you did, but it doesn't make it right."

"I know," he repeats, his expression sorrowed, even though it is still somewhat firm.

It becomes unreadable when I add, "I don't see Mikhail moving past this as easily as I have. I don't know if he will be as forgiving. You are the *only* person he trusts, and you broke that. He may not forgive you."

"I know," Andrik parrots, his heartache undeniable despite his hard expression. "But that is a sacrifice I am willing to make to fix my mistakes."

Mikhail and Andrik endured years of abuse together. They assisted each other through it, and it made their bond unbreakable. I don't want this to tear them apart. Enough heartbreak has already occurred. I would give anything for it to end here, and I think I know a way to achieve that.

"I don't think we should tell him yet." Zoya and Andrik gasp in sync. As my eyes bounce between theirs, I say, "He deserves to know the truth, and I will tell him, but I don't think now is the right time."

They see what everyone does when you look at Mikhail—a cocky, confident man. That isn't what I've seen reflecting in his beautifully tormented eyes over the past few days. I see the boy hiding behind the cloak his grandfather and father forced him to wear when he was a toddler. The facade all men wear to stop them from getting hurt again.

Mikhail was told for years that he was unlovable, and his belief that I had left him at the altar would have validated their lies.

With Zoya and Andrik still needing convincing, but unwilling to share parts of Mikhail he has only ever shared with me, I say, "You're his family, his one constant. I don't want to take that away from him." I lock eyes with Zoya. "He only just got you back. I don't want anything to take you away from him either." I drink in their bond not even the massive pain in my chest can discount. "This could affect that."

"I understand," Zoya says. "That's why Andrik made the decision he did. But I don't think keeping this from Mikhail is the right thing to do. He thinks you broke his heart, Emerson. He thinks you left him."

"He does," I agree, fighting not to cry as Zoya's hormones forced her to do during her caution. "But even believing that, he still helped me. He still went through with this..." I mimic her earlier wave, my hand freezing halfway when I recall how he helped me last night. "He still held back my hair despite his dislike of vomit."

When Mikhail was a child, he mistook a bowl of vomit for a bowl of porridge. His mother couldn't make it to the bathroom in enough time, and since Mikhail was in a hurry to rush back to Andrik's side, he scooped and swallowed too fast to be cautioned by the kitchen staff.

As memories of Mikhail wiping a smidge of vomit from my bottom lip last night filter through my head, I shift the tension by saying with a laugh, "I also have ways I can encourage his forgiveness in a manner neither of you can."

"That is true." Zoya giggles, wiping at her wet cheeks, the humor in my tone lifting some of the tension hanging heavily in the air.

Our plan seems as firm as concrete until Andrik says, "And if he finds out before you tell him?"

I take some time to deliberate. It is nowhere near as long as it deserves, but I've lost too much time to dilly-dally now. "We will cross that bridge when we come to it. Until then..."

I leap to my feet like my legs aren't as wobbly as Jell-O before shooing them out of Mikhail's office, doubling their shocked expressions.

Chapter 29

Mikhail

My stomach riots as I stumble through the front door of Zelenolsk Manor. What should be a familiar scent of home is tainted and murky. It stirs up bad memories and has me grateful I left the first bar I came across with a recently opened bottle of whiskey.

The whispered murmurs of the staff not accustomed to seeing a Dokovic so out of sorts blend into the cacophony that matches the mayhem in my heart as I dismiss them with an arrogant wave of my hand.

Whiskey sloshes out of the bottle and onto the floor when I jack-knife toward the owner's suite.

"Mik—"

"Leave!" I shout, cutting Kolya off before he can get in a single word.

He looks like he wants to argue but chooses life instead.

After a brief dip of his chin, he gestures for the housekeeping staff to leave before he follows their brisk exit, leaving me as alone and isolated as I feel.

My feet drag, heavy and uncooperative, as I make my way down the hallway. The dim lighting from the overhead fixtures cast long shadows, making the narrow space feel even more constrictive.

My shoulder clips the edge of an antique hallway table halfway down, sending a vase crashing to the floor. The sound of shattering glass echoes through the quiet, and I curse under my breath.

"Fuck," I mutter, rubbing my shoulder.

The pain is sharp, but it is nothing compared to the ache in my chest.

I drank like a fish over the past several hours to both numb the pain and avoid the conversation my heart wants to have with my head.

No matter how many shots I downed in a dingy watering hole five clicks from Zelenolsk, my heart's begs didn't lessen. Its rebelliousness meant I downed liquor too fast to be responsible and uncaring that I had to leave my custom Irbis in the unsecured lot of a rundown bar.

I'd give a shit if I hadn't learned again, only hours ago, that a man's most prized possession isn't materialistic.

After dumping my bottle of whiskey onto the hallway table, I lean against the wall, trying to steady myself. The wallpaper, with its horrid floral pattern, blurs before my eyes. I close them for a moment and take a deep breath. The room spins, but I stay upright—just. I drank so many shots so quickly that my veins are filled more with alcohol than blood.

When I open my eyes again, the shattered vase is still there, mocking me. I should clean it up. I hate leaving my messes to anyone else, but the thought of bending down makes my stomach churn. Instead, I kick a piece of glass out of my way, cursing again when a sharp pain hits my foot.

Looking down, I see a large piece of glass embedded in my shoe. There's blood, too. A lot of blood. But no pain.

I laugh. *Finally, the alcohol I consumed in excess has reached its desired strength.*

I'm about to pull the shard out, when a voice at the side stops me in my tracks—a highly recognized and stupidly highly craved voice.

"Don't yank it out yet. We need to make sure the area is sterile before exposing a wound to the elements and ensure that the shard didn't nick anything vital," Emerson says, kneeling to inspect my foot.

Even though I am sloshed, my cock hardens at the image of her kneeling before me. It pisses me off how quickly she can weave herself under my skin, but cut me some slack. I didn't lie when I said this woman could stab me in the heart repeatedly and I'd still come back for more.

I'm a fucking simp.

"There's too much dirt on your shoes to remove the glass here." Emerson peers up at me, her eyes full of concern. "We should do it in the bathroom. Can you walk?" Although she's asking a question, she leaps to her feet and then bands her arm around my waist, accepting the brunt of the weight the wall was supporting.

Although she is here, helping me, it does little to drown out the last words she spoke to me.

I don't want to be remembered as a dud.

Her voice was hazed with lust, and a fire burned in her eyes I've not seen in a decade that I would have given anything to squander with hours beneath the sheets, but the definition of remembered is to bring to one's mind an awareness of someone or something from the past.

Past.

Not present.

Not future.

Past.

Spit flies in all directions when I *pfft* my stupidity at how easily I fell under her spell again. The flirting, the connection, the whizz back in time, were nothing but a ploy for payment.

"Why are you here, Emerson? They paid you, so you should have left hours ago."

Ignoring me, she continues our slow and careful walk down the hallway.

I grit my teeth, the pain and alcohol making it hard to think straight. "I don't need your help."

I pull away and stumble two steps before falling face-first through the door of the owner's suite.

Emerson chokes back a sob when I hit the floor with a thud. It makes her voice crackly when she pleads, "Please let me help you."

"No," I reply, shaking my head enough to rattle my brain. "You are only here because you're worried about losing your mother's placement in the trial program. You're not here for me."

"That isn't true."

I continue as if she didn't speak. "You have no reason to fret. I will continue with our agreement as per the terms cited in our contract. Kolya drafted a media release that announces you had to return to Lidny to take care of your mother. I will take Emmy up a handful of times over the next twelve months to make it seem as if I traveled to visit you. Then, once our first-year wedding anniversary slips by unnoticed, we will announce our separation. We don't even need to be in the same room to pull this ruse off."

Her voice is a croak. "That isn't what I want, Mikhail."

"Then what do you want, Emerson?" Even though I am asking a question, I continue talking, stealing her ability to reply. "Because we sure as fuck know you don't want me."

I see her anger glaring up, but she refuses to nibble at the bait I'm throwing out—goddammit!

We fight, then make up.

That is how we operate.

Or should I say, that *was* how we operated.

"Emerson..."

Her eyes are brimming with tears, but her voice is surprisingly firm. "Let's get your foot cleaned up first. Then we will talk."

"No," I shout. "You broke my heart, remember?" I spit out, my words slurred. "That's more important than this." I thrust my hand at my throbbing foot at the end of my sentence before ripping out the shard against her silent pleas for me not to. "It is more important than anything."

"It is—"

I grip the glass fragment, and it digs into my palm when I interrupt. "Then come clean! Tell the truth. Admit that *you* broke my heart!"

Her wet eyes drink in the droplets of crimson dripping from my palm before she shouts, "Yes! Okay! I will admit it. I broke your heart." Her chest rises and falls as she takes a deep breath, her expression unreadable. "I hurt you, and I'm sorry for that. But doing this..."—she jerks her hand at the shard of glass—"and acting this way won't fix anything. It won't take back what I did or how I hurt you. It will only hurt you more."

Her confession adds more sways to my steps than the alcohol coursing through my veins. I stumble toward the bed and sit on the edge, where I stare at her, unable to comprehend what I'm hearing but grateful she has finally admitted her part in our downfall.

After a beat, I try to mask the vulnerability her words stirred in me. "Saying you're sorry won't make everything right."

"No, it won't," Emerson agrees, her eyes never leaving mine. "But hopefully it is a step in the right direction, and it will prove to you that I'm here for the long haul."

I don't know how to respond to the last half of her reply. The hope in her tone has me speechless. I never expected her to take the blame, to admit that she was the one who broke my heart. But this, an admittance that she wants to stay, is shocking.

I honestly don't know how to respond.

As I stare at the woman I promised to love until eternity, the wall hours of drinking built around me feels like it is already cracking.

I don't like it.

I don't want to let her in. I can't. I won't survive a third round of heartache. But as she stands before me, vulnerable and raw, my guard drops.

"Why?" I ask, my voice barely a whisper, needing closure. "Why didn't you show up?"

Emerson looks down, her shoulders slumping as a handful of tears escape her drenched eyes. She is quiet for so long that I think she will never answer me.

When she does, it goes differently than the numerous scenarios I've run through my head over the past ten years. "I was scared. Scared of what I was feeling. Scared of getting hurt." Her eyes lift and lock with mine. "Scared that your family was right." She sees me shake my head, but she acts as if she didn't. "We were young, Mikhail—"

"And what we had was fucking perfect."

Her lips shift upward as she nods. "It was. It was perfect."

She moves forward, her steps cautious.

Her mouth tilts higher when I don't pull away this time. Don't look at me like that. The love we once shared has turned into a battlefield, and we're both wounded soldiers struggling to stay alive.

Even fighting with her, I've breathed more in the past three days than I have in the past three years.

As Emerson removes the shard of glass from my hand, she confesses, "If I could change anything, I swear to you that the first thing I would change is that I would walk through those doors instead of walking away from them."

Doors?

The truth smacks into me like a ton of bricks and pulls the world out from beneath my feet—not in a good way.

She was there.

Outside the church.

She made it that far but didn't enter.

That hurts to acknowledge.

It hurts so fucking bad.

It shouldn't maim as much as it does, but the betrayal cracks something deep inside me. It makes me a shell of a man I had hoped to be and has me lashing out.

"If you're handing out genie wishes, I guess I'd wish to have never wasted my last coin on a jukebox in a pub no one outside of Lidny had ever heard of."

I don't know what hurts more. The physical discomfort of ripping Emerson's heart out of my chest and handing it back to her, or the way she looks past me, as if she can't see me standing directly in front of her.

I shouldn't be surprised she can't see me. I don't recognize myself when I say, "You should go. There's nothing here for you anymore."

The alcohol dulls the pain in my foot as I race for the bathroom, but it can't numb the ache in my heart when Emerson doesn't come after me.

Chapter 30

Emerson

The darkness of the owner's suite matches the murkiness sloshing in the area my heart once sat. Tears threaten to stream down my face as I replay my fight with Mikhail and the cruel words he spoke for the umpteenth time. I would have given anything to hurt him as he had hurt me, to lash out with the same level of vindictiveness, but I made my bed when I suggested we keep quiet for now about Andrik's part in Mikhail's heartbreak, and now I must lie in it.

In my heart, I have to believe Mikhail didn't mean the words he spoke. Alcohol was making him ballsy, and his heartache added a touch of cruelty his usually free-going nature rarely displays.

Furthermore, I don't mind taking his wrath if it will spare those undeserving of it.

Zoya is a recent recruit for this circus, and as much as I can see how much she cares for Mikhail, the love a woman has for her soulmate far exceeds the lengths she will go to for her family.

I gave proof of that only an hour ago.

For years, I've prayed to go back and change my mother's work environment to a less smoky, less dangerous setting.

Tonight, I only wished to go back ten years instead of thirty.

The bathroom door creaks open, and I quickly wipe my cheeks to ensure they're dry before stilling my erratic breaths. The room is pitch black, but I know Mikhail senses my presence before he leaves the bathroom.

As he stares at the lump of my body under the bedding, I silently pray that he won't kick me out. The embarrassment that would cause after begging Kolya to let me sleep in the owner's suite is too much to bear, so I won't mention the heartbreak it would stir up.

After clearing his throat, Mikhail acts oblivious to my presence. He heads to the walk-in closet, his movements deliberate and detached. He dresses into slinky pajama pants and a plain white T-shirt before bandaging his foot at a dressing station in the closet.

I watch him like a hawk, my heart aching with guilt and regret. I want to tell him the truth, to explain that I didn't break his heart—his brother did. But I am a woman who keeps her word, even when it feels like it is clutching my heart, strangling it of blood.

Once dressed, Mikhail slips into the bed next to me, and silence stretches between us like an unbridgeable chasm.

We lay still for several long minutes, my decision making a mess of my stomach. It twists and turns as often as Mikhail does as he endeavors to get comfortable.

His breathing, slow and steady, makes the quiet even more unbearable. The room feels colder than usual, or maybe it's just me. Building the courage to face your fears head-on is as chilling as it gets. It makes sense as to why Mikhail never finalized the last dozen miles to Lidny.

As time slowly ticks by, I stare at the ceiling, blinking back tears. The room is dark and silent, incomparable to the cluster of confusion in my head.

Scenarios race through my mind, each one more troubling than the last. I can't shake the feeling that I'm in over my head, that I don't have what it takes to help Mikhail move past his hurt anymore.

It used to be so easy to talk to him. There was a time when there was nothing I couldn't share. We would sit for hours, talking about everything and nothing, our conversations effortless. But now, it feels wrong. The words get stuck in my throat, and I can't bring myself to say anything, not even an apology.

Even though I can't see Mikhail's eyes, I know the pain they hold and the hurt I caused them. But his suffering isn't solely my fault. Andrik played a part in this too. I'm just the only one capable of picking up the pieces.

Or so I thought.

The guilt is overwhelming, and I don't know how much longer I can keep this up.

Several long blinks later, I roll onto my side, trying to find a comfortable position, like the pain in my chest will eventually leave me alone.

What if Mikhail never forgives me? What if he finds out the truth and hates me even more? The fear is paralyzing, and I feel like I'm drowning in it.

The anger and betrayal in Mikhail's eyes when he wished to erase our relationship make me choke on a sob. I thought I was doing the right thing by protecting him from the truth, but all I've done is push him further away.

I don't know how to fix this, how to make things right. It feels like I'm carrying the world on my shoulders, and the heaviness of the load is crushing.

I want to tell Mikhail the truth, to unburden myself of Andrik's secret, but the fear of his reaction holds me back, not to mention the worry that he will lose more than just me when he retaliates.

I close my eyes and take a deep breath, trying to calm my racing thoughts. It does me no good. The guilt and fear are too strong. I can't keep this up for much longer. How can I pretend everything is okay when it isn't close to that? My world is falling apart before my very eyes.

Guilt gnaws at me for the next several minutes, the wish to confess almost overwhelming.

I'm about to break my suggestion in a shamefully quick time frame, when, unexpectedly, Mikhail tosses me a life vest.

With one arm between my legs and the other curled around my waist, he cranes me to his half of the bed. The tears I've held back for hours soak his shirt when he pulls me in close to his chest. He holds me like my sobs are as hard for him to hear as they were for me to hold back. Tears stream from my eyes as pleas for forgiveness fall from my mouth.

I don't confess, though. His comfort is a coping mechanism I didn't expect, and it kills my confession at my lips.

Even with the alcohol seeping from his pores strong enough to make me tipsy, I can't bring myself to shatter this fragile moment of peace.

Mikhail needs this as much as I do.

As Mikhail rubs my arm in a soothing manner, my mind races with the possibilities of what his comfort could mean. Maybe I can find a way to talk to him, to explain what happened in a way that won't fracture his relationship with Andrik and Zoya?

I push the thought aside and focus on the present when the thud of his heart lulls me toward sleep. *One step at a time*, I tell myself. I can't fix everything overnight, but I can start by making sure Mikhail knows how much I appreciate his comfort.

I owe him far more than that, but for now, it is all I can give.

The next morning, Mikhail is gone. The bed is cold, and its emptiness is a stark reminder of the gap I still have to bridge between us.

I sit up, my heart heavy with the secrets I still carry. Inevitably, Mikhail will learn the truth. I can only hope that when the time comes, he understands this was never about hurting him. I want to guard the minimal good memories he has of his childhood and ensure they're not tainted by the ill judgment of an adult.

After getting out of bed, I walk to the window and look out at the world beyond. The sun is shining brightly, casting a gold glow over everything. I had hoped this morning would be the start of our new beginning, but all I feel are the chains of our past shackling our progress.

I can't live like this forever. Hiding the truth and pretending everything is fine haven't gotten me anywhere fast over the past ten years. I need to make things right, to mend the damage years of silence caused. But how? How do I undo the damage that's been done?

As I turn away from the window, my resolve strengthens. The crumpled bedding is only on one side of the mattress, from the side Mikhail pulled me to.

That means Mikhail never returned me to my side of the bed.

I slept in his arms all night.

My heart beats wildly when I lift the bedding to my face to drink in Mikhail's scent. He smells like home, and his familiar scent has me replaying conversations we had before I learned the truth.

He said that he couldn't stand the thought of losing me, how it would kill him to live without me for another ten years. That proves he doesn't want to erase our past. He wants it reimagined, and I know the exact person who can help me achieve that.

I race for my phone, my fingers flying over the screen.

A huge smile stretches across my face when my call is answered after only one ring.

"I need your help," I say, too captivated by my quick thinking to issue a greeting.

"Of course," answers a familiar voice without pause for thought. "Anything you need."

Chapter 31

Mikhail

D im lights cast shadows on the bottles lined up like soldiers ready for battle when I enter the office of my first solo establishment. The clinking of glasses and the murmur of conversations add additional thumps to the mariachi beat of my hungover head.

I woke up with a pounding headache and the remnants of last night's splurge still lingering in my system. The thuds of my temples are nothing compared to the thumping of my heart when I recognized the fiery red hair splayed across my chest this morning when I woke.

I thought I had imagined Emerson's presence last night, and as much as this kills me to admit, I'm glad I didn't.

As I stroked Emerson's tear-stained cheek, needing to ensure it wasn't still wet, parts of our fight rolled through my head. The accusations and the pain came through clearly, but some details were hazy, blurred by the excessive consumption of alcohol.

Even though I couldn't recall all our conversation, I knew I was responsible for the tears she had shed last night. I felt it in my chest. But since I also recalled how her voice trembled when she confessed to leaving me at the altar, I slipped out of bed and headed to work like hours behind a desk is a cure for the unease clutching my throat.

It isn't, but tell me one man who is smart while living without a heart?

After sitting behind my desk, I take another mouthful of the burning liquid I keep hidden in my desk drawer, not bothering with a glass.

Guilt-erasing chugs don't require formalities.

I've not once intentionally set out to hurt Emerson, not even after she left me, but I don't feel confident declaring that anymore. I feel like I broke her heart, like I betrayed the memories that have kept me alive for the past ten years.

The whiskey scald hitting the back of my throat distracts me from the confusion swirling in my gut, but it does little to replace the security footage I watched earlier of Emerson leaving Zelenolsk Manor an hour after waking from replaying in my head.

Her eyes were somewhat wet, but there was a fire in them I've not seen in a decade. A fire that was once only able to be extinguished with hours beneath the sheets.

My teeth grit when my cock hardens at the thought of being her extinguisher of choice. I shouldn't be so hard on myself. Love is like a drug. Rational thoughts are nonexistent under its influence, and bad choices seem plausible.

When I lower the almost empty whiskey bottle, the edge clanks against my mouse, firing up my computer monitor. I never use passwords, so access to the emails I was scrolling earlier is immediate.

My dislike of delayed gratification meant Emerson always took off her panties as the last call for drinks was yelled across the bustling pub her family owned.

While trying to make out she didn't enter my thoughts for the umpteenth time this evening, my bleary eyes scan a recently received email.

The more I read, the more my blood boils. The email announces the cancellation of the order I placed while waiting for Emerson at her family's church for the second time in my life. The cause states the purchase is no longer needed.

How fucking dare they!

I push back on my chair harder than intended. The bang of its crash into the wall is half the wallop my office door does when I throw it open.

Waitstaff glance up when I enter the main hub of the bar, but I ignore them, uncaring if they think I'm a grumpy cunt. They don't understand what I'm going through. They will never understand, because I've only ever given them a fraction of the man I am when I'm with Emerson. The bare minimum.

Disgust gnaws at me as I walk past numerous patrons eyeing me with zeal, but I shove it down, refusing to acknowledge them or my once go-to coping mechanism.

Losing myself in a bevy of heavy-breasted women isn't the solution to my predicament. I have no clue what the solution is, but I know that isn't it.

I find Lynx, my operations manager, toward the end of the bar, serving patrons.

"I told you I wanted the electrostatic precipitator installed no later than the end of the month, so why the fuck was my order canceled?"

Lynx knows me better than anyone does. He's been on my payroll since my inaugural year, and we've been friends even longer than that, but going above my head like this is outside of his pay scale.

Lynx hits a generous-tipping patron with a flirty wink before cranking his head my way. "I don't know what you're talking about. I didn't cancel anything."

"The electrostatic precipitator that was to be installed in the Lidny pub next weekend." My voice is harsh, and my temper is frayed. "Someone canceled it."

His laughter frays my mood further. "It wasn't me. I'm not fucking stupid. I don't want to die."

"Then who canceled it?" I can't think of a single person dumb enough to go against me when it comes to something like this.

Except perhaps one.

The air dampens with an incoming storm as the hairs on my nape prickle. I peer past Lynx, my body's awareness of its mate's closeness still strong despite the amount of alcohol I've forced through my veins over the past thirty hours, just as the voice from my dreams floats through my ears. "That would be me."

Emerson is at the end of the bar, mixing cocktails and pulling beers like she owns the place. Her presence commands the attention of everyone in the space, and she has a lineup of patrons desperate to be served by her.

Shockingly, not all of them are male.

She is a girlie girl as much as she is a sexpot.

Tension spikes when our eyes lock, and electricity courses through my body. I should hate how her presence instantly places my defenses on the back foot, but I don't.

I can't let her know that, though, or she will eat me alive. Instead, I try to downplay her craved yet unexpected arrival, certain it will end in disappointment.

I lost count of the number of hours I wasted watching the entry doors of this very club, awaiting her arrival.

I didn't name my first establishment Ember's for no reason. I wanted Emerson to know how badly I wanted her.

How badly I still want her.

The honesty of my inner monologue keeps my expression impassive when Emerson says, "The outfitter was charging you double for a subpar unit." She hands a patron one of our most requested drinks—the Ember Fury—before she serves another client, still explaining. "That's the thing about looking preppy."

I scoff, disgusted by her analogy. Preppy boys aren't her type. She likes men who are rough around the edges and completely under her control.

"They think they can charge more by announcing it is *designer*." She air quotes her last word after wiping her sticky hands down her barmaid's apron. The drink, named in honor of her hair and fiery attitude, is so popular because we use fresh tangerines instead of bottled juice. "I got a better unit for half the price." Her eyes mist as they stray to me. "The new manufacturer will install it as per your request by the end of business next weekend."

I purchased the electrostatic precipitator for Emerson's mother's bar. Although doctors doubt Inga's cancer diagnosis resulted from working in a smoke-filled environment for three decades, I wasn't as convinced. It's too late to adjust the harm that has already occurred to Inga's lungs, but it will lessen the chance of Emerson facing the same horrifying diagnosis, and that is all I care about.

I tell a patron I'll be with him in a minute when he grunts about me standing in a high-traffic zone and not matching the workload of my staff before I ask the most obnoxious question I've ever muttered. "What are you doing here, Emerson?"

She takes my hard tone in stride. "Working." She winks before she pulls a beer for the patron pissed that he finally reached the front of the line only to be ignored. "Unlike you."

Her hip bump is playful, but it does little to shift my confusion.

"You got paid." Even with my GPA smashed from too much liquor, I know this because when Kolya couldn't get the payment approved by my grandfather's solicitors without documented proof by a medical professional that we had consummated our vows, I transferred the payment from my personal account five minutes later.

"I did." Emerson's face screws up, switching her features from sexy to cute.

Her expression matches mine.

I swear we've already had this conversation.

I shake my head, ridding it of the confusion clumped there when Emerson says. "But I organized a replacement electrostatic precipitator *after* returning the funds to your account, so I figured I should get a job to help pay for it." She flashes Lynx a grateful smile that he accepts too readily for me not to veer my fist toward his face the instant we close. "And Lynx was generous enough to offer me one."

"So that's why you're here? For a job?" I hate the devastation in my voice even more than I hate that she went to Lynx instead of me.

Lynx was there when we dated, but not in this essence. He was never the man she ran to when she needed help. Once, only I had that privilege.

I wonder if I slipped and hit my head when Emerson murmurs, "That... and..."

I could finish this game now, end it before it spirals out of control like I did yesterday, but I can't. I've been out of the game so long that plays like this should be foreign to me, but since it involves Emerson, it is as if time stood still for ten years.

"And...?"

Her prolonged sweep of my body sends a jolt through me that hardens my cock, and I'm not the only one noticing.

Emerson's face reddens with jealousy as her narrowed gaze scans a group of women in front of her. My bulging crotch has attracted admirers, and their vocalized desires make Emerson furious.

"Seriously?" Emerson mutters, eyeing them with disgust. "He's wearing a ring." She thrusts her hand at the ring not even two bottles of whiskey could coerce me to remove. "That's a clear sign he's taken."

"And...?" The blonde at the front of the trio mimics, mocking our exchange as if it didn't smother years of hurt.

This is the bar I bought by using the family pub of the only woman I've ever loved as collateral. The establishment I named after the only woman I would ever marry. Everything about it is a remake of the establishment that ignited my love of the retail industry that serves alcoholic beverages, and my love of the woman who breathed air back into my lungs and made me burn.

I wouldn't be who I am without Emerson.

I wouldn't be here—period.

Shandi Boyes

That grants Emerson the right to stab me in the heart over and over again *and* not to be mocked in front of me.

When I signal for the bouncer at the door to move closer, the blonde scoffs. "That wasn't your response to my proposition at the Broadbent Hotel last year." As she drags her teeth across her bottom lip and lowers her lustful gaze to my body, she reveals a side of me I never wanted Emerson to see. "Kitty and Jasmina aren't here to equal your stamina, but I'm sure Kova and Mariya will happily take their place." She thrusts her big-breasted friends forward, their gawks as demoralizing as that of their evil counterpart. "We won't care if you call us the wrong name like you did with Jasmina." Her eyes shift to a custom wedding band that matches mine—just with a heap more diamonds. "Or that you're married."

Lynx laughs when Emerson's anger boils over. She tosses a lemon drop martini into the face of the blonde—who was so unmemorable that I can't recall her name—before reminding her of the sanctity of marriage.

"Marriage is a sacred and inviolable union. It is *not* something you interfere with to get your rocks off."

Lynx's laughter stuffs into the back of his throat when Emerson climbs over the sticky bar in preparation to retaliate to the blonde's snickered, "Remind me of that after I've sucked your husband's dick... *again*," comment with her fists.

Since I'm closer than the bouncer paid to handle these types of situations, and always on duty to protect Emerson, I hook my arm around Emerson's waist and drag her away from the suddenly fretful blonde.

Emerson thrashes against me like crazy as I walk her toward my office, her fight coming out with a heap of angry words. "Let me go, Mikhail. Let me fucking go! I'm not going to hurt her. Death isn't painful. To some, it is the only time they'll truly be at peace."

The lighting above our heads sends rainbow hues across the glossy surface of the bar from the diamonds in her wedding band. That's how hard she fights to get out of my hold.

When her endeavor is unsuccessful, she returns to yelling. "I don't give a shit what you did to him when he wasn't mine! But when Emerson Morozov claims it, you don't have permission to look, much less touch!"

She kicks out her legs and claws at my arms until we're in the safety of my office, and even then, it is still an effort to keep her contained. She's a wildfire, furious enough to burn through everything in sight—including my heartbreak.

The disrespect for monogamy and the continued attempts at seduction after being told someone is taken always infuriate her. It's a fight she took up within days of us meeting, and one I grew to love as much as I did her.

With my thighs, cock, and nuts nursing injuries, I free Emerson from my hold in the middle of my office before standing guard at the door.

Either aware she won't get past me, or not wanting to, Emerson paces the short length of my office while rambling under her breath. "Did you see the way her friends looked at you? We won't need to wet the mop tonight to scrub the floors clean. Their drool will soak it through."

Her jealous expression shifts to miffed when my lips furl at one side, and then she shoots daggers at me.

"Why are you laughing? Did you see their nails? They would have shredded you to pieces. And the bitch leading the 'let's seduce Mikhail train' had fangs instead of cat's eye teeth. Even if her friends reneged, you weren't getting out of her clutch in one piece."

When my smirk shifts into a full smile, she whacks me in the stomach before she endeavors to sidestep me.

I say endeavors because I beat her to my office door and slap it shut before she can race through it. Then I crowd her against the gleaming black wood.

I say nothing for several long minutes. I simply relish how fast my prayers were answered this time around, and how her jealous outburst is guiding me through the noise deafening me.

While I peer at my favorite shade of green, the fog of a long night of drinking lifts. I recall the pain and betrayal in Emerson's eyes when I lied about wanting to erase our past, and how she showed up for me last night, as she has again today. But instead of being grateful that she's matured enough to enter the battlefield, I shattered our memories with cruel, vindictive words.

My chest expands as I draw in a sharp breath. It isn't solely the cruelty of my words weighing heavily on my shoulders, but the realization that I'm capable of inflicting such pain on the woman who brought me back to life.

I should have never pretended I wanted to wipe the slate clean or that our past meant nothing. It means everything to me. Every moment, laugh, and corny jukebox dance are what have kept me breathing for the past ten years.

Yes, Emerson hurt me, but I hurt her too.

I didn't fight for her—for us. I let ten years slip by without a word being spoken between us. I tried. Believe me, I did. But after numerous failures, I started to wonder if fate was trying to tell me something, and I gave up.

I've never felt more stupid.

This is us. The fights. The passion. The love that can weather any storm.

This. Is. Us.

I draw in closer to Emerson, wishing I could take back what I said, but aware the damage has already been done. Scars are visible on both our hearts, and they will remain, but they're not solely signs of a vicious battle.

They are also a sign of healing.

"Em," I murmur at the same time Emerson whispers, "She wants you. Even knowing you're married doesn't stop her from wanting you." Her tone is defeated, as slumped as her shoulders. "And she's had you."

"No," I disagree, shaking my head. "She's never had me. Not once."

"She—"

"We fucked. That was *all* we did." Her shoulders slump further until I add, "We didn't make love or tilt the axis of the world. We didn't create fireworks that can still be seen a decade after they erupted. We didn't even kiss. We did nothing but have meaningless sex that meant *nothing* to me. It was an emotionless transaction, a chore. It was nothing close to what you're imagining."

I feel her resolve weakening, but she still makes sure she's not misreading what I'm saying. "You don't want her?"

"No," I answer without pause for thought.

"Why?" she asks, disbelief echoing in her low tone.

I throw down the gavel, choosing honesty. "Because she isn't you. None of them were ever you. I fucked them purely because it was the only time I could go an hour without thinking about you." I push in closer when she mistakes my words, making her one with the door. "Because we never fucked. We made love. We made memories. We made every other exchange outside of ours a mundane trailer of a love story too pure for the masses."

She chokes back a sob, but that is the start and end of her reply.

"I also never kneeled in front of them." I inch back before pulling her away from the door and spinning her around. It is time to let bygones be bygones, to push the ghosts of our past back into the closet and move forward from the hurt. "But you... I will *always* kneel in front of you."

Her gasp when I fall to my knees is liquid gold. It rolls through my veins, clearing out the whiskey and replacing it with lust.

I stare up at her for a moment, the noise of the bar fading into the background. It's just us, two soulmates caught in a moment of raw emotion, and the entanglement grows when Emerson joins me on the floor. She butts her knees with mine and cups my cheeks before she accepts the victory of her win in true Emerson Morozov style.

She kisses me.

Chapter 32

Emerson

The tenderness of our kiss and the emotions fueling it reveal that feelings don't fade. They evolve, becoming more manageable and functional, yet they never truly disappear. Each lash of our tongues and nip of our teeth are a reminder that love, once ignited, continues to burn within us, despite the heartache we endured.

The warmth of Mikhail's lips against mine is a reminder of our past, while also being a promise of a better future. Moments like this remind us that feelings aren't fleeting. They are eternal, woven by the fabric of our souls.

The remembrance sees me raking my nails through his hair. I pull his mouth closer to mine before dueling our tongues together. Through touch, I express my sorrow for the pain he suffered ten years ago, without taking all the blame, and Mikhail does the same.

We communicate without words, and unsurprisingly, things move forward fast when forgiveness is issued in less than a nanosecond.

One minute, I'm kneeling on the carpeted floor near the entrance of Mikhail's office. The next, my back hugs the plush sofa across from his large desk and my jeans are wrangled down my thighs.

Mikhail trails kisses from the seam of my printed cotton panties to the sensitive skin behind my knees. His curved lips trace the grooves my skinny jeans forever imprint on my thighs before his focus shifts to the damp patch in the middle of my panties. His kiss made me wet enough to shadow the cotton, and I'm too horny to act ashamed.

His groan when I sweep my thighs open rumbles through to my clit, and then his hand makes the situation even messier. He backhands my pussy, doubling the throbbing of my clit and forcing my eyes toward the back of my head.

I could come now. I don't purely because the tension is too blistering to tap out now. I need at least a few more minutes to relish its goodness.

My thighs shake when Mikhail's thumb finds my clit not even two seconds later. He circles the nervy bud with slow, purposeful swivels before he lifts and locks his eyes with my face.

"Christ, Emmy," he murmurs after taking in my flushed cheeks and dilated eyes. "You're almost there already."

The rasp of his voice almost sets me off, but I hold on tight, confident the reward will far exceed the effort.

The fight almost becomes unwinnable when Mikhail slides my panties to the side and blows a hot breath over my pussy. Watching the way he worships every squirm he demands from my body is thrilling. It has me gripping the back of his head like I did earlier. Except this time, I don't veer his mouth toward my lips.

I mash it with my pussy.

"So impatient," he murmurs against my drenched pussy lips before he spears his tongue between the delicate lines and pokes it inside me.

He eats me like he will never grow tired of my taste while bombarding me with a ton of praise. He tells me I taste like heaven, that he knew no one would ever taste as good as me, so he never gave them the chance to prove him wrong. He eats me like he's starved, and I can't get enough.

I rock against his mouth and murmur his praises like there aren't hundreds of people just feet from our hookup location. Mikhail's talents at giving head make my vision hazy and my stomach quiver in anticipation of what is still to come.

Within minutes, an intense orgasm builds low in my core. I'm so close to falling that my body stills in preparation for the battle it is about to endure.

My zombie-like state doubles Mikhail's efforts. He licks me, fucks me with his fingers, and grazes my clit with his teeth, lips, and nose until I thrash against the sofa like I'm possessed.

When he sucks my clit into his mouth, an orgasm rips through my body so hard and fast stars form in front of my eyes.

I can't stop screaming.

Can't stop coming.

Can't. Catch. My. Damn. Breath.

My climax is the longest I've ever had, and it sucks everything out of me.

Lust clouds my head so ruefully that it takes several lengthy blinks for my brain to register the enticing visual in front of me. Mikhail's trousers have slipped down his thick thighs, and he's fisting his fat cock. The veins of his impressive manhood are throbbing, and its cut head is glistening with pre-cum. He's the thickest I've seen him, and I stare unashamedly, hungry and wanton.

With his eyes locked on my spent face, Mikhail does a long, determined stroke. My insides clench as a ferocious fire burns through me. I've never seen such a stimulating visual. The image of him stroking his cock while his other hand cleans up the mess I left on his face is panty-drenching. It re-sparks the fireworks not close to diminishing and has me more than ready for round two.

"Please," I beg, my voice returned as hunger rips through me.

Smiling, Mikhail lengthens his strokes until a blob of salty goodness pools at the tip of his swollen knob. After returning his hand to the base, he jerks up his chin, encouraging my approach.

I pounce like a tigress protecting her cub. In under a second, I replace his hand at the base of his impressive cock with mine and slide my tongue over the slit at the top, tasting him again.

When his delicious flavors swamp my taste buds, I moan.

He tastes so good.

I squash my ear to the leather when he inches closer, and then open my mouth, wordlessly inviting him in. The corners of my mouth burn when he stuffs a handful of inches in, his patience as frayed as mine.

As he rocks his fat cock in and out of my mouth, his pace exceedingly calm considering the fire burning through his eyes, I maintain eye contact. I watch every expression crossing his deliriously handsome face and relish how at peace he appears to be.

It hurt when he admitted he had fucked the blonde, but this is a level of intimacy I am confident she never experienced with him.

It is too intimate, too special.

It is the weaving of two souls into one.

Mikhail's hips buck when my tongue flicks the piercings down his shaft. The coolness of the metal sends spasms down my spine and increases the strength of my sucks. I take him deep in my throat, spurring on more pre-cum to leak from the crown.

As I suck, lick, and graze the head with my teeth, Mikhail guides his dick in and out of my mouth. He pushes in far enough for my eyes to bulge, but not far enough for me to gag. He's not a fan of vomit—even the suggestion of it.

A moan vibrates on his knob when he returns his hand to my clit. He toys with it until my thighs are as shaky as his, and the veins feeding his magnificent cock work overtime.

"Fuck..." he groans, his grip at the base of his cock now more about calming the beast than enraging it.

His nostrils flare as an animalistic groan rolls up his chest when I slide my tongue over the sensitive slit in his cock, lapping up the droplets of his arousal. Then he increases the pressure on my clit. He rubs and strokes it in rhythm to my sucks, and within seconds, a familiar tightening sensation hits the lower half of my stomach.

My cheeks hollow from the pressure I apply during my next handful of sucks. I suck him faster. Greedily. I push him to the brink as his fingers do me, and I can't get enough. I lick, pump, and suck him while watching him unravel before my eyes.

I love the burn of taking him deep and savor every frantic grunt as he struggles to maintain control. They reveal he is no longer in charge of our exchange.

The power has once again been handed to me.

I won't fuck it up this time. I refuse.

While swiveling my tongue around the base of his cock, almost gagging, I watch him over the rise and fall of his chest. He's breathless and panting. I love that I get to see him this way—raw and unguarded. It makes our gathering much more intimate and reminds me that this type of tension can't be replicated with a stranger. It can't be manufactured. It is an artform only a select few can master.

I moan at the taste of him when the trekking of my tongue along the veins coursing down the length of his thick cock produces more pre-cum. I lap it up eagerly.

"Yes, Emmy," Mikhail moans, hissing. "Suck me hard and fast. Make me come."

I milk him with my hand while sucking on the crown of his engorged knob. Over and over again, my tongue flutters across the slit, gathering the droplets of pre-cum pooled there. I work him so hard that my mouth aches, and it pays off in the most brilliant manner.

It isn't as you suspect. Instead of flooding my tongue with his cum, Mikhail slams two fingers back inside me before swiveling my aching clit with his thumb. His cock muffles my screams when he hits the nervy bud with rapid-fire flicks at the same time his fingers massage the sweet spot inside me.

My tingling pussy clings to his fingers as his cock demands every inch of my mouth. I love the feel of him, the hotness and heaviness, and the sense of rightness that comes with every one of our exchanges.

"Please," I beg through a mouthful of cock a few seconds later.

I'm dying to taste him again, for his cum to ignite my senses. The urge is as blinding as the frantic buildup of my next climax, which is seconds from erupting.

I whimper when Mikhail brings me to the edge with a perfect amount of pressure and dedication while saying, "I want you to come with me. I want your juices dripping off my hand as my seed slides down your throat."

My screams are louder than the music pumping out of the speakers of his club when Mikhail switches from two fingers to three. The somewhat painful intrusion is the final push I need to reach climax. I come with a moan, my entire body shaking.

Mikhail is right there with me.

Thick spurts explode into my mouth, and I swallow them greedily while increasing the length of my strokes. I lure more salty goodness from the crown of his swollen cock with frantic, desperate pumps, hooked on his taste.

It appears as if I am not the only one addicted. Mikhail's cock pulls from my mouth with a pop half a second before his mouth lands on the cleft of my pussy.

After soaking his cheeks with evidence of my arousal, he plays with my clit until I lose count of the number of times he makes me come.

I'm so pliable by the time he's done I can barely talk. "Mikhail..."

His breath is hot against my neck when he says, "I've got you, Ember."

He hums softly when the tip of his cock pierces between the folds of my pussy. Then, slowly, he enters me. The burn is excruciating, but I tighten my legs around his waist before I lift my hips off the couch, opening myself to him more.

Once he is fully seated, he groans, the sound both erotic and peaceful. His cock flexes as one of his hands slides beneath me to tilt my ass higher while the other moves to my clit. I mewl, still sensitive, when he rolls the delicate bud between his index finger and thumb.

Only once he is confident that I won't tear does he inch back.

I suck at him, my pussy rippling as it silently urges him to lose control.

When their wordless pleas only get him halfway over the fence, I add words to the mix. "I want you to take me *hard*. I want to feel where you've been for days."

Cursing, he thrusts back in.

I moan, wildly aroused by how fast I can coerce him to the dark side.

I know what he's trying to do. He's trying to prove his theory that we've never fucked. We make love. He's just failed to remember it isn't the pace of an exchange that rates its authenticity. It is the emotions displayed and a connection that can't be made up on a whim.

When I tell Mikhail that, his jaw tightens before instincts take over. He slams into me, making me cry out and grip his shoulders. I clench around him, thrilled by the snippet of pain from taking a man so well endowed. It is a welcome relief from the bad experiences I've faced over the past ten years, and it has me encouraging more recklessness.

I beg him to take me hard and fast, to reclaim me as his.

My pleas are answered at a record-setting pace.

Mikhail's biceps flex as he drives in and out of me on repeat. He fucks like a god, and I'm singing his praises only minutes later. My back bows as heated pleasure treks through my veins, but our pace doesn't slow in the slightest. I move my hips and match Mikhail's thrusts grind for grind. I drive him to the brink of hysteria as rapidly as he forces me to surrender to the insanity.

"That's it," Mikhail murmurs, his teeth grinding. "Take it. Accept me. Swallow my cock like a good, obedient wife."

After watching me quake through his "wife" title, he adjusts the incline of my hips, sending the temperature to excruciating. I'm taking all of him now, every delicious inch, and it feels amazing.

Over the next several long minutes, he gives me everything and takes just as greedily. We can't stop touching. We grope, moan, and kiss, each touch more searing than the last.

I come in a long sequence of moans, grabs, and thrusts. My legs shake as the rush of release tingles from the roots of my hair to the tips of my toes.

Still, Mikhail doesn't stop.

He drives into me, making my pussy convulse. It isn't back-to-back orgasms, more an endless climax. The ultimate summit of desire.

As I clutch at him, the pulses of my climax thicken him further. His rough grunts and the throbs of his cock announce his release is close, the chase almost complete, but he refuses to relent.

My clit aches with every impact of his V muscle against my pelvis, and the couch's feet skid across the carpeted floor.

Within a handful of thrusts, I am at his complete mercy again, mindless with the desire to climax again.

The sounds of our bodies moving together like a well-oiled machine drown out the awareness of clubgoers only feet away. Our bodies slap and sweat glistens on our skin when he digs his knee into the couch and uses the springs to power his thrusts.

He takes me so hard and deep that his balls slap my ass and screams rip from my throat.

I come again with a hoarse cry of his name. Blood roars in my ears as tremors explode through me.

When I finally return from the lust clouds, I sink into the couch and enjoy the splendid visual of Mikhail suspended above me.

He's undone his button-up shirt to the third button, revealing inches upon inches of glistening skin. He is minus the tie his pompous competitors wear, and his hair is damp at the roots and mussed from the number of times I've run my fingers through it.

He is deliriously attractive, and I can't help but stare.

I should have nothing left to give. I've lost count of the number of times I have orgasmed, but there's something about this man that has me craving the impossible.

I want him at my mercy, too, and I think I know a way to achieve that.

With one foot on the couch and the other lowered to the floor, I prop myself onto my elbows before brushing my mouth against Mikhail's.

Pain spasms in my core when his next lunge stabs my uterus, but a low moan still escapes me. The sting reminds me of the brilliance of our exchange and how it is about to get even hotter.

My breathing saws my lungs when I brush our mouths together again, but this time, my tongue gets in on the action as well. I slide it across Mikhail's sweat-dotted lip, moaning when our combined flavors swamp my taste buds.

While holding his jaw in my hands, I kiss him passionately. I lick at his lips and stroke my tongue along the roof of his mouth until the heat I was seeking earlier erupts from his cock.

The gush of lubrication filling me sets me off again. Waves of ecstasy sweep across my skin. They add a layer of emotions to our lush, decadent kiss and make me realize Mikhail's long-awaited release isn't the cause of my latest orgasm.

It is the love displayed in his kiss that pushes me over the edge.

Chapter 33

Mikhail

Fiery red hair tickles my chin when I rest my cheek on top of Emerson's head and flare my nostrils to drink in her scent. She's half asleep, half comatose. Our night was long and filled with moments I will replay on repeat for many years to come. But this, having her in my arms again, smelling like me, is a comfort I've missed more than anything.

We lost so much time that I shouldn't be wasting it, lying on the couch in my office, but only a fool wouldn't relish the quiet after a storm. The air is fresher after a deluge, almost pure. It is the best time to gather your bases and work out which direction you should head next.

Today, my needles all point the same way.

In any direction Emerson goes.

Tonight was so magical that the hurt is gone, the anger dispersed. It is time to leave the past in the past and make every second she's willing to share with me count.

A knock on my office door disrupts my silent deliberations on how to achieve that.

I grit my teeth, unwilling to let this moment end just yet.

222

"Go away," I growl under my breath when the intruder knocks again, louder this time.

Whoever it is can wait. I have ten missed years to make up for. I'm not yet close to having my fill. If Emerson wasn't on the cusp of exhaustion when her kiss forced me to release, I would bury my head back between her legs. I don't care that I spilled my load inside her only an hour ago. Kissing Emerson's pussy is as enticing as kissing her mouth. I will never get enough.

Another knock sounds.

"For fuck's sake." I bite back a growl while sweeping my fingers through my hair. It's still damp, and the reminder as to why frustrates me as much as when I carefully peel Emerson off my chest and onto a pillow before I cover her with a blanket all my establishments have for this exact reason.

An oversized leather couch isn't as comfortable as a mattress on the floor, but it saves queries from people undeserving to learn the cause of my offices' designs.

From the rusted filing cabinet in the far-right corner to the bulky desk, everything about this office is a replica of the one in Emerson's family's pub.

I'm a fucking simp.

As a hazy memory of the last time I spoke those words ring through my head, I tug on my trousers, pull a shirt over my head, and head for the door. I only crack open the gleaming black material half an inch. Emerson is covered, but I'd never let anyone see her in a vulnerable state. Snoring with your mouth slightly ajar could be perceived as vulnerable.

My defenses lower a smidge when the face on the other side of the door registers as familiar.

"Hey." Lynx smirks while shifting from foot to foot. "Is Emmy in there?"

I block the doorway with my frame, too exhausted to waste a single morsel of energy on him. "She is, but she's busy."

"Too busy for me?" He rethinks his *pfft* when I work my jaw side to side, my jealousy streak long enough to be obvious even from a distance. "Courier arrived with a package for her. She needs to sign for it."

Curiosity echoes in my tone. "Sign it for her."

"Already have. Just figured I'd give her an out if she wanted one." He twists to his left and then shouts. "You good, girl?"

I realize I'm doing a shit job of guarding Emerson when her giggle sounds through my ears. "I'm fine, Lynx. But thanks for asking."

My back molars crunch when Lynx says, "You sure? If I recall correctly, wasting alcohol was instant toilet-cleaning duties. He's better at showering now than he was in his teens, but you should still consider a wet wipe."

After snatching the small box Lynx pulls out from behind his back out of his hand, I slam my office door in his face.

I hear his laughter all the way down to the gallows of my bar, his howls only ending when he says, "It's about time you rubbed some lubricant into that couch. The leather was getting stiff."

I spin to face Emerson when she says with a yawn, "Was stiff? It still is." She drags her hands over leather on the verge of cracking. "Did they not give you care instructions when you forked out for real cowhide?"

I shrug. The saleswoman spurted off a range of features, but I paid attention to the length and girth the most. It is an inch longer than Emerson and almost my width, making it the perfect size to force a close snuggling session.

When Emerson's curious eyes bounce between the rusted filing cabinet, my desk, and the couch, I wiggle her package in the air. "A package arrived for you."

"For me?"

Nodding, I toss it to her, and she catches it—even with her curiosity still paramount. She isn't curious about the contents of her package. Her eyes haven't left my desk.

Even if I deny it until I am blue in the face, she'd still know who I got the inspiration from for my office space.

Determined not to waste time, I confess. "The leather is hard because I refuse to let anyone sit on the couches in my offices. I didn't buy them to sit on them. They were purchased—"

It is a fight not to kiss her when she interrupts. "Because a couch is less suspicious than a mattress on the floor." She's always been able to see right through me and past the mess years of abuse hide me behind.

She is the only one who has ever been able to do that.

My pulse quickens when she stands before padding over to me. The sway of her hips effortlessly seduces me, so I won't mention the reaction of my body when my sluggish brain remembers how she fell asleep.

She is naked from head to toe, and I stare like a dog in heat.

As she returns my watch, her stare equally greedy, I drink her in as if it is the first time I've taken in her gorgeous features. The curve of her reddish brows, the plumpness of her lips, and the silky smoothness of skin that makes her appear far younger than thirty-two. Her nose is slim, her eyes are bright, and although she will never admit it, a handful of freckles dot her nose—they, too, adding to her youthfulness.

Her body is taut and slim like a runner, but her tits defy the logic of hours thumping the pavement. They're far more than a handful and taste as celestial as her decadent and almost bare pussy. Only the slightest trail of thin hair guides me to the splendor I plan to devour daily until the end of time.

She's fucking beautiful, and she's mine.

Too impatient, and still vying to make up for lost time, I finalize the last handful of steps between us. Air rushes from Emerson's mouth when I snake my hand up her back and lose it in voluptuous red waves before I seal my mouth over hers.

I kiss her with everything I have, her feet lifting from the floor and curling around my waist. I'm hard in an instant, my blood too hot for a flimsy T-shirt and designer trousers.

225

Pleasure brightens everything around me when, a second after unbuttoning my pants and sliding down my fly, Emerson's focus shifts to my shirt. She pushes it up past my six-pack before ripping her lips away from mine, as desperate to drink in my naked form as I was hers only minutes ago.

"Whoever invented shirts should be shot."

My husky laugh slides around the room and doubles the warmth of the heat between Emerson's legs. As she guides my shirt over my head, she returns her mouth to mine, her kiss teasing and deliberate.

We make out like teens at the prom as I shuffle toward my desk. Just like our impatience earlier tonight, my trousers don't even reach my thighs before I place Emerson on the edge of my desk and fall to my knees.

"Mm," she moans when I blow a hot breath over the cleft of her pussy.

Her excitement is infectious, and before I can query what's in the box left dumped on the couch, I press my mouth to her pussy and lick her from the base to her clit. Emerson arches with a moan, her bare feet digging into my shoulder blades.

"Oh god," she murmurs, breathing heavily. "Your mouth... there... *heaven.*"

I wrap my lips around her clit and suck gently, ramping up her moans and driving her toward release. Her thighs quiver when I hit her clit with back-to-back rapid-fire licks. She tugs at my hair, stinging its roots, before she climaxes with a mangled groan.

As she shakes through a ferocious orgasm, I continue feasting on her. I poke my tongue inside her, feeling her quivers, before I replace my tongue with my fingers.

Emerson grows slicker when I slide two fingers inside her while my lips and tongue nuzzle her clit. My cock is aching to sink into her, but I keep my focus on her pleasure, satisfied even if I don't come again.

Her pleasure is my pleasure, and she is my drug of choice.

Desire sparks through me when she moans my name as she returns from the clouds. Her grip on my hair is softer now, almost nurturing, but the tension is still insane. It crackles in the air and has me eating her more hungrily. I can't get enough. I rub at her clit with my thumb while furling my fingertips, milking the sweet spot inside her.

I need her to come again. Badly. Not because our exchange will move toward sex once she is pliable under my touch. But because I need to hear her shout my name, to watch her unravel above me.

"Please," Emerson begs, her hips grinding in rhythm to my fingers' thrusts.

I switch from two fingers to three, assuming she needs something to grip while riding the waves of ecstasy about to pummel through her, but I am proven wrong when locks of red slap her cheeks when she shakes her head.

"I need... I need..." Her hips churn relentlessly as she grows slicker and wetter.

A rough sound leaves me when our eyes lock and hold. She's there, on the cusp of climax, but she needs more.

"Tell me what you need. Tell me and I will give it to you."

I fuck her faster, harder. I tease her until her body coils tight, and the struggle to resist the overwhelming sensation swamping her is visible on her beautiful face.

"Tell me, Ember!" I shout, the need to fuck clawing at me, making me desperate.

My hips drive forward as I hump the air, and pre-cum leaks from the crown of my cock. If I were still wearing pants, they'd be soaked through by now.

A rough grunt emits from me when she replies, "I need you to call me your wife again, to give me the title I know you'll never give anyone else."

I come hard and fast, the spurts of my release shooting far enough to reach the far leg of my desk. Cum leaks from my crown when I rise to my feet, cup her ass, and drag her to the edge of the desk until my still-firm cock braces at the entrance of her pussy. I use it to lubricate her further before I thrust in fast, bulging Emerson's eyes and forcing her to gasp.

Her breathlessness worsens when I say through clenched teeth, "Take me, *Wife*. Let me in."

Steam curls around us as I twist Emerson to face the faucet. The moan she releases when I commence removing the conditioner I massaged into her scalp is similar to the one that rolled up her chest when her pussy clutched at my cock, strangling it. It's just fainter.

Our second marathon romp was as long as our first foray. The club-goers are gone, the staff has left. It is just me and the girl I fell in love with on sight.

"Mikhail."

"Hmm?" My voice hints at my exhaustion, but my cock has yet to get the memo. It is digging into Emerson's ass like its release an hour ago didn't have me coming with a violence that's still shaking my thighs now.

A smile lifts my lips when she murmurs, "I think I need to have a word with your interior designer." She spins to face me, her ass brushing my groin enough for me to groan. She acts oblivious, though. "Peach tiles went out of fashion years ago."

"Decades, actually," I correct. "I had to have these fuckers imported because white, off-white, and a shade of gray one step up from white was all they were stocking at the time of the build."

She laughs as if I'm joking. I'm not. The bathroom in Emerson's pub has peach tiles. I followed its theme to the wire. It is, after all, what made me rich—both professionally and personally.

"But if you want to consider a redesign, I'm open to ideas. It's your bar. You can do what you want with it."

I boink her nose before her adorable confused expression has me taking her hard and fast without foreplay before I exit the shower to fetch us a towel. They're the same scratchy material that more shred your skin from your body than dry it, and they double Emerson's smile.

She loves that I held on to a piece of us for so long, and I love it too.

"Why change something that isn't broken?" Her mascara-smudged eyes glisten with mischievousness before she darts into the main part of my office, not bothering to dry herself.

When I follow after her, I find her digging through the couch, seeking the box she dumped earlier. Her nose crinkles when she flips it over to learn the origin of the sender. Then her smile turns blistering.

"I can't believe she found it already."

I'm curious as to what is in the box, but the high praise in her tone —even with it being directed at a member of her sex—has my focus altering. "Who?"

I feel like a dick when she lifts her eyes and murmurs, "My mom."

I've only ever spoken highly of Inga, but I'd be a liar if I said I wasn't cursing her right now. Her package, though small, has Emerson dressing for the first time in twelve-plus hours.

I shove my feet into the legs of my sweatpants before following Emerson into the main section of the bar. It is different experiencing the bar at this hour, but not foreign. Emerson and I spent as much time at the pub outside of opening hours as we did during peak periods.

Curiosity envelops me when her steps lead us to the jukebox in the corner of the empty space. Then understanding takes hold.

"It took me longer than I care to admit that I had the definition of reimagining wrong." She rolls her eyes before a spark darts through them. "It isn't about copying an already done scenario. It is about striving to make it a better, more improved version."

The silver coin she pulls out of a tiny wooden box isn't a standard run-of-the-mill coin. It is worth a small fortune since it had an extremely limited run at the mint. When my grandfather tried to convince the federation to place his face on a ruble coin, he bribed someone at the mint to make it a reality. Only five coins were produced. One was given to the federation for consideration, and then the other four were distributed to high-up members of the Dokovic realm.

I somehow ended up on that extremely short list.

My father, Andrik, and our grandfather placed their coins in guarded vaults across the country. Mine was used more wisely. It was the coin I placed into the jukebox before asking Emerson to dance, confident the fifty-thousand-dollar loss would return tenfold if she said yes.

It's worth more now that my grandfather has passed. If sold, it would get Emerson's family's pub out of the red, pay her mother's mortgage in full, and fund Inga's participation in the immunotherapy trial.

Does that mean what I think it does? Was Emerson's agreement to marry me never about the money? It must not have been. She could have sold the coin. Its skyrocketing value was broadcast across the world in the week leading to my grandfather's death. Collectors are willing to pay in excess of seven figures.

She could have funded everything I offered with one sale.

When Emerson says, "It was never about the money, Mikhail," my theories are resolved. "It was always about us." She wipes at her cheeks like they're wet before veering the coin toward the slot in the jukebox. "And a reimagination so worthy of the record books the producers of *The Shawshank Redemption* are paying close attention."

Not speaking another word, she slips the coin into the jukebox, selects the corniest song on offer, and then asks the man who will never stop loving her, no matter how furious the storm, to dance.

Chapter 34

Mikhail

As the last call for drinks bellows over Ember's packed floor, I glance over at Emerson. She's mixing a cocktail, her skills still as apparent now as they were when I first laid eyes on her. The shock of her unexpected confession last night has worn off, and now it feels like no time has passed since we eagerly waited for the final call to be issued.

We move in sync, passing bottles and glasses back and forth, our hands brushing occasionally but with purpose. Each touch sends a spark through me, and I can't help but smile like a simp.

"Nice pour," I say, leaning in close enough to catch a whiff of her perfume that's barely noticeable through our combined scents. "Have you done this before?"

Emerson grins, her eyes sparking with mischief. "Once or twice." She hands a patron a frothy drink before twisting to face me. "You're not too bad at mixing cocktails yourself... for a stiff who sits behind a desk all day."

I scoff, but there's no real disdain behind it. I have a hands-on approach with all my establishments, preferring to serve alcohol than order it. Not even counting profits comes close to the joy of working behind the bar and the friendship each shift creates.

It is easy banter, and it's comforting to fall back into it with Emerson.

The bar is a constant buzz over the next hour, but we handle the rush with ease. Our chemistry is undeniable—as strong as our work ethic. The patrons seem to sense it too. They tip generously and linger at our side of the bar until the bouncer announces the bar is closed before guiding them outside.

"That was insane," Emerson murmurs, tossing a dishcloth onto the battered wood she just finished wiping. "I haven't worked this hard since..." Her eyes flicker as heat creeps up her neck. Her thoughts are far from her family's pub. They are solely focused on me and the numerous hookups we've had over the past twenty-four hours.

I toss my dishcloth into her face, momentarily distilling her lusty expression so I'm not forced to scrub toilets, before calling it a night. When I twist to face Lynx, he reads my mind before I can speak a word. His head bob is all the approval I need to snatch my bike keys from under the bar.

As much as I have enjoyed the past thirty-six hours, an almost cracked leather couch is only a temporary spooning station. We need room to move, room to explore. I need hours to reimagine the best sex I've ever had, and I know the perfect place for us to do that.

Emerson's smile is infectious when I twist to face her. It is cold as fuck outside, but she'd rather risk pneumonia than give up the opportunity to get on my bike again. She will even set aside her unquenchable thirst to fuck for another hour or two.

Although the winds have settled, I still assist Emerson into a wool-lined coat and a beanie before guiding our walk to the parking lot at the back of Ember's.

Soon, we're speeding through the city streets with her hands in my pockets to keep them warm, and her body pressed firmly against mine.

Although Zelenolsk Manor is closer, I take a left at the first T-intersection after Ember's instead of a right.

This, Emerson, is home, so it doesn't feel right to take her to the one place where I've always felt like a stranger.

We arrive at my penthouse apartment a little after 2 a.m. Emerson is quiet when I lead her inside the sleek and modern building with floor-to-ceiling windows offering stunning views of the city. But she takes in the space, her expression curious and too adorable not to respond to it.

As the elevator doors snap shut, I grip her sweatshirt and tug her close before sealing my mouth over hers. I kiss her for several long seconds, tasting the meal we shared earlier and a flavor that is uniquely her.

It is a rough, needy embrace, but my remembrance of the last time someone got frisky in this elevator sees me pulling back before I've had close to my fill.

In case you're wondering, I was *not* a participant in that romp. I simply instigated it.

After scanning my thumb on the fingerprint scanner, I push open the door of my penthouse apartment. Emerson enters first, her eyes wide with eagerness and a look I've missed the past ten years. She's jealous. Why? I'm not sure. I'd just recognize that expression anywhere.

I thank god for a woman not afraid to speak her mind when Emerson asks, "How many girls have you brought here?"

"None," I answer, meeting her gaze. "Except my sister. But she doesn't count. Right?"

"Depends."

Bile works up from my stomach to my throat as I silently grill her.

How can my sister not count?

Her expression is a cross of peeved and humored when she says, "Andrik and Zoya drove me to Ember's. Zoya shared a handful of stories during the commute."

I cringe while recalling how I handed Zoya my number and the keys to my penthouse last year. Cut me some slack. At the time, I didn't know she was my sister. I had an inkling she was someone special, but it was in a platonic, non-creepy way.

There's only one woman I've had an instant obsession with.

She is standing in front of me with furrowed brows.

After placing down an ornament on the mantel, Emerson twists to face me. "Did Zoya tell you what happened that night?"

"Not in explicit detail, but I got the gist."

She smiles at the disgust on my face before pacing closer. "Not the parts that include Andrik... though you're more than welcome to share if you need to get them off your chest." I screw up my nose, sending her laughter echoing throughout the penthouse. "More the events leading up to the main event."

"They're just as X-rated," I say with a laugh, willing to do anything to stop me from being sick.

Emerson continues as if I never spoke. "The scene where they arrived at your apartment to a woman on her knees, naked and eager."

I step back, shocked. "What?" When she nods, I speak at a million miles an hour. "A woman was here, in my penthouse, naked?"

Her nod continues. "And posed in an extremely submissive way."

She couldn't have shocked me more if she had slapped me. "I swear on my mother's grave..." My words trail off when I recall I can no longer use that analogy. My mother is alive. Not close to living, but very much alive. "I've *never* invited anyone here. Except Zoya, but she doesn't count, and it wasn't like that..." I struggle to finish what I had planned to be a lengthy plea when I realize it isn't jealousy now burning Emerson's cheeks. It is understanding.

What. The. Fuck.

"Why aren't you pissed?"

She saunters close, her swinging hips effortlessly seducing me. "Why would I be? You said you had no clue she was here."

"And you believe me?"

I'm confident I am dreaming when Emerson nods. "Yep." While smiling at my shocked expression, she nudges her head to the kitchen. "Hungry?"

Too stunned to speak, I nod.

"Good." I'm hard in an instant when she reaches for the crotch of my jeans and lowers the zipper. "Because once you've finished dipping my calories into the negative, you'll need to feed me."

She pushes me back until I land on the sofa with a thud before she frees my cock from my pants and arrows her lips toward the head.

Hours later, sexually gorged and in a carbohydrate coma, Emerson lies in the crook of my arm, rolling the coin I stole from the jukebox before Lynx could bank it through her fingers. She's naked—how she should be every damn day of her life—and a satisfied smirk is on her face.

Although I'm still curious about her earlier confession, I can get answers about the stranger in my house by requesting the video footage covering every inch of the penthouse floor. Only one person can answer this snippet of curiosity.

"Does that mean your mom knows about us?" I nudge my head to the coin frozen between her index finger and middle finger before lowering my eyes to her sweat-drenched face. We ate more than we fucked the past hour, but dessert is strenuous when the ultimate treat comes in body parts.

Rolling over, Emerson pops her chin onto my naked pec before peering up at me. I smile like a pig in a muddy hole when she jerks up her chin.

"I couldn't give them all the details, much to Aunt Marcelle's disgrace, but they got the gist of it." She hits me with a frisky wink that shouldn't make me hard but does. Her aunt Marcelle is the type of woman who will put a glass to a bedroom wall to make sure she doesn't miss a single moan. She is why Emerson and I spent so much of our time at the pub.

The fact she didn't drill Emerson is shocking. Marcelle lives precariously through her niece.

I learn the cause of her sudden change of demeanor when Emerson whispers, "Andrik isn't a man you can have a womanly conversation around." She huffs, blowing my hair away from my eye. "Zoya may get away with it, but the rest of us are a little wary."

Words leave my mouth before I can stop them, and they're shocking. "He's more bark than bite of late. Almost a pussycat." Curious, I ask, "Did you ask him to drive you to Ember's, or did he volunteer?"

"Um..." Her focus is shifty, and it places me on the back foot. Emerson can't lie even if it would save her life, so I'm a little put off by her sudden wish to be shady.

"It isn't a hard question, Em. He either offered or you asked."

"He offered," she answers, her tone low.

I rub her arm, assuring her I have no intention of fighting with her for at least a decade unless it is in foreplay, before asking, "Why was he near Zelenolsk?"

I assume to kick my ass for calling his wife sweetheart, but learn otherwise when Emerson answers, "Zoya had an appointment with her OBGYN." She's telling the truth. It's just what she's not saying I pay the most attention to.

"And?"

It takes a beat for her to reply. "And then they came over." Her eyes flicker as if she is recalling a memory instead of trying to make up one. "We talked, and during that conversation, I realized how much he cares for you. How much they both care about you. So, naturally, they were the first people I sought help from when I needed to find you. Andrik immediately offered to take me anywhere I needed to go..."—her eyes gloss with tears—"as long as I was going to you."

Andrik's empathetic side is still foreign, and it leaves me speechless.

As do the words Emerson speaks next. "He will never forget how you helped him when you were a child, Mikhail. And how you placed your life on the line for his wife and unborn child." She circles the bullet wounds in my stomach, accessories I never had when we dated, before her focus shifts to an area rapidly gaining its own pulse. "And neither will I. You make me burn, Coal. You are the reason I exist." I can't think of anything but her mouth on me, *anywhere*, when she circles her hand around my shaft and jerks it a handful of times. "So can we please stop focusing on everyone else and for once focus on us?"

"Christ," I bite out when her tongue treks across the slit in the crown of my cock a second after I dip my chin.

Chapter 35

Emerson

My smile bounces off my phone screen when my aunt Marcelle fans her cheeks. Her cheeks are the color of beets, and her eyes are dilated. Anyone would swear I shared in explicit detail how amazing the past few days have been. I only gave her a basic bullet-point rundown.

Alas, I guess a person without a sex life would be intrigued by the most mundane story.

Fortunately for Aunt Marcelle, my sex life isn't close to boring—anymore.

Excluding the slight hiccup during our first night at Mikhail's penthouse, the past few days have been magical. The reimagination of our relationship is a masterpiece, and I can't wait to share it with a broader audience.

Though I'll never get the chance if I don't get a wiggle on. I'm meant to be hunting down the dress Mikhail spent a fortune on, not steaming up my aunt's reading glasses like her raunchy romance novels usually do.

"If I don't hear from you before next Sunday, I will see you some time that afternoon." Mikhail wants to be in attendance when the electrostatic precipitator is installed at my mother's pub, and I want to be there too. It is exciting wondering how fiery the flames will become when we return to the place that sparked them. Ember's is a replica of my family's pub, but nothing ever compares to the real thing.

I startle when a voice from behind asks, "Any luck yet?"

Twisting to face Loretta, I shake my head. Kolya, understandably, assumed my walk out days ago was the end of my relationship with Mikhail and Mikhail's bid for his inheritance. He had the staff pack my belongings and store them in the attic. The sixteen-thousand-dollar gala dress I'm planning to refund was packed with my one lousy backpack.

As beautiful as the dress is, with the electrostatic precipitator being installed next weekend, and my earnings and tips this week not taking me close to half its purchase price, I must be cautious with spending on Mikhail's behalf.

It is easy to be overgenerous when you think you're about to inherit five hundred million dollars.

"Not yet," I answer, drawing Loretta further into the dark. "Are you sure this is where he placed my belongings?" Under the assumption his contract was over, Kolya returned to Moscow three days ago. The house staff has been in disarray ever since. Kolya is stern. He runs a tight ship. I don't see Zelenolsk Manor maintaining its pristine condition without him.

"That is where Kolya told Charles to place your belongings. It should be there." Loretta rummages through a handful of dusty boxes before sneezing. "Perhaps I should call Kolya and ask him?"

"No," I shout, a little too loudly. I startle Loretta. "It has to be here somewhere."

I grunt in frustration not even five minutes later. The dress bag is nowhere to be found, and my allergies will give me grief for a month if I don't leave the attic immediately.

Seconds after leaving the attic, I brush dust and cobwebs out of my hair and off my sweater and jeans before assisting Loretta in doing the same. She's not wearing jeans, but it is harder to tell which silver strands on her head are cobwebs and which are gray hairs.

"If you come across it, can you please call me?"

When she nods, I recite my cell phone number before thanking her for her help with a smile. I may not have gotten what I came here for, but Loretta has been nothing but kind to me.

As my feet tap the pristine floorboards on the grand staircase, my phone rings. I smile while staring at the image flashing across the screen. Mikhail's eyes are brimming with lust, but he looks content. Almost at peace.

That's why I've kept quiet on Andrik's secret for the past week. Mikhail is almost ready to handle the fallout of my confession, but he isn't there just yet. His ego is still frail from the years of torment and abuse he endured after we broke up, and I need it at its full strength before going at it with a sledgehammer.

After taking a moment to admire Mikhail's delectable features, I slide my thumb across the phone screen and press it to my ear. "Miss me already?"

Lynx rostered me off today because some of the other bartenders were getting crabby about the slimness of their tips on the nights Mikhail and I work together. Mikhail would have had something to say about it if I had told him. Instead, I made out I had stomach cramps and would rather spend my night in bed, recovering.

Mikhail looked set to join me until I dry heaved.

He was out the door fast, and I traced his steps only minutes later.

No wonder I couldn't find the dress. Its disappearance is my punishment for being a liar.

My heart warms when Mikhail answers my question. "Is the sky blue?" I listen for the noise of chatty patrons at Ember's when he adds, "It isn't the same without you at Ember's." I learn why I can't hear anyone when his laughter is chopped up by the high-powered revs of his engine. "So much so, I'm playing hookie. Wanna join me?"

I almost shout yes until I remember how slow the cab driver was.

Anyone would swear he was paid by the hour instead of the mile. I will never make it back to Mikhail's penthouse before him.

"Um." My gag is brutal. It almost makes me puke. "I'm still not feeling the best, so maybe you should—"

"You don't look sick," Mikhail interrupts, his tone somewhat stern but still playful. "You look mighty fine to me."

My eyes shoot in all directions before they land on the camera in the far corner of the foyer. "Are you spying on me?"

"There's no such thing as spying on your wife." My anger crumbles away during his last word. I love when he calls me his wife. "Protecting them, yes. Taking care of them, also yes. Spying on them... no such thing."

"Mikhail—"

"Get your ass outside, Ember, before I remember how your mother never spanked you, so you're more turned on by the thought than scared."

Excitement blisters for half a second. Confusion swallows it. "You're here? At Zelenolsk?"

His hum vibrates through my body before clustering at my clit. I'm so excited to see him again that I sprint through the main entryway doors, uncaring I am about to be called out as a liar.

As I reach the covered driveway, I sling my eyes to the left before veering them to the right. I'm seeking Mikhail's motorcycle, so it takes me longer than I care to admit to find him at the end of the lot, leaning against a flashy red sports car.

A *familiar* flashy red sports car.

Oh no.

The irony of my purchase isn't lost on me. I bought this ghastly monstrosity in a fit of anger and confusion. It was a knee-jerk reaction to the chaos swirling in my life. It is a flashing neon sign of how stupid I am, and I cringe more than I gleam when I join Mikhail at the side of a 1.2-million-dollar purchase.

Don't get me wrong. The car is beautiful, but just like the dress, I can't keep it. There's no way Mikhail will take Andrik's money once he finds out the truth about his inheritance, and as much as I wish I could keep Andrik's secret forever, cracks are already forming in my armor.

Furthermore, I don't want to form our reimagination on an unstable surface. It will crumble if I do that, and my heart won't survive a third demolition.

"I'm guessing it isn't as easy to refund a car as it is a dress... right?"

"You'd be correct." Smiling, Mikhail tosses a set of keys into my chest while saying, "So suck in your bottom lip before I bite it, get your ass in the driver's seat, and give me my money's worth."

When he slides his eyes down my body, his gaze hot and wanton, 1.2 million stops ringing through my ears. The same tingling sensation that hit me when we made our wish list for when he got his motorcycle license is racing through my veins now, and I'm too horny to think rationally.

While recalling how packed the floors of Ember's are every night—so I should earn a decent salary this year—I jog to the driver's side door, slip onto the leather seat, and then groan.

I should have paid more attention while wasting money I didn't earn. It's a manual shift, and I only learned to drive an automatic.

"Don't even think about it," Mikhail says while joining me in the low ride.

"It's a stick. I don't know how to drive a stick."

He *pffts* me. "Tell that to my cock. You've had no trouble driving it multiple times in the past week."

Electricity spasms up my arm when he grabs my hand, places it over the gearstick knob, then requests for me to engage the clutch.

"The what?"

Mikhail's laugh makes me hot all over, and it has me sizing up the backseat. It won't be as comfortable as a king-size bed, but I'm sure we can make it work.

My eyes flick from the red stitched seats to Mikhail when he says, "Lesson first. Then we'll test the softness of the leather seats."

Air whizzes from my nose, falsely displaying I hate how easily he can read me, before I pay close attention to his instructions. I engage the clutch, then glide the gearstick through the gears as shown by Mikhail.

He takes it slow, his patience as mesmerizing now as it is between the sheets.

We spend the next few hours in the driveway of Zelenolsk Manor, Mikhail patiently guiding me through the intricacies of driving a manual car. Moments of frustration surface occasionally, but they're quickly overshadowed with memories I will cherish for a lifetime.

Every time I stall the car, Mikhail's laughter echoes throughout the sports car's tight confines. It is infectious and warm and has me squirming in my seat more than his suggestion we take this circus on the road.

"I don't think that's a good idea."

He encloses his hand over mine and guides the shifts of the gears as we glide down the long driveway. His touch is so reassuring I veer toward the open road instead of completing a U-turn.

As he continues to coach me, I think back on the past few days. They've been wonderful, filled with moments like these—simple yet profound. We don't need to spend money to feel wealthy. It is in the connection we share.

We've grown closer, our bond tightening more with every second we spend together.

As the sun begins to set, casting a golden glow over the isolated road we're traveling down, my heart grows heavy with guilt. Not just for the secrets I'm keeping from Mikhail, but from how I reacted when I learned some of his.

"I shouldn't have spent money I hadn't earned," I confess, my voice barely a whisper. "I had no right to be angry. You had already given so much."

Mikhail's expression softens as he strokes his thumb across my hand. "I don't care about the money. It's yours to spend, and I'd give you the world if I could."

"I know that. Truly, I do. I just..." My words trail off, an excuse, the easy way out. "This car cost a lot. It will take years for me to pay it off, possibly even decades." He scoffs, and I grit my teeth. "The tips at Ember's are good, but not good enough to purchase a sports car."

"You won't feel that way in twelve months."

"I will."

"No, you won't," he argues, his tone still humored even with it having a slight hint of arrogance.

"Mikhail..."

He pulls the world out from beneath my feet when he confesses. "You won't because you don't know that I removed the top page of our agreement because I had it amended before presenting it to you."

My heart thuds wildly as I struggle to concentrate on both him and the road.

It is lucky we are on an isolated road or we may have gotten in a wreck by now.

I blink back tears when Mikhail twists to face me before confessing, "You won't get solely fifty million dollars at the end of our contract. You will get five hundred and fifty million dollars."

I stare at him, my mind struggling to process his words. "What?"

He suggests I pull over before we crash before he announces without the slightest bit of worry hardening his handsome face, "I signed the entirety of our combined inheritance to you."

"Why would you do that?"

Tears fill my eyes as I realize the depth of his love and how it has never waned. "Because a man's wealth isn't measured by the digits in his bank account—"

"It's from the memories in his heart," we say at the same time.

When he nods, my heart squeezes.

"Mikhail..." I should say more. I need to say more. I just can't.

I'm in shock, and it deepens when he says, "I didn't want his money, Emmy. I only wanted you." He tries to make out he's not the sentimental schmuck I made him out to be multiple times during our perfect but far too short three years. "Which means in a little over eleven months, you can buy this car or that car..." He points as if a random car is driving past. There isn't one. We're alone, and I realize he is in this for the long haul when he says, "Or any fucking car you want. As long as it is a manual and I'm your instructor of choice."

The horn honks when I use the steering wheel as leverage to lunge myself at him.

"Always," I murmur over his lips before sealing my mouth over his. "You will always be my instructor of choice."

One brush of our tongues and the world and everything in it fades.

As I rake my fingers through Mikhail's long, silky hair, I drag my tongue along the roof of his mouth before kissing him as if I am starved of his taste. I tug his hair, loving the moan it produces, before I straddle his lap and grind down slowly.

A shudder rolls through me. He's hard, but I know all too well that we won't be moving from home plate anytime soon.

Mikhail loves foreplay. Almost as much as me? I truly don't know anymore. I think I may have risen to the top of the pile after his confession.

The thought sees me rocking against him harder, the friction exquisite. I grind against him on repeat, stroking myself with the hard rod of flesh between his legs. My breathing labors as the tingles of an orgasm surface, but I can't stop. The buzz is amazing, and my horniness feeds off it.

"Please," I murmur breathlessly. "I need you." My nostrils flare as I breathe in his scent, my lungs deprived like we spent more than an hour apart.

"No, you don't," Mikhail denies. He adjusts his position, making us more comfortable, before he spreads his thighs wide and arches his pelvis. "You've got everything you need right here. Keep going, Emmy. Make me come in my pants like a virgin at a whore house."

I shouldn't laugh. His analogy isn't funny. Mikhail comes from an extremely bigamist family. Whore houses were very much a part of their welcome-to-manhood rituals. My laughter just can't be helped. I love how wide Mikhail's berth went when he steered his life down its own path. He skipped almost every horrid sacrament. I would like to say all, but unfortunately, not all of them were reserved for adults.

When my rocks slow, my thoughts trapped in the past, Mikhail shifts my focus back to him by rolling his hips ever so slightly. He's so thick and long, his piercings stimulating my clit seconds after the mouthwatering rub of the crown of his glorious cock. They make me ache, and strip everything back until only the insane need to orgasm matters.

I hug his thighs with my knees as a wildfire blazes through me. My nipples pucker as my breasts grow heavy with need. I can't stop grinding. Rocking. I take and take and take until Mikhail's body trembles as ruefully as mine.

"Yes," I moan, conscious Mikhail's release is almost as formed as mine. I want him to come with me, to surrender to the power stronger than any man.

And I know the perfect way to achieve that.

I am near mindless with need after a handful of grinds. The tension is blinding, and the friction can't be matched. My panties slick with wetness as goose bumps race across my skin, but the best is still to come. I just need him closer to the edge so I can force him over it with me.

"Christ, Emmy," Mikhail hisses between his teeth when my wetness is evident even through layers of clothes. "You make me so hard it almost hurts."

The need in his tone sets off an avalanche of touches and moans. We make out like teenagers in their parents' borrowed car, and I love every minute of it.

My vision blurs, my eyes losing their focus, as Mikhail's deliriously handsome face becomes ravaged with desire. His teeth graze his lower lip as sweat dots his temples, but our pace never diminishes. We're wild with desire and almost clawing at each other.

Over the next several minutes, we move in sync, dry humping with our clothes on. My pussy aimlessly seeks something to cling to as signs of a blinding orgasm race for the finish line. Every grind, thrust, and moan brings me closer and closer to the edge.

I'm there, on the cusp of riding the wave cresting in my stomach, but it is scary being in the clouds and having nothing to cling to.

"Keep going," Mikhail begs when the power of my impending climax startles me. It feels intense, like it will be the strongest I'll ever have, and he hasn't even removed his dick from his pants yet. "Just like that. Good girl. You're going to make me come so hard... in my fucking pants." He locks his eyes with mine, and the love in them places me an inch from the finish line. "But you like that, don't you, Ember? You love having the ability to make your husband come in his pants." I nod, unashamed, and it makes him smile. "Then do it, *wife*. Make me come."

I thrash against him as an orgasm pulses through me. My core cramps violently as my limbs shake, and Mikhail watches every shudder with beady, lust-filled eyes.

His cock thickens further, but that is the only sign of the excitement roaring through him. There's no stain on the front of his jeans, no scent of his release, because his wife reference sent me freefalling over the edge before I could force him to join me.

Needing him to feel the connection, I maintain eye contact while brushing my mouth against his. Spasms dart through me when I trek my tongue across his top lip before piercing it between them. I kiss him with everything I have, doubling the rock of his hips.

He spreads my thighs wide as he uses my body and my kiss to find his release. His pace quickens, and after several slamming thrusts, he climaxes with a hiss. I swallow his groan when he growls into my mouth. His orgasm is as raw and emotionally moving as his kisses will forever make me feel.

Chapter 36

Mikhail

As I enter the living room of my luxury penthouse, I adjust the cuffs of my tuxedo. The fabric feels cool against my skin, a stark contrast to the warmth that seeped into my trousers earlier today.

After handing me the Pants Jizzer title for the second time in a week, Emerson and I took our antics into the back seat. The confines were tight, but it made our make-out session the steamiest it's ever been.

I'm hard again now recalling how Emerson worked my cock in and out of her mouth while kneeling on the driver's seat, and the moans she released when I spilled my load down her throat. How she took control while riding me from above in the back seat and how she didn't push me away when my hunger to taste her again didn't have me caring about our combined flavors.

We christened our new car appropriately for newlyweds, and I plan to do the same tonight while we're chauffeured to my father's gala in a stretch limousine.

Emerson is sitting on the couch, her legs tucked beneath her. She's engrossed in the user manual that came with the electrostatic precipitator being installed in her mother's pub next weekend.

She wants to learn how the precipitator will help lessen the chance of bar workers facing the horrifying disease her mother is enduring, but also a way to make it cheaper so the lesser-known establishments aren't disadvantaged.

Sensing my presence, she says, "The setup seems pretty simple." She doesn't look up. "It is more about the unit not recycling the air circulating throughout the establishment and filtering it instead." She looks up, her eyes widening in confusion when she notices my swanky threads. "Budgeting hacks get you that worked up, Marshmallow Man?"

I roll my eyes like I hate how close she has become with Zoya the past few days, before entering the den further. Emerson looks smoking hot with flushed cheeks, mangled hair from giving me the best head of my life, and chapped lips, but since I need to be on my game tonight with members of my family in attendance, I think it is best that she changes.

When I say that to her, her confusion greatens. "Are we going somewhere?"

I can't help but smile at her daftness. It is endearing how oblivious she can be sometimes, but tonight, we don't have the luxury of time— not if I want her to spend the next hour naked and moaning beneath me.

"Tonight is the gala." I check the time on the pompous timepiece I was gifted on my eighteenth birthday. "We need to leave soon."

"The gala?" She swallows thickly. "I didn't think we were still going, so I didn't organize anything to wear."

Emerson looks peeved when I say, "Then what were you searching for in the attic at Zelenolsk this morning?"

Stealing her chance to answer, I walk over to the coat closet and pull out the midnight-blue dress bag she was seeking.

Her eyes widen in surprise as she stands, stepping closer. Her eyes bounce between the dress and me for several seconds before they eventually settle on me.

"I'm glad you found it, but I still don't think we should go."

"Why?" I ask, talking through a tight jaw and the pain of my clipped nails digging into my palm from when I ball my hands into fists. "If it is about my father, I'll—"

"It's not about him."

"Then what is it?" I don't mean to snap at her, but I'm truly confused. She sought out this event off a list of many. She approved it. So why is she backing out hours before the main event?

I know she's endeavoring to prove she isn't in this for the money, but this is about more than that.

It is something far, *far* greater than that.

I need my father to see I got the girl and the success, because then maybe he will accept one of my mother's many requests to see him. He could be the key to the shackles holding back her recovery, but he's refusing to see her.

I also want to commence crossing items off our list so my grandfather's estate lawyers won't have anything to fall back on if they try to deny our claim of matrimony.

Kolya's return to Moscow ruffled feathers, and his whispers about our marriage being fraudulent have extended further than the gallows of Zelenolsk.

Emerson bites her lip before she sinks back toward the couch and takes a seat. Her eyes search mine, seeking any signs of leniency.

I usually hand it over in a nanosecond, but this time, I clutch to it, my resolve undogged.

"Em—"

"It's just... this. Us. I'm not sure I want to take it to a wider audience yet."

My heart sinks to my feet, and its quick drop is heard in my tone. "You're embarrassed to be seen with me."

"No, Mikhail. Never." She races across the glossed floorboards, reaching me in less than a heartbeat. "I just don't understand why you want to surround us with these people. They're the same people who tried to destroy us, the ones who pushed our heads under the water when we fell. They are *not* the people we want in our inner circle."

"They're not," I agree, wholeheartedly understanding her concerns. "But they're the people I need to see us." *The ones I crave approval from the most.*

Since I can't say that, I remind her that the lawyers from my grandfather's estate will also be in attendance, so this is a good way to show unity.

She is mere months from a massive payday that will set up her family for life.

I don't want anything to ruin it.

I didn't lie when I said I would give this woman the world. Five hundred million dollars isn't close to the summit I plan to spoil her with, but it is a good start.

Emerson sighs softly and looks away. "Another reason we shouldn't go."

When I pull away from her, shocked by the weakness of her excuse, she follows me.

"You don't need your grandfather's money, Mikhail. You're wealthy in your own right." She thrusts her hand at the window displaying the twinkling city lights. "You wouldn't use a 1.2-million-dollar sports car as a sex chamber if you weren't." Her teeth gnaw her bottom lip again, this time in seduction. "So why don't we spend the night in, watching movies and feasting off each other's bodies instead?"

"Because this isn't just about me, Emmy, or the inheritance. It is about us!" I shout, too worked up to speak rationally and maturely. "And showing them fucks that they didn't destroy everything you once loved about me!" Emotions I'm not used to handling bubble to the surface faster than I can shut them down. "That you loved me back then. You were just scared."

She's taken aback by my outburst but takes it in stride. "I was scared."

"You still are."

She shakes her head, sending red locks bouncing across her face.

"Then why don't you want to do this? Why don't you want to stand at my side and tell everyone that you're finally mine?"

She searches my face again, her excavation successful this time.

This isn't about the inheritance or the pittance we will receive for our attendance tonight. It isn't even about my mother. It is about replacing the memories in my head where I was mocked relentlessly for "not controlling my woman" and being a jilted groom before the subsequent downgrade to shitkicker in the Dokovic realm.

That's what the naked stranger in my apartment last year was about. She was a gift from one of my father's biggest benefactors. A "here, have my leftovers since you can't get your own woman" taunt. It was a slap to the face.

Although one night won't erase a decade of torment, having a woman as refined and beautiful as Emerson on my arm will be the sweetest revenge. It will end their games in an instant and have them green with envy.

My eyes float over my wife's face when she asks, "How long do I have to get ready?"

"An hour." I smile to announce my gratitude for her understanding before adding, "If you don't want to fool around in the limo. Twenty minutes if you do."

My cock twitches when she replies, "I'll be ready in ten."

After snatching the dress bag from my hand, Emerson heads to the master's suite to change. She enters for half a second before she doubles back. The tension left lingering from my unsuspected moment of vulnerability slips away when she drinks in my tuxedo from the thread in the collar to the ankle of its pricy hem.

Her gawk is hungry, and I'm as equally starved when she says,

"Pack spare pants. I'll never get Aunt Marcelle off my back if you're photographed in cum-stained trousers."

Chapter 37

Emerson

I n front of the vanity mirror, I adjust the delicate straps of a gown that costs more than my first car. The soft fabric clings to my skin, its regalness a reminder of the significance of tonight's event.

Mikhail's father's gala isn't just another event. It is a testament to the world that the "unworthy" stamp the head of the Dokovic realm marked my forehead with ten years ago has faded, that we're now part of the same team whether they like it or not.

After learning how people in his inner circle treated Mikhail after we broke up, I should have realized how important tonight's event is to him. It is about schmoozing the billionaires who fund his father's campaigns for office. It is about taking back the power they tried to strip from him and showing them that even the strongest men occasionally stumble.

His father could learn a lesson or two from his eldest son.

The stories Mikhail shared over the past week broke my heart while also fortifying my decision to keep Andrik's secret for a little longer.

Mikhail's relationship with his father is beyond fractured, and

Mikhail believes our rekindling may be the only kilning capable of relighting the fire.

I'm confident Ellis doesn't deserve the lifeline Mikhail is handing him, but I understand why he is extending an olive branch. His father and Andrik were the only constants in his childhood. From someone raised with an absentee father, I know that makes you cling to the most mundane snippet of attention they grant you—both good and bad.

Mikhail needs his father's approval of our relationship more than anyone else's, but unlike the time I spent years of savings on a pretty dress and a bus ticket to the other side of the country, I plan to show Mikhail that the only approval he needs is his own.

Sixteen years ago, I left my father's hometown heartbroken but determined. His dismissal taught me that my worth consists of who I am, not what I have.

My mother's love is enough for me—as mine will be for Mikhail as well.

As I add a final coat of mascara to my lashes, Mikhail enters the room, looking suave in a tailored tuxedo that showcases every spectacular ridge of his body. Lust replaces the last of the angst in his now hooded gaze when our eyes lock and hold.

"Emerson..." The pride in his tone adds more rouge coloring to my cheeks than the blush I applied in a hurry. "You look stunning." Walking over, he presses his lips to my temple before breathing against my rapidly heating skin. "I can't wait to introduce you to everyone as my wife."

His wife comment already has me on edge, so I won't mention the butterflies that erupt in my stomach when we make our way downstairs. The limousine gleams under the soft twinkle of the evening sky, and its grandeur is a symbol of what awaits us.

The driver greets us with a dip of his hat before he opens the door for Mikhail and me. "Sir. Ma'am."

Smiling, I slide in first, eager to remove his flushed cheeks from my mind. I don't want to recall how rheumy his cheeks already are before

Mikhail orders him to circle the block. My thoughts will be far from embarrassed then.

Our plan to get frisky during the commute hits a snag when I look up to ensure the privacy partition has settled into place. We're not alone.

The virile, endorphin-enriched air makes sense when my eyes lock on Zoya and Andrik seated across from me. Zoya's blush also isn't synthetic, and the heady scent of lust makes the confines of the limousine seem half the size.

When Mikhail settles in next to me and closes the door, I can't help but giggle. The interior lights of the limousine expose a flaw in his tuxedo I didn't notice earlier. The suit pants he switched out to ensure he didn't greet his father's benefactors in cum-stained pants are more a charcoal gray than black, and the stitch is a whip stitch instead of a back stitch.

Zoya's laughter echoes with mine. "You didn't tell them we were chaperoning them to the gala, did you?" She doesn't wait for Andrik to answer her. "Why would he when he organized for the chauffeur to collect us first... an hour earlier than necessary." Her scald has no heat to it, and everyone knows it. After flicking her eyes to me, she greets us. "Hello... I'm sorry to have ruined your fun."

I wave off her apology as if I'm not gutted. "It's fine. Truly." I wouldn't be me if I stopped now. "As long as there is more than one storage closet in the ballroom, everything will work out fine."

I am a woeful liar. The further the limo travels, the more aware I become of how good Mikhail smells. He showered before dressing in his tuxedo, but remnants of our exchange in his sports car are clinging to his skin. I can smell my arousal on his mouth and taste him on my tongue, and it makes the sexual tension bristling between us excruciating.

Even something as simple as his thumb raking the top of my hand after gathering it in his could set me ablaze.

I'm horny as hell and struggling not to squirm.

Mercifully, I can excuse my writhes as nerves.

They're bubbling too, building with each mile we travel.

They are almost at the boiling point when we reach the venue, and we're escorted through a dark corridor by two security guards.

The air thickens with anticipation when Mikhail tells me he will be back in a minute before he disappears into the crowd with Andrik shadowing his fast and furious steps.

The room is brimming with elegantly-dressed men and women, but the energy is off. It feels odd, like we're once again sardines crammed into a conference room, awaiting the will reading of a man no one liked.

It feels like my heart is going to thud out of my chest, and the likelihood increases when Zoya announces the cause of the delay. "This is where we're meant to wait for approval before we can walk the gauntlet."

I peer at her in shock, stunned she needs approval to attend her own father's event.

She is his daughter, his flesh and blood.

Also, isn't that what invitations are for?

I realize it isn't solely our status being judged when a woman with a clipboard and a snarky *tsk* rakes her disapproving gaze down the dress of an attendee. She judges her gown as harshly as someone would the digits in her bank account, and it has me suddenly grateful Mikhail steered me toward this dress instead of the one I tried to pass off as acceptable.

Seconds feel like hours as Zoya and I wait for Mikhail and Andrik's return, the silence only broken by the occasional murmur of voices—raised voices.

I glance at Zoya, who gives me a reassuring smile when the voices register as familiar. Andrik isn't happy about the delay, and he isn't a man who will stand by and allow someone to rate his wife's acceptability via a spreadsheet printout.

Mikhail is right there beside him, demanding the same level of respect for me. "Emerson is *my* wife. My. Fucking. Wife. Disrespect her again, and more than your job will be on the line."

"*Oh...*" Zoya half moans, half purrs. "Perhaps Marshmallow Man wasn't lying when he said his heart is the only soft and gooey thing about him." She hits me with a frisky wink that lowers my angst in an instant. "His backbone seems extremely sturdy of late. Shall we go check it out for ourselves?"

When she holds out her hand in offering, soundlessly suggesting we go against the grain, I slip my hand into hers and then lead our walk toward the men defending our honor.

Mikhail beams at me when I arrive at his side, his pride unmistakable. His eyes are full of confidence, and the scent of a man in charge invigorates the lust in my veins.

Everything inside me twists into a mess of need and anxiousness when a second after replacing Zoya's hand with his, the doors three guards are manning open, and we're given the nod of approval to enter.

We step into the entrance of the ballroom, and the atmosphere is electric. The who's who of Russia is in attendance, but instead of the focus being on them, everyone's eyes are locked on Andrik, Zoya, Mikhail, and me.

Not even Ellis, Mikhail's father and apparent man of the hour, gets a look in. His benefactors absentmindedly shift to our half of the room, eager to greet the fresh blood needed to resurrect an overrun and stale realm.

Mikhail greets over a hundred guests in a matter of minutes. He introduces me to every one of them as his wife, his voice ringing with pride as he ensures I am included in each exchange.

The shift of power between the powerhouses of the Dokovic realm is felt across the room, and my hunger for the man finally demanding his worth feeds off it. I'm hot all over, my skin physically warm to the touch.

Mikhail looks every inch the powerful, brilliant man he was born to be, and I am honored to witness his resurrection firsthand.

Camera flashes dance white spots in front of my eyes when Mikhail places his hand on the small of my back to guide me toward the ballroom hosting the main event. Photographers shout a range of questions as we move through a gauntlet of media capturing tonight's event, but most steer in one direction.

Who is the mysterious redhead on Mikhail's arm?

Thankfully, they keep the rest of their confusion on the down-low. I don't need to be reminded of how many times Mikhail has been photographed with a busty blonde on his arm. All I need to remember is how he introduces me to the people capturing this moment in time for eternity.

Mikhail's fingers flex against my back as he peers down at me with a hint of a smile gracing his plump lips. "This is Emerson Morozov, my wife." Camera flashes burst around us as he commences spelling my name to ensure there are no misprints in tomorrow's newspapers. "E-M-E-R-S-O-N—"

His smile turns as blinding as the camera flashes when I interrupt, "Dokovic. D-O-K-O-V-I-C." I return his needy stare while speaking words I've practiced a million times already. "Emerson Dokovic, wife of Mikhail Dokovic."

Chapter 38

Mikhail

As my muscles burn through the aftermath of Emerson's umpteenth orgasm, I drive into her on repeat. The call for last drinks was announced only an hour ago, but when I walked in on Emerson slipping off her panties in preparation for close of business, I lost all sense of control.

One minute, I was stalking her from afar. The next minute, I hooked her legs around my shoulders, and buried my head between her legs.

I ate her until she screamed my name loud enough to warn the staff not to enter the storage room unannounced, and her juices flooded my tongue not once but twice.

Then I entered her slowly, almost torturously, like I did in the woman's bathroom of the gala a second after she proudly spelled her name for the media in attendance.

Contrary to expectations, she didn't retain Morozov as her surname. She didn't even hyphenate our names together. She gave them the name she had practiced signing for months before we had planned to elope, and she said it with pride.

"Emerson Dokovic, wife of Mikhail Dokovic."

The way she said "wife" echoes in my mind, and it shifts our exchange from calm and loving to wild and out of control.

I thrust in deep, growling when the walls of Emerson's pussy cling to my cock, milking me for my release. The neckline of my shirt is damp, my thigh muscles are aching, and my balls are hurting from how many times I've staved off my release, but I refuse to relent.

I love this. Fucking my wife. And I'm not close to having my fill.

Sweat runs down my forehead as my chest heaves with exertion. It is hot as fuck in the storage room, but it has nothing to do with the unghastly setting of the manufactured air.

I love taking her like this, nailing her to the shelves like I did when we were teens, while she moans my name on repeat. Except this time, I appreciate what I have more than I did back then.

Emerson was right. A reimagination isn't about making a shitty remake of an overworked storyline. It is exciting and fresh, better than anything I've experienced. The past two weeks have been magical, and it isn't always about sex.

We've talked, cooked, laughed, and reminisced.

And we showed those stiffs who ridiculed me last time that I'm wealthier than they will ever be. I got the girl, the success, and the envy of everyone in my realm.

I can't remember the last time I felt so at peace. It was honestly over a decade ago.

Emerson has always been able to do that—make me forget my worries. I had the world on my shoulders when we met, but she made it seem manageable. Weightless. She made it seem inconsequential.

When Emerson's back arches, bringing her breasts to within an inch of my face, I become even harder. While circling my lips around the bud of her nipple through the cotton fabric of her shirt, I stretch her wide.

I gently tug on it with my teeth, bringing her moans up from a whisper to a roar. Her arms wrap around my neck as tremors wrack through her. She is close to coming again, to surrendering to the madness that has kept our sleep at a minimum for the past week.

Emerson's mewls have me desperate to taste her again, to feel the quivers of her orgasm with my tongue this time instead of my cock.

Since I've never had the ability to deny myself of this woman, I move forward with my plans rather fast.

Banding an arm around her legs, I withdraw my aching cock and hoist her up the shelves, and then my mouth finds her drenched slit. I lick her possessively, each stroke of my tongue chanting the same word through my head.

Mine.

Mine.

Mine.

As her cries grow desperate, I eat her faster. I lick at her clit and bite it a handful of times before poking my tongue deep inside her.

Her cries grow more desperate when I spread her wide with my shoulders until her glistening pussy is displayed directly in front of me. Then I suck at her clit and lick it.

Her body tenses up with every timed flick. Then, just as the tingles reach a level of hysteria, I say the words I've spoken a minimum of four times a day for the past two weeks.

"Come for me like a good, obedient wife. Mark me with your scent. Make me yours."

Emerson climaxes with a breathless sigh, her entire body shaking. I poke my tongue inside her, giving her pussy something to cling to as she rides the wild ride. My cock aches to sink back into her, but this is more intimate, more us. It is a man kneeling at the feet of his woman, and him worshipping her how she deserves to be adored.

Once the shivers racking through Emerson's tight, fit body subside, I lower her back down the shelves before nestling the crest of my cock at the opening of her pussy.

I watch her while slowly entering her, absorbing every spark, glint, and glimmer darting through her impressive eyes.

I'm under her spell in less than a second and unashamed to admit it.

"I love you, Ember. I always have, and I always will."

When tears well in her eyes, I thrust hard, putting the weight of my body behind my pumps. Emerson's eyes roll backward, and my name leaves her mouth as her pussy convulses around me.

I grit my teeth, fighting to stave off my release, but lose the fight when the faintest whisper has me coming with a roar.

"I love you too, Coal. Always."

Sometime later, I enter my office with a warm washcloth and a satisfied smile. We moved to the office so the staff of Ember's could close without interference, and we've been going nonstop since. Emerson is exhausted, but that isn't the sole emotion she's displaying.

Something is bothering my wife.

I've noticed this expression a handful of times in the past week, but anytime I try to question her about it, she assures me she is fine.

I wonder if it has something to do with the name displayed on my phone screen when it rings. The groove between her brows deepens— as it does anytime I've brought up Andrik since the gala.

"You should answer it," Emerson says when I continue for her instead of my phone, aftercare a priority of mine. "It could be important."

"More important than you? Never."

She *tsks* me, but I see the flare darting through her eyes. She loves when I put her first, and it has me doing it more regularly.

"Mikhail..." Her laugh makes me hard, like I didn't just achieve release. "It is five a.m. Not even the sparrows are up yet." She snatches the washcloth out of my hand and barges me toward my phone. "Answer your brother's call."

I pout while snatching up my phone and dragging my thumb across the screen. "This better be important—"

I'm cut off by a man desperate to kill. "Zoya's water just broke."

"What?" I stare at Emerson as if she has supersonic hearing. "She's not due for another six weeks."

"I know, but Nikita said she'd most likely go early since her uterus will struggle to reach full term," answers a man pacing in frustration. "I don't know what to do."

That's a first. Andrik is the mastermind of our family. He's the brain—*and the brawn*. I'd just rather you keep that last part between us. I've been feeling like the king of my realm since the gala, and I'm not ready to return to reality just yet.

"Take her to the hospital." When my suggestion lands on deaf ears, I shout, "Now, Andrik!"

He's not accustomed to being snapped at, but he takes it in stride. "We're not home. We're at an onsite cabin at Zelenolsk." When I gasp, annoyed, he pushes out, "Zoya wouldn't leave until she was confident I didn't fuck this up for you."

"This?"

I'm interrupted by a woman in pain. Zoya's groan sounds terrifying, and it has my stomach churning like I vomit in sympathy.

"Breathe, *милая*." Andrik's voice is more controlled now, more in charge. He knows how to take care of his woman. He's just shit fucking scared about not being able to accept her pain on her behalf. I know this because I face the same issues with Emerson.

I sigh in gratitude when Emerson proves she has supersonic hearing. "Take her to this hospital." She twists a tablet around to face me. "It has one of the best obstetrics units in the country. They will be able to help her."

I recite the information on the screen of the tablet we use to order stock to Andrik before telling him we will meet him at Vlotz Private. He grunts his approval of my suggestion half a second before the line goes dead.

Chapter 39

Emerson

Despite being born exactly six weeks early, Zoya and Andrik's daughter weighs a healthy six pounds one ounce. She has a head of adorable dark-blonde locks, a slight cleft chin, and ten perfect little fingers and toes.

I swear I've not seen a child as adorable as her in almost a decade. Wynne was smaller at five pounds two ounces, but she had the same fight as Amaliya. They survived the odds, and I am hopeful Amaliya will be the glue that keeps the Dokovics together like Wynne was for me.

I felt like I was drowning those first few weeks of our breakup. Chaperoning my mother to medical appointments and weekly scans gave my life purpose.

As Amaliya wiggles in my arms, I can't help but marvel at the miracle of life. Her delicate features, her tiny fingers, and the way she nestles into my embrace are all so perfect.

When I glance at Mikhail, my lungs stop accepting air. His loving glance as he watches me hold his niece speaks volumes. It is a look of pride, love, and a hint of longing.

I can't wait to make him a father someday. The thought fills me with hope and excitement. He will be an amazing father, just as he has been an amazing spouse, uncle, and brother.

"Come, meet your niece," I say to Mikhail when our eyes lock and hold.

As I gently hand Amaliya, swaddled in soft blankets, to a man who will protect her until his dying breath, a sense of peace washes over me. This tiny miracle is another symbol of hope and healing for Mikhail's family. Considering how things were not that long ago, it is incredible to see the joy and unity this new life has brought.

Only months ago, Zoya would have disappeared off the face of the planet within a minute of finding out she had conceived a daughter. If she were fortunate to have conceived a son, she would have been granted a maximum of five years.

It is insane to consider how many changes Andrik has made to his family's bigamist ways in the past six months, and it has me hopeful Mikhail will have more understanding for the reason he made the mistake he did.

As I drink in the image of my man of great strength and power swaddling a newborn, I slip my hand into Mikhail's spare one. He squeezes my hand gently before tilting closer, the miracle of this day not lost on him either.

He only learned of Zoya's existence last year, so he's never held a newborn baby girl, much less one related to him by blood.

"She's beautiful," I whisper, my praise both for Amaliya and her parents watching our interaction with eagle eyes. I am aware of the cause of their gawk, but Mikhail is clueless. That doesn't mean he will hide what I mean to him, though.

He nods, his eyes never leaving Amaliya. "She is." The world's axis tilts when he lifts his eyes to mine and whispers, "And so are you."

This is the perfect time to tell him what's been gnawing at me for the past week, to soothe any possible troubled waters while his niece slumbers peacefully in his arms, but I can't do it.

Amaliya and her big brother are the bridge that will keep his family connected, but a story can only be written one word at a time. Mikhail will learn the truth one day. It just won't be during a moment that he's meant to cherish for eternity.

As we walk toward the exit of Vlotz maternity suite, a smile tugs at my lips. The last time I walked these steps, I did so with my baby sister in a baby carrier, and my first true smile in months spread across my face.

Mikhail's hand is warm in mine, and I can feel the slight tremor of his grip.

I'm about to ask him what's got him so nervous, when he blurts out, "Do you want kids, Emmy?" He twists to face me, almost walking backward. "It was on our list for a long time, but it was the only thing we didn't place a timer on."

"Because I was a hog." When he peers at me with crinkled brows, I laugh. "I wanted you to myself. I didn't want to share." He stops waggling his brows when I add, "But yeah, I think one day I'd like to have kids." I graze my lower lip with my teeth, keeping the tension high. "You?"

"With you..." I could kill him for the delay. "Yep." My heart pounds furiously when he says, "I've never had an interest with anyone else, though."

"So there are no mini-Mikhail lookalikes already running around?"

He laughs, loving my jealous tone before he boinks my nose. "Nope, not yet." He nudges his head to the maternity ward. "Might be one day soon, though. She's cute as fuck."

For the first time in my life, I don't get jealous about his immediate bond with his niece. I use it to my advantage to guide him toward a softer landing spot for when the truth comes out.

"You'd do anything for her, wouldn't you?"

He nods before saying, "Don't be jealous, Em. I'd do anything for you too."

"I know, but it's different for Amaliya. She's blood. Nothing is off the table when it comes to blood."

He looks like he wants to argue, but he's paying too much attention to the groove between my brows to remind me of how horrible he was treated by blood when he was a child. "What is this about? The groove between your brows I've not been able to shift for a week is back."

"I'm just trying to emphasize that sometimes, even if there is a possibility of them being hurt, we do things others may not approve of to protect our blood."

"It's almost noon, and I'm running on fumes, Em. You're gonna need to spell out what you're trying to tell me."

I weigh up my options. My deliberation is nowhere near as long as it deserves. It isn't my fault. This place is full of good memories, and since I want Mikhail to be a part of them, I need him to know the truth.

I've not yet told him about Wynne because I'm worried he will piece the puzzle together incorrectly as Andrik and his advisor did. The only way I can avoid that is by telling him what Andrik did before announcing that he isn't the only one with a baby sister.

"I—"

I'm interrupted by a highly recognized voice. "Emerson, finally. I was starting to think I'd have to deliver my messages in person."

My mouth dries when Aunt Marcelle joins us in the foyer of the hospital where I spent both the renovation budget for the pub and all its savings on my mother's prenatal care.

Her pregnancy was high-risk from day one, and she needed the best doctors in the country to make it through the harrowing odds unscathed. A two-hour drive wasn't ideal, but Wynne is proof that sometimes you get what you pay for.

"Aunt Marcelle, what are you doing here?" My aunt is well past breeding age. She has also never given up her "kids aren't for me" stance since she was nineteen.

Her rapidly whitening face has me gasping for air.

I can't catch my breath.

This can't be good, and my thoughts shift straight to my mother.

"Mom!" I shout, startling the people exiting next to us.

Pushing off my feet, I enter the emergency ward and search the closest cubicles. Memories of the first time my mother collapsed threaten to stream hot tears down my cheeks. She was nursing Wynne when she undertook a massive coughing fit. Like me now, she couldn't catch her breath. She fell awkwardly to avoid taking Wynne down with her.

I found her three hours later.

Doctors at our local hospital told her it was just a chest infection. It was only when I saved up enough money to bring her back to Vlotz did we learn the truth.

That means my aunt wouldn't be here unless it was something urgent. We can't afford this caliber of health care.

"Mom!" I shout again, my heart aching.

I have no clue how I'm moving. I put one foot in front of the other, my walk guided by the strength of a man shouting to be updated on the location of Inga Morozov.

"Inga Morozov!" Mikhail yells again, startling the desk clerk. "M-O-R-O-Z-O-V."

He tells me to take a left just as my mother's head pops out of the curtains of an emergency resuscitation bay three spots up. She looks well. Good, actually. Albeit a little panicked.

I learn why when I dart my eyes to the occupied hospital bed. Wynne is swamped by the oversized bed and plugged into multiple machines. She's smiling, though. Shockingly.

"It's okay," my mother assures me. "She's okay. It's just the tests Doctor Clestonv ordered. This is the hospital he suggested we attend for additional testing if we could afford the admittance fee." I feel the blood rush back to my cheeks when she twists to face Aunt Marcelle. "I thought you texted her to tell her we'd secured an earlier appointment?"

"I left my phone at Mikhail's penthouse," I say before Aunt

Marcelle can speak. "I don't have it with me." I pat my flat pockets to prove my claim before walking closer to Wynne, silently seeking the truth from her eyes.

She looks healthy, but I've been fooled before.

Even now, my mother still looks as fit as a fox.

"She's okay, sweetheart. I promise you," my mother assures again, cozying up behind me. "The doctors think she might have asthma. Her lungs didn't fully develop before she was born, and the smoky conditions at the pub when I worked throughout her pregnancy made them worse."

Asthma isn't a walk in the park, but the diagnosis is better than expected, and I can't help but sigh in relief.

The air I just released is sucked back in a hurry when the hairs on my nape stand up, my body's ability to sense its mate even during a crisis still paramount.

Mikhail greets my mother with a relieved smile, but it's chased away by confusion. Just like me, his eyes snap to the occupied hospital bed.

I see a million thoughts race through his head when he drinks in Wynne's dark hair, icy-blue eyes, and strikingly gorgeous face. She has the features of a super model, and she's only ten.

My heart launches into my throat when Mikhail briskly swallows half a second before he pivots on his heels and stalks out of the emergency ward.

This is exactly what I was worried about the past two weeks, and why even after the gala, I've kept secret on Andrik's mistake.

"Mikhail, wait!"

After telling my mother I will be back, I take off after Mikhail. His strides are so long I have to jog to bridge the distance between us, and even then, it's still too wide.

"It isn't what you're thinking. She's not your child."

Either not hearing me or deaf from the raging of his pulse in his ears, he continues walking.

"Can we please talk about this? It's not what you're thinking."

My heart rate surges into coronary failure territory when he doesn't head for the exit as anticipated. He enters the maternity ward at the speed of a bullet, and it catapults my panic.

I reach him as he flings open Zoya's hospital room door. A sickening crunch sounds from the room when he slams his fist into his brother's face. The power of his hit sends Andrik sprawling back and has him rearing up for a fight... until he realizes who the hit came from.

After wiping at the blood dribbling from his nose, Andrik tells the guard stationed outside Zoya's room to stand down before he holds out his hands in a non-defensive manner. "Mikhail..."

Mikhail didn't come here to talk. In a maneuver too quick for Andrik or the guard to ward off, he yanks a gun out of the guard's holster and points it at the crinkle between his brother's dark brows.

Zoya watches the spectacle unfold, unable to speak and somewhat contained since she is nursing Amaliya, and Andrik searches my face for answers since Mikhail's impassive expression is unreadable.

I don't know what he sees, but the truth settles on his face remarkably fast.

"It isn't what you're thinking." Andrik's words are calm despite the anger flaring his nostrils. He knows he brought this situation on himself, but at the moment, his only thought is the safety of his wife and daughter. As he moves so not even the dust of a ricocheting bullet could reach them, he says, "Wynne is not your daughter."

Mikhail's voice is on the opposite end of the spectrum. He sounds murderous. Villainous. "I know that."

Andrik's eyes shoot to me. Shock I got the situation so wrong is all over his face.

I shrug, a better defense above me. I thought he believed Wynne was his daughter.

I've never felt more confused.

Andrik's eyes slowly return to Mikhail when he says, "I know that because Emerson would *never* hurt me like that. She would never strip

271

the blood from my veins while standing directly in front of me, pretending to love me." The return of the hurt, scared boy I've been trying to protect the past two weeks forces tears to my eyes. "But you... my family... you would do that. You'd drain the blood from my heart if it meant you could skip the shit-fest they'd planned for you before you were born." He grits his teeth as anger overwhelms him. "I was the one who saved you from that, Andrik!" His shout startles Amaliya, but he acts oblivious. "I sat with you year after year, decade after decade, and faced countless forms of abuse, and *this* is how you repay me. You stripped me of the one thing I loved more than life itself. You destroyed my fucking life."

"No—"

Andrik's denial agitates him further. "She was there, wasn't she? She was at the church, for me."

He chokes on a shocked breath when Andrik nods, digging his hole further. "Yes. She was there for you."

"What did you tell her?" More babies cry when Andrik's silence forces Mikhail to shout. "What did you tell her!"

Andrik stares his brother in the eyes, his thighs unshaking, his jaw tight as he says with remorse, "I told our grandfather to tell her you weren't coming." When his confession forces Mikhail to curl his finger around the trigger, he speaks faster. "Because I thought it would be better to lose her for a while instead of forever. The gender scan was in her name, Mikhail. The federation would have made the same mistake as me."

He's telling the truth. My mother is the director of our company, and as such, doesn't have insurance. Back then, I was an employee with full benefits, so I booked her scan under my insurance details, as I had other medical procedures during my relationship with Mikhail. It isn't a hard ruse for my mother to pull off. People often mistake her for my sister.

Mikhail knows this. He's just hurting too much right now to think things through.

Andrik keeps chipping, though. "I thought I was protecting you, Mikhail—"

"From what?"

"This," Andrik shouts. "The pain in your eyes. The devastation I would give anything to accept on your behalf."

"The devastation *you* caused!"

Andrik nods, agreeing with him. "Because they wouldn't have asked questions first. They would have killed her, *then* sought the truth."

There's no denying the honesty in Andrik's tone, but Mikhail doesn't hear it. He is too swallowed by anger, buried with grief. He is shaking furiously as years of hurt and abuse spill from him in a brutal display of violence.

He appears seconds from killing his brother.

"Mikhail..." Zoya's plea is as painful to hear as the cocking of the guard's gun when Mikhail unlatches the safety. "Please. I love him."

"That isn't enough." I don't recognize Mikhail's voice or the words he speaks.

Love was always enough for him.

He said it is the one thing that can overcome any obstacle.

I learn the cause of his backflip when he says, "Because I loved her too, and *he* still took her from me."

"He made a mistake," Zoya says at the same time I deny his claim that love can't achieve the impossible. "Love is enough."

Mikhail's stance remains firm, but I know he heard me. His cheek muscle twitches as he fights like hell not to crank his neck to face me.

Tears burn my eyes when I force eye contact. I'm not wrangling a boy hell-bent on proving that he is a man worthy of affection. I'm fighting the demons of his past, the abuse that years of love will barely touch the surface of. I am endeavoring to break through decades of trauma with three short words. "Love *is* enough."

Andrik warns me not to, but I have no reason to fear stepping into the path of a gun. Not when the man holding that gun is the love of my life.

I fill the minute gap between Mikhail and Andrik, immediately decompressing Mikhail's compression of the trigger, and then I peer at him over the barrel of the gun. "It can overcome *any* obstacle."

Tears flow when I stare into the eyes of a man I will never stop loving. He's there, hiding behind years of pain and hurt. I just need to coerce him out of the dark.

"And if you give me the chance, I will prove that to you. I will spend every day showing you that love is the only thing you need to survive. It triumphs *everything.*"

I hear Andrik swallow thickly when I lower myself to my knees. He isn't fretful his cover is gone. It is from how Mikhail's eyes immediately follow my fall, and how the deviation of his eyes adjusts the aim of his gun. It is no longer pointed at Andrik's head. The bullet would barely graze his ear if it were to be dislodged now.

I shake my head when Andrik considers making a dive for the gun.

I've got this.

I'm confident I do.

A shaky breath rattles my lungs when my confidence pays dividends not even three seconds later. The gun clatters to the floor a second before Mikhail's knees butt mine. We breathe as one when he balances his forehead against mine, and then he closes his eyes as I brush our mouths together.

"I love you, Coal," I whisper over his lips as my relieved exhale breathes life back into his lungs. "Always have, and I always will."

Epilogue

~ **Emerson** ~

Almost one year later...

My hand slaps the roof of a limousine as ferocious tingles race through me. Mikhail and I are meant to be doing an innocent grind-up to pass the time during a long commute, but as per our last million romps, there's nothing innocent about it. My white lace dress is hiked up around my thighs, my panties are soaked through, and the front of Mikhail's trousers have a wet patch.

But I can't stop.

I refuse.

Mikhail has been teasing me relentlessly for hours, and it is about time he pays his dues.

"Please..." I shake my head, confident we can't do this.

Mikhail's tuxedo is custom, and I forgot to tell the tailor he may need a spare pair. If I give in to the tension, Mikhail will greet hundreds of guests in cum-stained trousers.

I can't humiliate him like that. He's faced enough abuse, and the respect he deserves is too fresh to test how powerful it is just yet.

"Keep going, Emmy," Mikhail encourages, rolling his hips. "Make me come by doing something as simple as rubbing my cock against my wife's drenched panties."

His "wife" statement tips me over the edge. I want him now more than ever, and I will have him. It just won't be like this. I need him inside me so I can tighten around him and milk him with my vaginal walls. I want to be stretched wide by him, and I know the perfect way for us to do that.

Mikhail groans a rough sound of delight that makes my mouth water when I fall to my knees and tug at his belt. He loves having his dick sucked as much as he loves giving head, but that isn't the cause of the gargle in the back of his throat this time.

It is his remembrance of the silent promise I issue him every time I kneel in front of him, and how I've proven over the past twelve months that love is enough.

It's been a challenging year, but I would be a liar if I said they weren't also some of the best months I've lived. Our mothers are in remission, my sister has her asthma under control, and every day, I've shown Mikhail that love is enough.

We've grown stronger.

Our bond is unbreakable.

I wish I could say it was as easy sailing for Mikhail and Andrik. Their relationship struggled for months. But as I suspected, Amaliya and Zakhar helped bridge the divide—Zakhar more than I could have ever comprehended.

Kids don't feel tension. They also don't have a filter. Zakhar has no qualms telling his uncle Mikhail when he is overdue for a visit, and he is as bossy as his father while demanding immediate ramification of Mikhail's mistake.

To begin with, their relationship grew outside of the home Andrik and Zoya created for their family. They went on motorcycle rides and trips to local landmarks and tasted every flavor of ice cream at a local parlor.

Over time, Zakhar gave Mikhail more understanding of why Andrik did what he did and reminded him that Mikhail was not the only one to have suffered under the hands of the federation. Andrik's son was stripped from his life for almost five years, and his mother still hasn't been found.

Having a better understanding of Andrik's thought process when he made his decision won't take away Mikhail's hurt, but it will help mend things.

The bridge is almost back to its pre-burned condition, and I see today's event adding a final lick of paint to the charred remains.

There's something magical about weddings, but they're even more wondrous when the bride and groom's big day was delayed for means outside of their control.

Upon spotting my admiring watch, Mikhail's thumb strokes my cheek. "You're going to make me come so hard," he murmurs, thickening further when I tug his trousers to his thighs like they didn't cost a small fortune. "I'm so fucking hard for you."

To prove his point, he fists the base of his girthy shaft and squeezes it. The soft rasp of his moan nearly sets me off. I'm so desperate to have him, taste him, that I lunge forward and swipe my tongue across his engorged crown without warning.

As his delicious flavors swamp my taste buds, I float my lips over the wide crest before slowly lowering them. Groaning, Mikhail's teeth catch his bottom lip as one of his hands tangles in my hair. I suck harder when our gazes meet and then swivel my tongue along the vein feeding his magnificent manhood.

Over and over again, I draw him deep into my mouth. His hips grind with every suck as the movements of his hand in my hair guide the speed of our exchange.

He watches me through hooded lids when I take him to the back of my throat.

"Ah, god." His words are hisses. "I love the way you suck my dick. It's like you can't wait to swallow my cum."

"I can't." I pump him with my hand while talking over the wide crown of his cock. "So stop delaying the inevitable and come in my mouth. We have guests waiting for us."

I would care more that there are hundreds of people waiting for us in the ballroom of one of Andrik's many hotels if anyone could steal my devotion from this man.

Since they can't, I continue sucking Mikhail's dick like I was born to do it. It isn't a hard feat. His pleasure is my pleasure. The wave close to cresting in my stomach is a surefire sign of this.

Pre-cum leaks from his crown when Mikhail's hooded gaze rakes my wedding dress. My gown is almost custom. A designer who bid to be featured in the wedding of the year didn't sew it, though. It was made by the woman who made my first dress. My mother.

"You want me to come?" His gravelly, unrestrained voice is enough to bring me to climax, but I hold back, desperate to see where the flare darting through his eyes will take us.

When I nod, he smirks.

"Then you ought to thank your mother for the split in your dress, because I sure as fuck ain't coming before my wife."

His wife comment already has my core clenching, so you can imagine how hard it is to stave off my orgasm when he plucks me from the floor, spreads me on the leather bench opposite him, and then loses his head under layers of lace.

My hands seek something to clutch when he blows a hot breath over my pussy seconds before his lips find my clit. Through the delicate material of my panties, he circles my clit with his tongue before sucking it into his mouth.

I climax in a rush that burns through me like wildfire, setting me alight. I buck against his mouth as I sing his praises like our limousine is unmanned. My climax is unending. It lasts forever, and I can't stop moaning.

"One more." Both my dress and the frantic thud of my pulse muffles Mikhail's voice, so he repeats his request. "One more, then you can make me come."

My back arches when he tugs my panties off like he knows I packed a spare pair, and then I sink into the sticky leather when his tongue flutters over my sensitive skin in rapid succession.

He eats me with a hunger that hasn't dispersed a smidge over the past twelve months, and I surrender to the madness.

I grind my hips upward, mashing his face with my pussy and increasing the friction. The tingles racing through me turn blinding, and I am at his complete mercy in a shamefully quick time.

I need this orgasm more than my lungs need air, but it won't relent. No matter how hard he sucks at my clit and tongues my pussy, the storm doesn't roll in.

Don't get me wrong. It feels amazing, but the needy clenches of my pussy, desperate for something to cling to, are frustrating. I need him inside me. Now.

When I tell Mikhail that, with the added word of *husband*, he turns feral. He thrusts my dress up until I'm almost lost underneath it, wets the head of his cock with the evidence of my arousal while scrubbing at his drenched lips with his free hand, and then enters me with one forceful thrust.

The sudden intrusion is painful, but it is also explosive. I come with a mangled scream of his name, my body convulsing as relief splinters through me.

Through a hooded, lusty stare, Mikhail continues lunging forward, fighting through the squeezes of my pussy, coercing him to join me on the dark ride.

He extends my pleasure by adding a heap of wicked words to the thrusts of his hips. He makes my orgasm last forever. I can't stop coming. Screaming. And they make Mikhail even more unhinged.

He spreads me wide with his hips while sinking into me deeper.

Over and over again. His pace is manic, and I lose my mind more with every precise pump.

Mikhail's eyes are locked on my face, his lips glistening from my earlier arousal, his nostrils flaring with every breath. He looks so beautiful above me, so powerful, it is almost unfair. His personal development has grown in leaps and bounds over the past year as well. He is more confident and self-assured and not tempted to hide it behind a cocky, arrogant demeanor. He loves fiercely and honorably, and I'm so fucking grateful I am the one he loves.

"I love you, Coal," I murmur, my voice heavy with sentiment. "You're the reason I burn, and I am honored to call you my husband... for real this time."

He bottoms out at my uterus as a rush of pleasure sears his gorgeous face. I climax again when the hot spurts of his cum fill me. His release takes everything out of him. He collapses on top of me with his lips on my cheek and his hot breaths gusting over my bone-dry lips.

I don't see him staying down long when he feels my body's response to his reply. "I love you too, Ember. Always have. Always will."

Fifty minutes later, round two a necessity when emotions spill over, I lay sated and bleary-eyed on the back seat of the limousine. Mikhail sits on my left, seemingly unruffled. His hair has the sex-mused look all women crave, and his expression announces complete satisfaction.

When I harrumph, disgusted at how perfect he looks after a marathon romp session, his lips curve into a smile. "We can skip the church and go straight to the reception if you're tired."

I'm overwhelmed with post-orgasmic endorphins, but nothing will stop me from shaking my head. We need this, and I won't have anyone take it away from us this time.

"All right," Mikhail murmurs, effortlessly reading me. "If you're sure?"

When I nod, he pushes the intercom button at his side and instructs the driver to take us to the church.

Anticipation builds the further we travel. This is the first time we've done this route together. Although I doubt anyone will try to intervene this time, it feels right doing it together. It makes it more special. Unique. It is us creating our own waves as it always should have been.

My nose tingles when our arrival at the church has me spotting familiar faces. Since we're already technically married, we were meant to "elope" before joining our guests to celebrate our one-year anniversary. No one knew we were renewing our vows.

Mikhail's smile bounces off the tinted windows of the limousine when he says, "They're important to you—"

"So they're important to you, too," I interrupt, almost sobbing.

Mikhail nods and then grunts, the force of my kiss knocking the wind out of him.

Before things get out of hand, I thank him for his kindness with nothing but my mouth before I slip out of the limousine to greet our guests.

It is an extremely intimate affair, with only my mother, my aunt Marcelle, and my baby sister in attendance from my side of our soon-to-be joined families.

The guest list doubles when it is exposed how similar our brain waves are. Mikhail looks a mix of shocked and uneased when Andrik assists Zoya out of a custom SUV that looks more like a tank than a family mover before he straps Amaliya into a baby carrier.

The unease becomes manageable when Mikhail's mother takes Zakhar's hand in hers before she joins us at the front of the church. She looks well, and her glossy blonde locks announce which side of the family Zoya got her fair hair from.

"They're important to you..."

I leave my sentence open for Mikhail to fill it.

He follows along nicely.

"So they're important to you, too."

He accepts the hand Andrik holds out when they join us on the sidewalk, kisses his mother's and sister's cheeks, and then noogies Zakhar's head, disgusting him. Zakhar looks like he worked on his gangsta part for hours. It is a replica of his father's hairstyle.

Any tension left hanging fades to nothing when Zoya says, "When Konstantine announced you were circling the same block for over an hour, I assumed we had plenty of time to get here. Traffic was a bitch. Does everyone go to lunch in this town at the same time?"

My hand shoots up to cover my smile as my family's giggles echo in the gardens of the church. I love how quickly our two families are becoming one, and I can't wait to make days like today a permanent fixture in our lives.

"Are you ready?" Mikhail asks when Father Loroza signals for us to join him inside the church.

"Yes. I just have one quick thing to take care of first. Go ahead, I'll catch up." He looks worried until I add, "Nothing will stop me from walking through those doors. Not even a tornado."

"Russia doesn't have tornadoes," Zakhar murmurs, leading his family's entrance to the church. He doesn't just look like his father. His personality is as commanding as well.

"Actually, they do," Wynne corrects, jogging to catch up to him. "Although they're not as often or as strong as tornadoes in the US, they're still common." Zakhar looks up at her in awe. If we were a cartoon, love hearts would be bouncing from his eyes. He doesn't snarl when Wynne ruffles his hair in a similar fashion to Mikhail while saying, "I'll tell you more inside."

Nodding, Zakhar spins back to face Mikhail. "Are you coming, Uncle Mikhail?"

I squeeze his hand in silent support when he nods, then brush my mouth against his, my promise issued without words.

Once he disappears inside the church, I twist to face my aunt. "Did you bring it?"

Confusion fills my mother's face when my aunt nods before pulling my surprise out of her oversized purse. It is quickly chased with unspoken anger.

~ Mikhail ~

As I stand at the altar, my heart races with anticipation. The moment I've been waiting for is finally here. Emerson Morozov is about to become mine—officially.

The church doors open, and I swallow in relief. I only left Emerson's side thirty seconds ago, yet here she is, standing in the doorway of her family church, holding a bouquet of daisies and smiling softly.

My breath catches in my throat as I take in her beauty. Her dress is a vision of elegance I failed to notice while banging her senseless in the limousine. Its hem floats gracefully over the floorboards with each step she takes, and the delicate lace and intricate beadwork shimmer in the soft afternoon sun. Their sparkles make her look like a goddess, and I can't believe I get to call her mine forever.

Her hair is styled in soft waves, compliments to the clutch I had on her hair, and they are cascading down her shoulders. Her eyes, those mesmerizing eyes that will always be my favorite color, are fixed on me, and I can see the love and happiness reflected in them as she moves them between our guests.

Emerson's smile lights up the room when her eyes lock in on my family hogging the front pew on the right side of the church. She's forgiven Andrik already. Mine has been harder to come by.

I understand the mistake he made, and the consequences of what could have happened if anyone in the federation reached the same conclusion, but his betrayal hurt. He could have spoken to me. He could have manned up and told me his concerns. I probably wouldn't have listened, but I only remember that when Emerson is moaning beneath me.

It is easy to forget the cruelties of the world when the very reason you exist is breathing life back into your lungs.

I'm sure I will get over it eventually, but my forgiveness will have nothing to do with the five hundred million Andrik is refusing to let me return, and everything to do with the woman who made decades of abuse disappear with a single glance.

As our eyes lock again now, the magic that spell-bounded me fourteen years ago hits me again. Andrik did try to warn me. He told me again and again how dangerous my plans with Emerson were. I didn't listen. I thought I could dodge the federation's rules as he had most of his life. I had no clue how fucking stupid I was being.

My stubbornness is the reason Andrik was forced to take matters into his own hands.

I am to blame for losing Emerson from my life for ten years, not my brother.

Actually, no. It was neither of our faults. It was the cruelness of a world too corrupt for young love to survive.

As Emerson reaches the altar, I take her hand in mine. The warmth and softness of her skin tell me what I need to do. After holding my finger up, requesting Father Loroza wait before commencing our vows, I twist to face Andrik.

He looks humble when I gesture for him to join us on the altar as Wynne has on Emerson's side. It isn't a look I thought he could pull off.

When Emerson's cheeks turn a red hue in support of my attempt at reconciliation with my brother, I flare my nostrils, eager to capture the scent of her heated skin.

Confusion bombards me. A unique scent is bounding out of Emerson's mouth. It wasn't there when we fooled around in the limousine, but before I can query about it, Father Loroza requests for me to read my vows.

With my eyes locked on Emerson instead of the card Father Loroza is trying to hand me, I say, "I, Mikhail, take you, Emerson, as my lawfully wedded wife. I promise to support you, honor you, and stand by your side through all the challenges life may bring. I vow to respect you and to fulfill the commitments we have made to each other today until death do us part."

Emerson's smile is radiant, lighting up my life as she returns my vow. "I, Emerson, take you, Mikhail, as my lawfully wedded husband. I promise to support you, honor you, and stand by your side through all the challenges life may bring. I vow to respect you and to fulfill the commitments we have made to each other today until death do us part."

Memories flash through my head at the speed of a bolt of lightning when mischievousness darts through her eyes at the end of her vow. The priest, however, moves the ceremony forward like we didn't black out his calendar for the entire day. "These rings are a symbol of marriage, a tangible reminder of the promises you've made today."

Father Loroza hands us the rings that will weave together with the rings we've not removed once in the past twelve months before he requests we place them onto each other's fingers.

I go first, grateful that we're finally here, ready to start our lives together as husband and wife.

As Emerson does the same, I look into her eyes and see my future—a future filled with love, happiness, and endless possibilities. I can't wait to spend the rest of my life with her, to cherish and protect her, and to build a life together filled with joy, love, and countless orgasms.

Father Loroza's voice breaking through the wicked thoughts in my head keeps my cock half-mast. "In the sight of God and the power vested in me, I now pronounce you husband and wife." His narrowed gaze is unexpected when he turns his eyes to me and says, "You may kiss your bride."

Emerson leans in first, her eyes brimming with lust. In this moment, everything feels perfect. I am the luckiest man in the world, and the scent that wafts out of my wife's mouth when she opens it in preparation for my kiss makes my assumptions undeniable.

Her mouth, tongue, and lips are coated in peanut butter.

There's enough greasy residue to kill me.

Doesn't mean I will back away, though.

My wife wants me at her mercy, she wants me on my fucking knees, and her wish is my every command.

Air hisses from Emerson's mouth when I band my arm around her waist and tug her in close. Her nipples scratch my chest as my erect cock digs into her already drenched panties. I can smell how aroused she is, and how hopeful she is that I will make true on the threat I delivered the last time she denied me at this exact location.

Emerson trembles—voluntarily this time—when I press my lips to the shell of her ear and say, "Are you sure this is what you want? I will never deny you, but your momma may never look me in the eye again when I show Father Loroza, on this very fucking altar, that a mouth isn't the only place a man can kiss *his* wife."

From the spark that lights up her eyes, I get my answer, but she adds words to the mix. "You didn't think we really hired the church for the entire day for a ten-minute ceremony, did you, Coal?"

When lust burns through her body, making her cheeks glow, I step back, ready to empty the church with an arrogant wave of my arm.

Shock rains down on me for the umpteenth time over the past twelve months when I find nothing but empty pew after empty pew. Not even Father Loroza is in attendance anymore.

It is just me and the woman I would go to the end of the earth for.

Emerson lazily falls to her knees, deliberately enticing me, before she removes an EpiPen from her bra and stores it on her right for safekeeping. "What do you say, Coal? Shall I make you burn again?"

By the time we leave the church, I make true on my threat not once but twice.

Andrik, Zoya, and Nikita already have books. You can find them on Kindle Unlimited.

If you enjoyed this book, please consider leaving a review.

Facebook: facebook.com/authorshandi

Instagram: instagram.com/authorshandi

Email: authorshandi@gmail.com

Reader's Group: bit.ly/ShandiBookBabes

Website: authorshandi.com

Newsletter: https://www.subscribepage.com/AuthorShandi

Also by Shandi Boyes

Denotes Standalone Books

Perception Series

Saving Noah *

Fighting Jacob *

Taming Nick *

Redeeming Slater *

Saving Emily

Wrapped Up with Rise Up

Protecting Nicole *

Enigma Series

Enigma

Unraveling an Enigma

Enigma The Mystery Unmasked

Enigma: The Final Chapter

Beneath The Secrets

Beneath The Sheets

Spy Thy Neighbor *

The Opposite Effect *

I Married a Mob Boss *

Second Shot *

The Way We Are

The Way We Were

Sugar and Spice *

Lady In Waiting

Man in Queue

Couple on Hold

Enigma: The Wedding

Silent Vigilante

Hushed Guardian

Quiet Protector

Enigma: An Isaac Retelling

Twisted Lies *

Bound Series

Chains

Links

Bound

Restrain

The Misfits *

Nanny Dispute *

Russian Mob Chronicles

Nikolai: A Mafia Prince Romance

Nikolai: Taking Back What's Mine

Nikolai: What's left of Me.

Nikolai: Mine to Protect

Asher: My Russian Revenge *

Trey *

Nikolai: Through the Devil's Eyes

Nero: Shattered Wings *

The Italian Cartel

Dimitri

Roxanne

Reign

Mafia Ties (Novella)

Maddox

Demi

Ox

Rocco *

Clover *

Smith *

RomCom Standalones

Just Playin' *

Ain't Happenin' *

The Drop Zone *

Very Unlikely *

False Start *

Short Stories - Newsletter Downloads

Christmas Trio *

Falling For A Stranger *

One Night Only Series

Hotshot Boss *

Hotshot Neighbor *

The Bobrov Bratva Series

Wicked Intentions *

Sinful Intentions *

Devious Intentions *

Deadly Intentions *

Martial Privilege Series

Doctored Vows *

Deceitful Vows *

Vengeful Vows *

Broken Vows *

Omnibus Books (Collections)

Enigma: The Complete Collection (Isaac & Isabelle)

The Beneath Duet (Hugo & Ava)

The Bad Boy Trilogy (Hunter, Rico, and Brax)

Pinkie Promise (Ryan & Savannah)

The Infinite Time Trilogy (Regan & Alex)

Silent Guardian (Brandon & Melody)

Nikolai: The Complete Collection (Nikolai & Justine)

Mafioso (Dimitri & Roxanne)

Bound: The Complete Collection (Cleo & Marcus)

Made in the USA
Las Vegas, NV
31 July 2025